The Would-Be Virgin

AND OTHER TALES

The Would-Be Virgin

AND OTHER TALES

THE COLLECTED SHORT FICTION OF
SUSAN SURMAN

PROSPECTIVE PRESS
Winston-Salem

PROSPECTIVE PRESS LLC

1959 Peace Haven Rd, #246, Winston-Salem, NC 27106 U.S.A.

www.prospectivepress.com

Published in the United States of America by PROSPECTIVE PRESS LLC

↑ TRADEMARK

THE WOULD-BE VIRGIN
AND OTHER TALES

ISBN 978-1-943419-59-3

First PROSPECTIVE PRESS trade paperback edition

Printed in the United States of America
First printing, December, 2017

1 3 5 7 9 10 8 6 4 2

The text of this book was typeset in Minion Pro
Accent text was typeset in Marienda

PUBLISHER'S NOTE

Some content previously published.

Contents

Kaplan's Crisis

"Doctor Sidney Kaplan, I'm gonna kill you." Came a roaring voice from the other side of the closed door.

Ah, my eleven o'clock is here.

Like a flash, she made a fierce entrance into the office, not unlike the running of the bulls, holding a glass vase in the air where it then hung over his head dangerously close to his skull.

Intuition, common sense, nearly twenty-eight years experience, and a keen will not to die this way, came together in an instant. As a psychotherapist in a business overcrowded with disturbed and dysfunctional beings, it was not an unusual morning.

With a slight uplift of his eyes, his only movement, keeping the glass vase, the hand of the threatener, and her facial expression in view, Sidney Kaplan said in a soothing, yet firm tone, "You, Princess Rose Berman, an aristocrat, would kill me with that cheap piece of glass? At least use Steuben." Just the ticket to disarm the would-be attacker, he used that split second to stand away from his desk, thus removing himself from harm's way.

This was not a new event. She had made other attempts on his life. Once with a lethal letter opener directed at his chest; once with her enormous handbag filled with rocks aimed for the back of his neck. Carefully, he took the vase out of Rose's hand, guided her onto the couch, and took his usual place in the matching leather armchair facing her. He slipped the weapon under his chair, at the same time Rose apparently lost interest in the episode.

Miss, never Ms. and definitely never Mrs., Rose Berman was one of the many long-term patients who made a way of life out of seeking professional help. Sidney liked Rose, felt sorry for her, and genuinely wanted to help this middle-aged, overweight, overwrought, overanxious woman whose sessions with her therapist were, in her mind, the only legitimate excuse to temporarily escape from an overbearing mother with whom she had lived all her forty years. Inherited wealth from a grandfather's real estate holdings had allowed her the very expensive ongoing treatments. Sidney would have given anything to get the mother on his couch, but that hadn't happened up to now, and didn't seem likely to ever happen, such was the nature of Rose Berman's mother.

After a respectable lapse of time, Sidney began the session as he had been beginning their sessions for two years, now once a week, although for the first year, it had been three times a week, a referral from their mutual dentist.

"Anything new, Rose?" He had perfected over the years, and very much liked, that part of his voice to exude reassurance in his patients. After a few seconds of silence, he repeated the question. "Anything new, Rose?"

Rose mumbled something.

"What did you say? Something? Nothing?"

"That's what I said."

"Nothing?"

"Rose Berman needs no sermon. A rose is a rose is a rose. Anything else is just cheap prose. John F. Kennedy rose and Rose froze." Without taking a breath, she said flatly, "I made you a chocolate cake. But I left it in the taxi."

Ah, today, the manic part of manic depressive. To him, the definition said much more than the current phrase: Bi-polar. Manic was when he got poetry, oil paintings, baked goods, and chicken pot pies. When Rose was depressed, nothing he said, or did not say, could get her to open up. "That's too bad. About the cake, I mean. I hope the taxi driver isn't allergic to chocolate." His sarcastic attempt at humor was unfunny.

"I'm depressed."

"You seem very *up* today. You just tried to kill me. If you were depressed, you would have killed yourself." His direct approach took some people by surprise. He could count four patients he lost to another practice because of his candid ways. "Any dreams?"

"You don't wanna hear my dream."

"Okay."

"You wanna hear my dream?"

"Sure."

"Well, I'm not gonna tell ya, so there."

Sidney waited. They'd been through this routine before.

"Okay, I'll tell ya. She won't let me make any decisions."

"Is that the dream? Who is the *she*?"

"Her. Rose."

"*Rose*, Rose?"

"I mean Marjorie." Rose made a face.

"Your mother. Go on."

"I hate you, Kaplan."

"I know. Tell me about the dream."

Rose spat out something about a boxing match, a brown canvas tent, Jay Leno, and a metallic blue Chevrolet convertible.

"How did you feel when you woke up?"

"Hungry for meatballs in tomato sauce."

"Is that what you ate when you woke up?"

"Spaghetti. With the meatballs. It's the same, always the same, what's in a name, same name."

"And when you ate the spaghetti and meatballs, how did you feel?"

"After or during?"

"Both."

"Nauseated."

"You felt sick?"

"What did I just say? Are you deaf?"

"We are here to discuss *you*, Rose."

"Show me your spleen. Don't be mean, jelly bean. Oh, jelly bean mine."

Sidney was beginning to wish she *had* conked him out with that glass vase.

"Then I ate a Hershey Bar. No... a Twix. No... wait... Three Musketeers."

"You've been watching *Adam's Rib* again," he interrupted.

"So?"

Her chatter about food was making him slightly queasy. "I've told you many times, it's a movie, Rose, just a film, nothing to do with real life. And all the actors in it are dead." He caught himself. Who was alive and who was dead in Hollywood had taken up three sessions. He didn't want to go there again. "It doesn't matter. You know you're allergic to chocolate."

"I am," she said, as if just making the discovery. "Yes, I am. Is that why I can't get enough of it? I saw on television the food you eat a lot of is the food you're allergic to."

You're driving me nuts. He might have said that out loud. Wasn't sure.

"I'm allergic to nuts, too." She began citing her list of allergies.

None of this was new. Sidney had developed certain techniques to stay awake during the ramblings which went on for ten or fifteen minutes. Just as some people recite baseball scores under certain circumstances, just as some count sheep under other conditions, Sidney's thoughts went to data from various medical journals. Today, however, was different. It was rare he let his personal life enter into a session, but today was not like any other day in the life of Beverly Hills' psychotherapist, Sidney Kaplan.

Twenty-five years Hazel and I have been married. We eat together and sleep every night together in a king-sized bed in our house with ten rooms and four and a half baths, ten minutes from my office. In our service, we employ a full-time cook, a full-time maid, and a gardener who comes in three times a week. Neighbors come in the movie star and plastic surgeon variety. We are referred to as the ideal couple. Three children. Twenty-two year old Suzanne, never Sue or Suzie, lives with her boyfriend in a small apartment in Hollywood. Both aspiring actors with some talent judging by the two or three showcases Hazel and I attended. Twenty-four year old Eric, a computer programmer, lives and works in San Francisco. While he never told us, we know about his sexual preferences. The youngest, Mark, eighteen, will eventually become a doctor. He lives at home sometimes. The 'sometimes' because his girlfriend, the twenty-two year old jazz musician, Butternut—real name—has a pad in Santa Monica.

"Dr. Kaplan? Are you all right? Dr. Kaplan?" she asked, genuinely concerned, gently tapping him on the shoulder. "You seem a little, I don't know, like you're sleeping. Was it something I said?" She was standing in front of his chair, hovering over him. "Are you all right?"

Had he blacked out? He pointed to the couch. "Sit, sit. It's the biological factors that give the driving force to the personality through the id. This source of psychic energy is manifested as the person's wishes correspond to specific needs. Pre-dispositions in human personality refer to the biological history of man as an animal species. The analysis of parts cannot provide an understanding of the whole. It is necessary to analyze from the structure of the whole to the characteristics of its constituent parts."

"I love when you talk shop."

"Rose, please! Sit!"

Rose did as she was told. "Should I buy a dog? My mother wants a cat. But I don't like cats. I like dogs."

Something clicked in Sidney's brain with the word. Dog. Time to step up to the next plateau in Rose's treatment. "You ask if I'm all right. Ah. Where do I begin?"

"The beginning is always good," Rose said as if it were the most normal thing to say; as if it were a normal thing coming out of the mouth of a normal human being which she really wasn't.

Sidney cleared his throat. Did he dare? Was she ready? He cleared his throat again.

"Go on, Sidney. I'm listening."

"Thank you, Rose." *Sidney? She has never called me anything but Doctor or Doctor Kaplan or Doctor Sidney Kaplan or sometimes just Kaplan. This is a new development.* "This could be the beginning of an incredible breakthrough, Rose."

"Remember, you're not alone."

Was this the same woman who thirty minutes ago held a glass vase to his cranium? He began. "I have always had a particular affinity to animals. When I was younger, I wanted to be a veterinarian. When I watched *Lassie* on TV, I didn't identify with the kid, I identified with the dog."

"Wait. Should I make notes?" She glanced around for a notepad.

Sidney shook his head. "Just listen." He waited until he had her complete attention. "Dogs don't have to worry about the mundane chores that humans must carry out. Haircuts, lawyers, taxes, tailors, cooking, laundry."

"Unless they happen to be in show business, in which case their agents take care of all that." She pointed her index finger at him to put an exclamation point on the matter.

"Right. Right. Just listen, Rose. A dog accepts he's a dog. It eats, performs natural functions, sleeps, and feels emotions."

"Have you noticed how many dogs are working now? Every ad on television has a dog."

"Just listen, Rose." His eyes widened and he tilted his head a little to the left.

Rose caught the look and nodded, the way he had often done with her. "Go on, I'm listening," she said.

"The first transformation took place in Scotland in 1881. A dog, not dead two hours and preserved in a special fluid, was brought to the surgery. Under deep anesthesia, Sir Lancelot Alexander's pituitary gland was replaced. One hour later, the dog's testicles replaced the human testes." The words spilled from Sidney's mouth with authority.

Rose sat wide-eyed, closed mouth, and all ears. Certain subjects and certain words were positively taboo in the Berman household.

Sidney continued. "It took fifteen operations to complete the transformation. The technical term is canine transincision homeoectomy. Observe." He got down on the floor on his hands and knees to illustrate the position. "Today, they can do it in five."

Rose studied him. "You know, Kaplan, in that position, with that expression on your face, you look just like a dog."

"Thank you. I take that as a great compliment."

"That looks like a very comfortable position."

"It is comfortable. It's common knowledge that upright positions are unnatural. Backaches, feet malformations, and even toothaches are common symptoms. In this position, back pain is non-existent. I feel weightless, self-assured, and not in the least bit tired or hungry. And it's easier to take deep breaths, the essential life ingredient."

"My back always aches, I'm always hungry, and I'm always running to the dentist. Do they do many of those trans thingy things?"

He was elated at her engagement. "An excellent question. And I shall happily respond with a question. Who do you think won Best in Show in 2016 at the Westminster Dog Show?"

"I love that show!" Rose thought a moment. "No! R-e-a -l-l-y!"

"You bet. She wasn't just any ordinary Scottish deer-hound. Half the entrants were transincisions. And they only lost one. I shouldn't even mention it. It was a fluke. A miniature poodle was poisoned backstage." The words were pouring off his tongue. If he hadn't chosen the medical profession, he would have been a screenwriter.

"No kidding. Too bad." Rose was fascinated. "Would it be okay if I tried that?" she asked, pointing to his position on all fours.

Hoping for this, he swept his hand out. "Be my guest. It's a free floor."

Slowly, Rose got down on her hands and knees.

Now, both human beings on all fours, foreheads nearly touching, eye to eye, Sidney said almost in a whisper, "Just think, Rose, as transincisionees, we'd be able to go to the park, play ball, take long walks in the rain. And just imagine what it would be like checking into a hotel. 'Welcome,' they'll say. 'Your basket is ready on the third floor front, as requested. The Cockapoo will take you up.' "

There were tears in Rose's eyes. "Is this what health feels like?"

"What do *you* think, Rose?"

She smiled and looked at Sidney beseechingly. "Woof."

Tilting his head slightly to one side, he barked back. "Woof."

A gurgling sound escaped from the back of Rose's throat as she curled up on the floor. She closed her eyes. A soft snore followed by a puffing sound came from her lips. Snore, puff, snore, puff.

Sidney stood up. He had done a good job. She would wake up totally refreshed, having made some strides in her treatment, but only remembering that she had helped someone in distress by listening. Sidney's colleagues thought his methods were way outside the lines. More than once the wheels had been set in motion to get his license revoked. He was of the opinion that their readily doled out drug prescriptions were the extreme. He had woven what appeared to be a fictional account but in reality, the truth. His truth. His own life was in shreds and it was killing him. He looked at Rose. She would be down for at least another half hour. He stretched out on the couch.

No warning, no tell-tale signs. Hazel simply announced she was moving out. Why? Why would a woman do that? She has everything. Another man? No. Not Hazel. I'll go home tonight and she won't be there. How the hell am I going to get through that?

The Noble Thing

1

Elegant Tastes

IT WAS A BOLD MOVE FOR CATHERINE STEWART TO RIDE South West Trains some eighty miles north from the security of her birthplace in Hampshire in the south of England to an unknown life in London. Thanks to the financial aid from affluent mummy and daddy, she was able to purchase a smashing ground floor flat in Kensington overlooking a lush green park and enroll in the London branch of *Le Cordon Bleu* for two years. The flat provided ample space for living, a home office, and had more than enough room for stewing, frying, roasting, baking, and storing pots and pans and miscellaneous equipment required for the day to day running of a catering establishment, all perfectly legal, once she had graduated. No one in the family had ever demonstrated any aptitude for cooking, and while support was forthcoming, her news was a mixture of shock and surprise to her parents, with whom she had lived all her twenty-four years.

Elegant Tastes officially began when a friend hired her to cater a luncheon for his soliciting firm in the city. It became an ongoing weekly event and led to other high profile lunches commissioned by directors of banks and law firms. Referrals came in for business dinners from bankers, solicitors, and physicians. It didn't take long before she was hired to cater dinner parties in Mayfair, Belgravia, and Hampstead, prime locales where the crème de la crème resided. Then came the occasional wedding of the daughter or son of an existing client. It wasn't unusual for clients to invite her to join the family at their country house for a weekend to plan and prepare the meals; thereby, freeing them up to do whatever took their fancy.

As sole proprietor, with three on-call assistants, it appeared that Catherine Stewart, thirty-three, single, a successful business woman, had it all; *appeared* being the operative word. There was one missing ingredient, as serious as leaving the eggs out of an omelet. The old clock was ticking away and she desperately wanted a family of her own.

"I'm slowly becoming convinced I will be chopping onions, garlic, and parsley for other people's families forever and, at the end of the day, curling up with a book about someone else's life," Catherine reported to her parents at one of their monthly Sunday lunches at the house in Hampshire.

Mary Stewart was sympathetic, but only to a point. "The trouble with you is you're too finicky. No one is perfect, my dear Catherine. If you are looking for the moon and the stars, you'd best give up the notion." She glanced over at her husband slumped in his armchair in front of the muted telly, pretending to read his day-old Financial Times, while listening to every word between the two women in his life. Mary rolled her eyes upwards. For all his inherited wealth, he was underneath it all just a man.

Charles Stewart looked up from his paper and piped in, "Not finicky enough, if you ask me." He couldn't understand why his daughter, who had such a good head for business, fell short in her personal life. "No one can bake a chocolate soufflé like our Catherine, but if there were one hundred men gathered together for a boat trip on the Thames, and one of the hundred was rowing upstream with only one oar, that's the one to whom Catherine would gravitate."

Charles and Mary dove into conversation as if their daughter were somewhere else.

"Truth be told, I don't know what she wants, Charles."

"Eroticism is first stimulated by the eyes which then, transmitted to the mind, creates certain havoc. She's met dozens of men. No one to my liking. There was Mark Hall, the Australian hotel and travel executive based in London. Turned out to be gay."

"Bi-sexual. I think there's a difference," Mary said. "And he admitted it once Catherine confronted him."

"Throw another shrimp on the barbie, mate, before you exit. *Ta-ra*, Mark Hall." Charles chuckled at his Australian imitation.

"There was that import/exporter, Stefano Bardino, Italian, *pied a terre* in Hampstead. I thought he might be the one," Mary said.

"It was never quite clear what it was that was imported or exported."

Catherine remembered Stefano very well. He was bright, funny, responsive, considerate, and very romantic; especially when he spoke Italian which was a lot of the time, especially in the bedroom. They both loved food. They both loved children. They both liked to laugh. She even learned a few Italian phrases, not to communicate with him, as he spoke perfect English, but just for fun, just because she wanted to. The relationship seemed to be going well; that is, when he was in England and not in Italy. She absolutely refused to believe the wagging tongues who warned her he was probably married and had a family stashed away in an Italian villa in Naples. She'd read somewhere that a man would rather go to war than break up with a woman, so Catherine brought up the subject. There was indeed a family in Italy. A loving wife who lived in Milan with their three adorable children. Divorce was not an option. He honestly believed he and Catherine could continue as they were. All that had changed was she now had more information about him.

Feelings hadn't changed. He would even be willing to father her child should she require his services for such a blessed event. In a weak moment, Catherine imagined the whole scenario. She'd have his child; the father would come and go; she wouldn't have to be out there dating anymore; she would be able to continue her business. Mainly, she'd have a child of her own. When logic returned, Catherine was able to say, *Abbastanza, caro. Arrivederci*, Stefano Bardino.

Mary continued, "What about Nikko Cortez, the nephew of a former South American Ambassador to Britain who lived in Kensington practically next door to Catherine?"

"He lived and breathed soccer. Turned out he was already married. To soccer. *Adios* Nikko Cortez." That was Charles.

"What is the attraction for foreigners?" Mary went on. "I like Will Waddington. They know the same people. Both love the theatre and the opera and the ballet and Covent Garden and all that. We know the parents. As a member of British peerage, he will one day inherit his father's domain near Cornwall."

The idea of becoming Lady Waddington appealed to Catherine, but, and here was the ugly truth, it was evident that Willie boy, who was as sweet as could be, was an alcoholic. It was impossible for her to go on in any capacity with Will. Neither as friend, companion, or most definitely not lover. She could no longer watch him destroying himself. And she couldn't help him, not that he wanted any help. His love of the bottle made conversation, and everything else, very difficult indeed. Difficult? Impossible would be a more apt description. So it was, toodle-oo to Will Waddington.

Charles got up from his chair. "Will Waddington? Christ, Mary, Waddington's father is a bungler. Look how badly he handled that thing with Churchill."

"A bungler who only inherited half of Cornwall, thank

you very much. Besides, Charles, dear, she's not marrying the father. And wasn't that thing with Churchill with the great grandfather? Years old and forgotten."

"No matter, the apple doesn't fall far from the tree. Or should I say, the apricot, as in Apricot Brandy, if you get my point, and I think you do."

Catherine had heard all this over and over. "Hello, you two," she said, raising her voice, so they could hear over their chatter. "Hello! I'm right here, in case you hadn't noticed."

"Another country heard from," said the father. "Don't ever forget, your grandmother's the true benefactress. *Elegant Tastes* would never have happened without her."

"She knows all that," Mary said. "She'll marry whomever she pleases."

"I'm not marrying anybody," Catherine said. "Or what have I been telling you half the afternoon? Nothing is working out in that department."

"We'll see," Mary said, winking at her husband and mouthing the name, *Will.*

"I saw that," Catherine said.

Catherine adored both her parents. Their verbal exchanges were positively exquisite and a thousand times more entertaining than any British sit-com on television.

2

Holiday Plans

Elegant Tastes was typically dead from mid-December to late January. It was the time of year when the category of clients Catherine serviced took their holidays. She had always been content to go down to Hampshire and spend time with the parents. If there was a current gentleman, he was included depending on his own obligations. And thinking back over the array of men, they always had other obligations, except for Will Waddington. Catherine was convinced it was because of the galloping supply of spirits provided by her dear father.

But this year, she didn't want to go down to Hampshire. Without work as a distraction, the crowds of Christmas shoppers, brightly lit Christmas decorations, and clutching couples visiting from the Continent depressed her. She had to get away, out of Britain. The search for a holiday spot online began. Most of the better places were booked already but with perseverance, the Canary Islands seemed likely. Spanish, off the coast of northwest Africa, it attracted mainly British and German tourists. The larger islands, Tenerife and Las Palmas didn't have any decent vacancies, but there was hope for the smaller island, Lanzarote, sometimes described as lunar. Catherine liked what she saw on the virtual tour of the five star hotel and booked three weeks before she changed her mind. Fortunately, her passport was current so all she had to do was prepare her wardrobe, pack, and in twelve days get to the airport. Breaking the news to the music hall team in Hampshire that she wouldn't be spending Christmas with them was not a pleasant task.

With great disappointment, her mother said, "But it is tradition. Traditions shouldn't be broken. For years, we've lit up the homestead. We're known for miles for our fairy lights. You'll miss everything, Catherine. Everything."

Her father was equally unhappy. To his wife, he said, "Why does she have to go away at this particular time? And to, of all places, the Canary Islands." To his daughter, he said, "Lanzarote is rocks, sand, desert. That's all it is. You know it was formed by a volcano. It isn't safe."

"The island was formed thirty-five million years ago," Catherine corrected her father.

"By a volcano," he insisted.

"Thirty-five million years ago," she repeated.

"A volcanic eruption is a volcanic eruption."

"Isn't it awfully close to Africa, darling?" Mary Stewart was truly fretting.

"It is seventy-nine miles off the northwest coast of Africa, not exactly on the border."

"If you must travel over the holiday, why not go to a civilized place?" Mary asked. "Rome might be nice. More like our winter weather, I mean. What's the weather going to be like on the island? Are you prepared?"

"It's been years since I've seen Rome," Charles Stewart said, lost in his memories.

"Wouldn't you be worried the Coliseum might come down on my head?" Catherine said goodheartedly.

"Don't talk nonsense," her mother said.

And without pausing, once again, her father brought up the fact that Catherine might win prizes for her chocolate soufflés, but choosing a mate was not her strong suit.

"That isn't the topic right now, Charles."

"I thought we were talking about volcanoes," Catherine said.

"If there were one hundred men in a room, and one of them was operating without a full deck, that's who Catherine would be drawn to."

"Rubbish, Charles. We're not talking about Catherine's choices in men now. Our daughter is flying abroad for Christmas. She's going alone on holiday to a desert island near Africa. Do you understand? She will not be here with us in Hampshire. She will miss the tree and the fairy lights." Mary spoke to him as if he were a child.

"Mother. Father. I'm exhausted. I've been working hard. I need a change more than I need tradition this year. That's all it is. My business is quiet now. It's the only chance I'll have to take a real holiday for who knows how long."

The conversation finally ended with her mother telling her to bring her own face flannels with her.

"Face flannels?" Had Catherine heard her mother correctly?

"To remove your make-up, darling. You don't want to mess up the hotel towels. Maids talk to one another, you know."

Catherine hugged her mother for all the nonsense of it. Fairy lights and face flannels. "I adore you, Mother. I'll bring you a nice souvenir." A costly and elaborate present, perhaps for the mantel, would salve her conscience and hopefully suffice for her non-presence this holiday season. It was a frightful responsibility being an only child.

3

Lanzarote

WHEN CATHERINE STEPPED OFF THE PLANE IN ARECIFFE, the first thing to hit her was the intense heat. She literally couldn't breathe. It took a few minutes to get her bearings helped by the thought that she had left behind the icy, not quite thirty degree weather in London.

Only ten miles from the airport, Hotel Canaria was an older hotel which could explain the availability at the last minute. However, the rooms had been refurbished with balconies, bathrobes, slippers, marble and granite bathrooms, and satellite TV. Half-board, which meant breakfast and dinner, were included. A poolside restaurant provided lunch or a light snack. And if she felt bored, the town of Puerto del Carmen was nearby with shops and bars and restaurants.

Her room, a suite really as it turned out, was decorated in traditional Spanish earth tones of burnt orange and deep reds. Stepping out onto the balcony, a feeling of well-being swept over her. The unidentifiable sweet scent that wafted up from the garden below was heavenly and spoke to her, enough so that she was convinced all would be well. A couple, walking hand in hand along the beach, reminded her that she couldn't remember ever walking on a beach with anyone. She quickly erased the negative thought and focused on the satisfying aroma surrounding her.

The sudden sound of the ringing doorbell startled her. She looked through the peep hole in the door before cautiously opening it to a waiter carrying a small round tray with a solitary drink of unknown origins.

"No, no. There must be some mistake. I did not order a drink." When he didn't respond, Catherine tried to make it simpler. "Mee-stake," she said, pointing to the glass of liquid. "*No por yo,*" she added, tapping her chest with her forefinger and shaking her head.

Half in English and half in Spanish, the waiter said that it was the custom of the hotel to welcome all new guests with a complimentary beverage. He held the tray out to her. She took the drink and tried to explain she hadn't yet exchanged her English money. Even though her package deal promised an all inclusive holiday, she had the feeling extra gratuities would not be frowned upon. The waiter took the British coin she handed him, looked at it with disdain and as he went down the hall, he could be heard muttering something about the English tourists. It didn't sound like a compliment. Catherine took a careful sip of the pinkish colored liquid, unable to tell if it was watered down alcohol or alcoholed down water with added color. It didn't matter because she had no intention of drinking it.

Somewhat fatigued from the flight and the sudden extreme change in temperature, she didn't feel up to facing the dining room that evening. She would miss this first night's meal and opt for her walnuts and sultanas, the emergency food she carried in her handbag. It would hold her until morning at which time she promised herself to indulge in a hearty breakfast in the dining room.

As she unpacked and organized her toiletries in the marble bathroom, she rang reception and booked a tennis lesson for eleven in the morning. She took a shower and slipped on the light terry bathrobe provided by the hotel. She grabbed a light blanket from the cupboard and arranged herself on the chaise lounge on the balcony. It was December and all she knew was she wasn't huddled around a blazing fire to keep warm. She took in a deep breath and let it out slowly. She kept up the rhythmic breathing and felt her body totally relax. No need for phone calls, no need for television, no need for people. Never could she recall seeing a sky with so many stars. The sliver of a moon beamed down at her. Not concerned in the least that she wasn't in bed, her last thought before dozing off was that she remembered reading somewhere that one should begin new ventures with a new moon.

4

Tennis, Anyone?

THERE WERE FOUR TENNIS COURTS AND SEVERAL BENCHES lined up facing the courts. A sign indicated that courts C and D were for hotel guests and A and B were for the coach. There were two middle-aged women playing on Court C. Catherine watched the man she assumed to be the tennis coach, on Court B, speaking to his present pupil in German. She hoped he spoke English. He didn't look German. Maybe Italian or of Middle Eastern origin. Perhaps thirty-nine, no more than forty-two, about five foot ten, a beautifully shaped head of the blackest, thickest, straightest hair Catherine had ever seen, a muscular build, well-defined against his light green polo shirt and matching shorts. Her eyes, out of habit, dropped to his left hand. No wedding band. Nothing on the right hand, either. She didn't detect any jewelry other than a wristwatch. Maybe he just didn't wear anything at the tennis court. Not that any of it mattered one iota. Being ten minutes early for her lesson, she was just passing time. He saw her and shouted that he was almost finished. In English. His accent was unfamiliar. She nodded and put up her hand in a sort of wave.

Catherine felt old-fashioned in an obviously out-of-date white tennis dress. The others looked quite modern in assorted colors and short shorts. When she played on the courts in London's Regent's Park, she hadn't felt dowdy, but here she felt extremely self-conscious, with milk-white arms and legs that hadn't seen the light of day in years.

Having finished his lesson, the coach sat down next to his new student. He reached underneath the bench and took a pack of Camels out of a small brown leather pouch. He held out the pack. "Cigarette?"

"Thanks, no. I don't smoke," Catherine said, surprised that he did.

He moved his sunglasses onto the top of his head. He lit a cigarette, taking a long drag. Holding the cigarette away from his face and twirling it in his fingers, he said, "I know it's bad for me, but I like it too much to stop. Almost a pack a day. Maybe one day I will stop," he said not very convincingly while taking another drag.

He had the loveliest hazel green eyes she had ever seen. No one's eyes could be that green. Colored contacts? She wondered how his teeth stayed so white with all that smoking. His voice came from back in his throat with a gruff tone. It was kind of sexy. His accent wasn't anything that she could make out. Not European or German or Middle Eastern. Maybe a combination of all three. It wasn't unpleasant, just different. And sometimes he would drop the article, omitting *a* or *an* or *the* before nouns, but not all the time. She wondered if it was intentional; if he was aware of it. Probably not. Why was she so concerned about any of this, she wondered. Enough wondering. She was here for a tennis lesson.

Sailing in with details of her checkered tennis history beginning with, "I haven't played tennis for many years," her words were halted by the coach who held up his hand.

"There is no need to tell me. I know where someone is in their tennis as soon as they stand on court." With the cigarette between his teeth, he picked up her tennis racket, turned it over a couple of times, fingered the strings, shook his head, and let out a long, deep sigh. "Wrong one. No good."

"I've had it for years."

He checked his clipboard. "Catherine Stewart."

"Yes."

"English?" As he spoke, he wrote something down, never taking his eyes off her.

"Yes." Was he making notes about her archaic costume?

"My name is Unal Aslan. I am Turkish, but I went to Germany when I was twenty and got good job with American company in Frankfort because I could type and speak English. I speak Turkish, German, English, a little Spanish."

"Oo-nahl Ah-slin," she repeated, wanting to get the pronunciation right.

"You got it. Okay, let's go. You need sun." He slipped on his sunglasses, took another drag on the cigarette, stubbed it out in a makeshift aluminum ashtray under the bench, and led the way.

Following behind, Catherine found the back of him just as attractive as the front and mentally gave herself a gentle slap on the cheek to remind herself, again, she was here for a tennis lesson. On the court, he stood behind her and reached around, standing a little too close, while showing her the correct way to hold the racket. The heat of his body mixing with whatever cologne he was wearing was quite heady, the intoxicating scent making her tense up.

"Relax, relax, Ms. Catherine. You are not playing world tournament," he said laughing, but not moving away.

"Sorry." She let her body ease into position.

"Good position. Much better. Now I explain. Tennis is very old game. The big tournament is in Wimbledon every year. Famous players from all over. You get tickets?"

The way he said it into her ear could go down in history with all the great seduction scenes ever played. Three words. *You get tickets*? Forcing herself to focus on the business at hand, she replied, "Yes, Wimbledon. I mean, no. I've always wanted to, but I've never been able to attend, for some reason. I don't really know why." She stood very still, not sure which way to move.

"One day, I'll be there watching my son play."

She was not going to ask about his son. This hour, for which she was paying, was supposed to be about her.

"Okay, today I explain some easy basics." He moved around to face her. "Tennis can be played with singles, doubles, or mixed doubles."

"Yes, I know."

"You know this?"

"Yes, I understand all that. At least, I understand the theory of the game."

"So I can move on. *Gut*. Good. With forehand, you need to swing the racket back near the body." He demonstrated. "You hit the ball a little in front of your left leg. Short backswing and long forward." He demonstrated. "With backhand, it is the same way like forehand, except you change your grip and swing the racket back." He demonstrated. "Best to learn from professional tennis coach. Not good to teach yourself."

"Quite. I understand that." It felt very different with a private coach than with her cronies on the public courts in London where it had always been non-competitive friendly games.

While explaining and demonstrating the different tennis strokes again, this time standing beside her so she could get the angle from another point of view, Unal casually asked a lot of questions. "Are you married?"

The question momentarily threw her. "Uh… no."

"You here for vacation?"

"On holiday. Yes."

"Alone?"

She wasn't sure what to say. With hesitation, she managed, "M-hmm." Maybe she should have said she was with a friend. She was beginning to think this handsome, divine smelling man was a little strange. She'd have to be cautious. This was no way to take a tennis lesson.

"You live in England?"

"Yes."

"London?"

"Yes."

"Big city. Expensive. Lots of hotel guests from England. What work you do?"

These questions were really too much, but she didn't want to come across as the ugly Brit, unfriendly and difficult. "I'm a caterer." When he questioned her with his eyes, she added matter-of-factly, "I prepare food for people. Private lunches, dinners, parties."

"Ah, yes. We have that at hotel for special functions. You work for big company?"

"I have my own business." Now he would think she was rich. Oh, dear. She quickly added, "It's a small company. Very very small. Very."

"That is good. So you are good cook?" he asked. "I like good food."

"I suppose I am." Catherine wasn't sure if this approach he was taking was professional. With all the talk, she was having difficulty focusing on the correct way to hold the racket and was greatly relieved when he walked to the other side of the net.

"Now I will throw few balls. Your job is you hit them over the net back to me," he explained. "You got it?"

"Backhand or forehand?" she called out.

"As you see it, but don't try to do an overhead smash," he said laughing. "That's the advanced lesson. The main thing, you must always keep both eyes on the ball."

Catherine tried her best to hit the balls that came her way, but she missed every time and felt utterly foolish waving her racket in the air. This kept up for a while, but she was totally winded before the hour was up and had to stop. "It's enough. I'm sorry, Unal," she called out across the net. I must stop." She went back to the bench and sat down, slowly catching her breath.

"It's okay. Time almost up." He joined her on the bench and told her, "This is normal for someone in your shape who isn't a regular player. You should see what some of those people are like who come from Germany. They play in many indoor courts all year round and think they are tennis stars. But it is big joke. Many of the same people come here every year just to take lessons with me."

Someone in your shape. She knew she wasn't twenty-five, but she wasn't forty-five, either. And she certainly wasn't falling apart. "I'm just out of practice." She reached into her sports bag and pulled out a bottle of water.

"Very good," he said, referring to the bottled water. Drink slowly," he cautioned.

"Thanks for reminding me." She followed his instructions.

"All part of the lesson. So, Miss Catherine, you are here how long? One, two weeks, ten days?"

"Nearly three." She watched his reaction, not sure if he was drumming up business or if it was personal. Either way, he was making her very nervous.

"Ah, that is good. To play well, you will need lesson every day, and I can arrange for you to play with other hotel guests at your level, maybe slightly higher level. You learn better with someone better than you." He consulted his reservation sheet. "Make the appointment direct with me, not with hotel. Best if you buy new tennis racket, new tennis shoes, and new tennis outfit. Don't worry. I am part-owner of small tennis shop near hotel. I will give you good price. Don't buy in the hotel shops. They charge double for everything. All new stuff will help you play strong tennis, get in shape, firm up, and look good. I can bring everything tomorrow. No need for you to come to my shop."

Not wanting to get in too deeply with lessons, she booked for the next two mornings only.

"Two not enough. People come from all over the island, not just the hotel. I am always booked up."

"I'll take my chances," she said, remembering how easy it had been to get this morning's appointment. All she wanted right now was to get out of the heat and back to her air-conditioned suite. *Damn his green eyes.*

Back in the privacy of her rooms, she didn't feel quite so disoriented. She spent the rest of the day lazing about the suite. It was madness to believe she could remain cloistered forever. Besides, she was quite hungry and needed a meal. She showered, dressed, did her hair, put on make-up, and steeled herself to go downstairs to the dining room.

Catherine stood as inconspicuously as she could, not an easy task, at the arched entrance of the Mediterranean style dining room. It was a mere second before the *maitre d'* appeared in front of her and learning she was alone, showed her to a small table in a corner. Catherine felt self-conscious, certain that everyone was staring because she was alone. She was also smart enough to know that deeply absorbed in their own scenarios, absolutely no other diner cared a fig about the woman dining solo.

By now, she was famished and while there were some interesting dishes on the menu she would have loved to sample, she wanted to put the restaurant experience behind her as swiftly as possible, so she ordered the specialty knowing it would be served quickly. No sooner had she declined the wine that was offered, her meal was placed in front of her. After gobbling down the *paella* without tasting it, she made a hasty exit, not looking left or right. She needed desperately to talk to people who were on their own as she was. If there were any single people, they would be in the cocktail lounge. Heading that way across the lobby, she heard a man's voice calling out to her.

"Most beautiful English lady."

The voice was easily distinguishable. She halted and turned to face Unal. Catherine was struck at how handsome he looked in a white linen suit, pale pink shirt, and a pink and black silk tie. Out of tennis attire, she felt definitely more confident. In her black and white sundress and black patent leather high heel sandals, she knew she looked quite attractive.

"Hello," she said cheerily, genuinely happy to see a person she knew.

"You want join my table in cocktail lounge? Bunch of tennis students. All German. Their English is so-so," he apologized, flapping his hand back and forth.

She didn't care if they spoke Swahili. "I'd love to," she said quickly. She was ready for company and it would be preferable to sitting by herself at the bar pretending she cared about striking up a conversation with a stranger.

After some chit chat in broken English and German, most of which escaped Catherine's comprehension, the group of three young men and two women were ready to move on to the hotel's nightclub on the lower level taking it for granted that she would be joining them. Catherine hesitated, but at Unal's insistence, she agreed to join them, stressing that it would be only for a short while.

Over an hour later, having been deserted by the inebriated entourage, Catherine and Unal sat side by side on a banquette at a table in the dark and noisy club. As these things go, they had slipped into a conversation about intimate subjects.

"How did you come to the Canary Islands? To Lanzarote, I mean," Catherine asked.

"I was married to a German woman and have one son. He is in the private American School here."

Was married. Had she died? That would explain why the son was with him. "So you were married. Not now, I gather?" He hadn't answered her question.

"Divorced. I got the boy," Unal said firmly, without offering any further explanation.

"There is an American School here?" She wanted to know, not really, but more for a reason to change the subject.

"Of course. It is small school, but is very good. Only the best teachers come here. My son is a big tennis player. Junior Amateur Tennis Champion in our region in Germany."

"I see. That's interesting."

As if he had been mulling over how much to tell her, after a pause, he said, "I got divorced eight years ago. I had house in good area in Germany." He let out a sigh. "*Yah, yah*, big house."

"Oh. You had a house." It was difficult to think of him anywhere else but on the tennis court at the Hotel Canaria.

"I had business, too."

"You had a business?" It surprised her. "What kind?" she asked hoping to eke out more information.

"What difference now? I lost everything."

Catherine sensed some regret in his tone. She was curious, but didn't want to pry. Yes, she did. Besides, he was right. It was gone now, so what difference did it make what it was. However, it might tell her more about the man. But did she really care? Despite her inner red flag, yes, she did.

"I was big tennis player at our club. Big." He shook his head up and down as he remembered. "So I decided to get a license to coach. Why not? That way, I figure I can coach my son until one day he becomes professional tennis player. That's when I hear they need good tennis coach here at Hotel Canaria. So I got in touch and I got job. I come every year in winter. About eight months. Four months in summer, I go back to Germany and teach at a private tennis club. Since he was seven-years-old, my son is playing many tournaments in Germany, Austria, and now Canary Islands. He is strong player. One day, he gonna be world champ. You will meet him tomorrow." His face lit up when he talked about his boy. "Miss Catherine, you are good listener. I told you my story. Now is your turn."

"My turn?"

"To talk about Catherine."

How she would love a young boy to be proud of, to brag about. She cleared her throat. "Well, I come from the south of England. Hampshire." Catherine intentionally kept it simple as she told about her business, *Elegant Tastes*.

As if he hadn't heard a word, he said, "You are most beautiful woman. Like Grace Kelly, the American actress. Why beautiful woman like you not married?"

"Well, it just hasn't happened."

"In England, the men must be blind."

It was her cue to change the subject. "I'd like to ask you a question."

"You can ask. Maybe I don't answer." He smiled.

"Earlier, at the cocktail lounge, one of the girls referred to you as *chuk* and everyone laughed and clapped. Was it a tennis award? Why were they laughing?"

Unal let out a lecherous grunt. "It big joke in Germany. *Chook*," he corrected her pronunciation. "It means little. I am not little. You know what I mean?" He smiled as if he had a big secret. "I am here to serve. Serve on tennis court and off tennis court." He moved in closer and put his arm around her.

Catherine wasn't fond of off-color humor and he was way too close for comfort and she was feeling lonely and she wanted him to put his arms around her and hold her. Why didn't she say goodnight and go to her suite? She knew why. Because he was totally, utterly charismatic and unlike anyone she had ever met.

Taking her two hands in his two hands, he said, "Four hands better than two."

Catherine didn't know what he meant. But she knew. He'd had quite a few beers while she had been nursing a glass of bad white wine that went down like razor blades. Maybe it was the alcohol speaking and he wouldn't remember any of it. There was a big part of her that hoped that was the case.

A trio playing recognizable popular tunes had replaced the disc jockey. Unal took Catherine's hand and led her onto the dance floor. She fell in with him as though they had danced together their whole lives. It came as no surprise that he was a good dancer. She liked the way his hands, not to mention the occasional thigh, guided her during a slow number. It was much more fun than sitting on the balcony of her suite watching others having fun. Maybe, just maybe, she could get him to walk on the beach with her. That's all it would be. Just a walk. They would hold hands as they walked. Maybe this was the reason why she had met Unal. He would be her beach walker.

All that thinking caused her to miss a beat and she slammed down hard on the top of his foot with the heel of her shoe. "Sorry, Unal. I'm so so sorry."

"Hey, English, war is over. Be cool," he said lightly, looking into her eyes.

They continued to dance. He held her tightly. As pleasant as it all was, she was afraid of giving him the wrong message and pulled away. "It's late. I'm rather tired."

He was a gentleman. He didn't object or try to change her mind. "It takes time to get used to the Lanzarote weather. I will walk you to your room. Strange people sometimes in hotel corridor at night forgetting where their room is."

"No, please, I'll be fine." There would probably be the attempted kiss at her door and much more. She didn't need that hassle.

"Just to the elevator, most beautiful lady." Unal knew exactly what she was thinking. And he knew what he was thinking, and he didn't want to frighten her away.

Much to her relief, he didn't become difficult. At the elevator, she thanked him for a nice evening and as an after-thought said, "Well, maybe just to the door would be all right. It is late, and you never know who might be lurking in the elevator or in the hallway on holiday. You know what men can be like when they've had too much too drink on holiday. I'm going to stop talking now." She was acting like an absolute fool.

There were others in the elevator, so she didn't have to worry about him getting too personal. When they got to her floor, she directed him to her door. It was all very formal. "This is it."

He didn't move.

"Well, goodnight," she said, putting out her hand for him to shake.

He ignored the gesture. "Let's make sure you get in," he said.

Oh no, here it comes. She made no attempt to open the door. "Well, see you on the tennis court in the morning."

He glanced at his watch. "In a few hours. It is now three a.m." He stepped closer to her and put his hands on her shoulders.

She thought she would die from his divine scent. She could feel his body heat. This was precisely why she didn't want him to get this far. She should have left him at the elevator. "Goodnight," she repeated, hoping to sound calm even though her insides were wound up.

He felt her body tense. "No. Don't be frightened." He kissed her on both cheeks. "Now it is goodnight," he said softly.

He made sure she got in her room, but never made a move to enter. She appreciated that. "Goodnight," she said again. "I had a lovely time. Really, I did." She lingered in the doorway. The evening that had spilled into night was over and it was now morning; yet, she was having difficulty letting go.

Slowly, she closed the door. *Oh Lord, what have I got myself into?* She leaned against the door and fanned her face with her hand. "Lord oh Lord. I'm way too young for hot flashes. Damn him."

Tossing and turning in her bed for the next five hours, she told herself it wasn't personal on his part and that it was probably part of the job. Most likely, he had been told by the hotel to court women traveling on their own. Well, she wasn't going to be his next victim. To assure her feelings of separation from him, she went over some of the negative things that had been said, the things that made her stomach churn. That comment about serving on and off the court. And his accent got on her nerves. She was going to have to keep it professional on the tennis court and no matter how lonely she felt, she wasn't going to socialize with him and his crowd in the evenings. She was sure a brief affair with her tennis coach while on holiday was not what the doctor ordered. She didn't care how he smelled.

5

Arif

Catherine hit day two like a pro. Semi-pro? This assumption was based solely on her new tennis outfit and not that she had become an ace player overnight. Unal had equipped her with tennis gear from head to toe. It was too late to worry about what the bill would be. The items were well-chosen and in navy blue shorts and a light blue tee shirt, she did feel more of an insider. How did he know her exact size? The shoes were the latest style and felt so much lighter on her feet than what she had been wearing. The racket was the most expensive item. When she questioned the weight of it, because it was as light as a feather, he reassured her it would allow her control and power. All the pros were playing with it now and the good thing is it was guaranteed to last a lifetime. Before beginning her lesson, they watched a young boy and a middle-aged man in the middle of their game on Court A.

"That's Arif," Unal said. With great pride he went on to explain, "That man he is playing with is top player in our tennis club in Germany and still, my son beats him every time."

"Ah-riff?" she said slowly. She wanted to be sure of the pronunciation.

"Arif." He spelled it. "Very old Turkish name. "My grandfather, my father, same name. They skipped me." His attention went to the game. It was match point and Arif won. Both father and son let out a cheer. "See? I told you. One day, he gonna be tennis champ of Germany, then the world."

Unal called out to the boy in a loud, gruff voice, "Arif, come on over. You gonna speak smart English."

"Doesn't he speak English? I thought you said he went to the American School."

Misunderstanding her, he said, "Today Saturday. School Monday to Friday. In two days, he will get Christmas vacation."

"Lovely." She would have to phrase her sentences more carefully.

"How would you like to teach him smart English?"

"Smart English?"

"British English with good accent."

Catherine didn't know what to say. She was on holiday. Did she want to get involved this way? Did she want to spend that much time with the boy? With Unal?

"I thought about this last night. A business deal. In exchange for English lessons for the boy, I will give you tennis lessons. No charge. Good deal?"

Before Catherine could respond, she was being introduced to a tall, lean, very good-looking thirteen-year-old boy, who looked more like fifteen or sixteen, with longish medium blonde hair who didn't resemble his father in any way. He kept his eyes on the ground, obviously very shy about meeting the English lady. Catherine nodded, not wanting to overwhelm him with a gushing speech. However, she did congratulate him on a good game. He kind of shrugged, but she could tell he liked being praised.

While the son appeared very low key, the father had enough enthusiasm for all of them. "Hey, I got another great idea. Me and Arif are supposed to eat lunch with staff from hotel, but since I am professional tennis coach, I get special privileges and can eat anywhere in hotel same as hotel guest. Everything special for us. We have a good hotel apartment on second floor facing tennis court." She followed his pointed finger in the direction of the hotel. "It's a good deal all around. You eat lunch with us today. Is okay. No problem. I can fix it."

Catherine hesitated, not sure what to say. She would feel obligated to the two of them. She didn't want that. "I have a half-board plan. It includes breakfast and dinner, but not lunch. I have to pay for lunch if I want it."

"All the people have half-board. You don't pay if you eat with us." Unal reassured her he could get as much free food as he wanted, so it was no problem for her to eat lunch with them.

"Well, that's it, then. I'm not going to look a gift horse in the mouth." She hoped it didn't sound like she was looking for a handout.

"Is perfect. Here's plan. Arif, you get in the buffet line half past twelve and get food for three. I take my break at one, so is perfect. Outside near pool is good place to eat. Big plates. Lots of food." He put out his hands and mimed lifting a heavy plate.

Arif shook his head. "No, Papa," he said half under his breath. He was reluctant to do it. Then he said something in German.

Unal translated. "He's afraid they will see him taking too much food and stop him."

Catherine understood. The boy was embarrassed. She had an idea. "Why don't I go with you to the buffet, Arif? I can help carry the plates of food."

Arif shook his head and looked down at the ground. Unal insisted it was a good idea. Finally, Arif gave in. She found the boy so appealing that she forgot her own earlier reluctance about spending too much time with them.

Unal was pleased. "Okay. Problem solved. See? Catherine, you won the point. I told you. One night dancing, new tennis racket, new tennis shoes, new outfit, and you are new woman."

"New everything," she said. The meaning of her remark went way over the heads of her two new companions.

Standing in line at the buffet table, Catherine asked Arif, "Should we speak in Spanish, English, or German, not that I'm a linguist." She laughed and said, "Actually, I only speak English."

Arif thought it was funny, too. The shared laughter loosened his tongue. "I am not so good in Spanish, so we can speak in English because you do not speak German."

His speech was halted, not because he didn't know the language, but she knew it was because he was thinking of the correct way to say it. His accent was very different than his father's. It was more European, and his enunciation was very good. And so was his grammar most of the time; no doubt a result of his education at the American School.

"What does your father like to eat, Arif?"

"My father eats everything."

They piled their plates with food and Catherine explained each item to Arif. At least with the subject of food, Catherine was on her home turf. Onion soup, broccoli soup, roast beef, roast chicken, shrimp, salads, rice, pasta, cold food, hot food, relishes, garnishes, cheese, fruit. The desserts included cakes, pies, puddings, do-it-yourself ice-cream sundaes. All very attractively presented.

"You know the subject of food very well," he said.

"That is my business. Like tennis is yours."

Unal was already seated at a table and didn't get up to help them even though they were juggling three huge plates of food, napkins, utensils. It was a bit of a challenge, but they managed to fit everything on the table. Unal didn't wait for them as he dug in.

It was the first time Catherine had seen Unal eat a meal. Up to then, it had only been drinks and snacks. His eating habits were uncouth, to say the least. He grunted with every mouthful, talking, and chewing with his mouth open, not aware that pieces of food dribbled on his chin. Catherine caught Arif's look to her. Some kind of bonding? He was aware of his father's coarseness, but did his best to conceal his self-consciousness. Catherine was embarrassed and looked away. She remembered her mother once saying that if one ate with anyone for any length of time, one would find something disgusting about the other person's eating habits, no matter who the person was.

Unal was oblivious to everything but his food and the sound of his voice. "It is wonderful life. Canary Islands eight, nine months, and we got three, four months in Germany. That way, Arif plays tennis all year round, and I coach all year round. It is best of all worlds." He gave his son an affectionate light tap on the side of his head. "Eh, Arif? One day, you gonna be champ of Germany, then England, then United States, then the world."

The boy turned bright crimson.

"Arif, do they give you much homework at school?" Catherine asked, wanting to somehow save him.

"Yes. Lots." Quickly discovering a way out of his current situation, he announced he had to go do his homework so he could play tennis later in the day and help his father on the court. He nodded at Catherine, mumbled a quick goodbye, kissed his father on the cheek, said something in German, and ran towards the hotel.

Unal lit a cigarette. "I need this now. Good after big meal."

Catherine was intrigued by his smoking etiquette. It was strange how, as sloppy as he was with food, he was particularly immaculate with the cigarette ritual. First, the way he removed a cigarette from the pack and then the way he lit the cigarette. He didn't dangle it from his lips. He made sure it was out properly and put in an ashtray, not just stubbed out on the ground. His fingers weren't stained brownish-yellow from the tobacco. His teeth did not have that brown tell-tale sign of a smoker. She hadn't heard him wheeze on the tennis court. He didn't have a smoker's cough. He never smelled of stale smoke. Catherine found it all fascinating. More than that, she was fascinated that she was so fascinated. In London, she abhorred second-hand cigarette smoke and definitely would not go out with a man who smoked.

Despite the fact that she was relishing feeling warm in December, she could not drink the iced tea in a pitcher that was automatically served. Old habits die hard. She ordered hot tea. "I need this now," she said with a big smile, referencing his comment about needing a cigarette.

"So we have agreement? You help Arif with English lessons, and I give you tennis lessons. No charge. Tennis lessons cost a lot of money."

She was well-aware how expensive tennis lessons were, and she quite liked the idea of getting to know the boy better. Being busy in this way might prove a little more interesting than vegetating around the pool even though that was the purpose of a holiday.

Before she could give her answer, Unal explained that since it was Arif's vacation time, he would give her a tennis lesson early in the mornings while Arif played with a guest on the other court; then she would do the English lesson until lunchtime. They would all have lunch together by the pool. After lunch, Arif would help him on the tennis court for a couple of hours. Then he could study with Catherine until dinner. "And then after dinner…" Without warning, Unal effortlessly pulled her chair along the cement closer to him. His strength amazed her. Looking into her eyes, he said, "A woman without a man is no woman. Life in the sun with one man, no worries, is best life in the world. Make you fit. Make you look ten years younger. Great life in Canary Islands and Germany. You will feel good with Doctor Unal."

He totally brought up another subject, but maybe it wasn't another subject. Maybe she was missing the point. Maybe it was all the same subject. It wasn't a question. It wasn't a demand. What he said was a solution. And it startled Catherine. She wasn't aware she gave the impression she needed to be saved.

"Unal, I want to say something to you." She made sure she had his full attention. "I have a life and a home and work in London, thank you very much."

"You are not getting younger. Old man can always get a woman. Not the situation for woman. You must use your brain. I am alone same as you. Women come here, and even if the husband is here, they want to be with me. It's true."

"I don't need to know that." His presumptuousness disturbed her. "Unal, listen, I have a good job, a life in London, a family, and many many friends. I have a life."

"And yet, you are on holiday alone."

He hit a nerve. "It was a last minute decision," she said too quickly; too harshly.

"I got great idea. Tonight, you come with me to most special party. Friends I know many years live here in big villa ten minutes from hotel. Good food. Good music. You will see different world from people who come for vacation. No problem to get there. In my contract, I can drive hotel car anytime."

"What about Arif at night, if you're not here?"

"All arrangements with hotel. He not baby. He knows what to do. So is okay. We will go out, you and me." He stood up. "You a special lady. You wear nice outfit. I show you off. These people very high class. Best friends of mine." He didn't wait for her answer. "Okay, I got student now. You drink as much hot tea as you like. Do not leave tip. Everything is included. See you later." And he moved off.

Catherine didn't know if she felt comfortable or uncomfortable. She opted for slightly embarrassed which was the English stock in trade. She lingered over a second cup of tea and thought about what she had brought that she could wear to the party.

6

The Party

"HERE IN THE CANARY ISLANDS, LIFE GOES ON PEACEFULLY with respect and love. What else should life be required to give?" Christie told Catherine.

Christian and Christina Steifel. He was Chris. She was Christie. A gracious couple in their late fifties. They had retired from their teaching positions in Frankfort eighteen-months ago and following a visit to the island, bought a charming villa. Ten days was all it took for them to fall in love with Lanzarote. Catherine found the couple most charming as they talked about how much they loved the tranquility of their new lifestyle and adopted home, never regretting their decision.

Catherine hadn't expected the cosmopolitan group that comprised Spanish, German, and Turkish men and women, she being the sole Brit. Everyone was well-dressed in dressy casual attire. Her simple outfit of white silk slacks, a summer-weight light blue sleeveless sweater, and flat silver sandals had been a stellar choice. Unal was positively movie star handsome in light tan linen slacks and a black silk shirt. Seeing Unal through his choice of friends raised him up quite a few notches in her estimation.

Everyone spoke English. For her benefit? She couldn't be sure. There was a lot of tennis talk since they all took tennis lessons from Unal and played in the island tournament he arranged one Sunday a month. All the ingredients needed for a successful party were here: good conversation, laughter, music, wine, beer, and excellent food including some interesting German specialties that Catherine planned to incorporate into her repertoire when she got back home. While Catherine made her one glass of Chardonnay last, which meant it was rapidly moving from ice cold to lukewarm, Unal had four bottles of beers. Once again, she noticed and had to turn her eyes away from Unal's gross eating habits.

What seemed to be his only flaw was quickly forgotten when he took her in his arms and danced with her around the patio to the seductive tunes of Julio Iglesias. Unal up close and personal. As close as pages in a book. She couldn't help wonder if this is what the tennis coach did with the female hotel guests who were single. Was it part of his job? While the others at the party were polite to her face, were they snickering behind her back with know-it-all glances? If it was part of his job, he was a success. He danced only with her. He made sure she had enough to eat. He whispered sweet nothings in her ear. He didn't hide the fact that Catherine was number one. The hotel was a fairy land where people were determined to be happy whether they were happy or not. But here, at the Steifel's villa, away from the pseudo gaiety, there was a security; that maybe it was real; just maybe his attentions weren't part of Unal's job description.

The evening came to an end at one in the morning. People who were complete strangers a few hours ago filled her heart with unexpected warmth. All the goodbyes included an invitation from her host and hostess to visit again while she was on the island, with or without Unal.

This time, when he walked her to her suite, there was no goodnight, thank you for a lovely evening, I'm tired, see you in the morning on the tennis court. Despite being worlds apart intellectually, and she knew it was her own snobbish definition about what intellect was, the physical attraction between them couldn't be ignored. And so, intimate pleasures began without any thought of the ending.

7

Then Came Love

CATHERINE AND UNAL WERE TOGETHER FOR LUNCH, TENNIS, parties, evening walks along the beach. She felt an energy she had never felt. Their lovemaking often took place in the water. Under the stars, it was all so sensuous, so unforbidding, and so utterly agreeable.

Along came love with all its madness. Along came love with all its sadness. The tune and words of the song had haunted her ever since hearing the Australian composer/pianist, Grant Foster, at Wigmore Hall in London one evening a year ago. His song certainly applied to her now. She wondered what had happened in the composer's life to inspire such an emotional and moving piece.

Why are dreams so hard to find... from one bed to another... I found you... then came love with all its madness... with all its sadness. Then came love. But what comes after?

There was Unal. And there was Arif. Especially Arif. Their little life together included reading lessons, walks, talks, swimming in the sea. He had warmed up to her. He carried around books in English, showing off to all what he knew. He insisted they speak only in English. He wouldn't even speak to his father in German anymore. Catherine and her two men had become a tight threesome. There was one caveat that all the intense love-making with Unal couldn't erase. She was becoming painfully aware it was the son, not the father, who made her heart sing. Not in a romantic way. Heavens, no. It was a different feeling, something she had never felt before. All her deep-rooted maternal instincts were coming to the fore.

One afternoon, at the American Ice Cream Parlor in town, over sumptuous hot fudge sundaes loaded with chopped walnuts and whipped cream, Arif opened up about his early life. Dipping his spoon into the whipped cream in his dish, he said suddenly in a low voice, "My mother go away."

"Went. Went away," Catherine quietly corrected him, surprised at his openness. Usually they talked about words, about tennis, about swimming, about school, about books. She waited for what might come next.

"She went away one day and never come back. Came. I don't remember her too much. Very much."

"How old were you, Arif?"

"I think I was four or five. I'm not really sure. I remember, but I think I'm forgetting."

"That must have made you sad when she left." Catherine wanted to stay engaged in the conversation and wanted to keep him engaged because she thought it was healthy. It wasn't that she was being nosy. She truly felt it was good for the boy to talk about it.

"I was very young. My father was always there, so I don't remember too much at her. Of her. About her."

Catherine nodded. "Yes, that one. About."

He went on. "I'm getting bigger now and older. I am worried because I begin forget her."

Catherine didn't want to interrupt him by correcting his grammar. She just wanted him to talk.

"Sometimes, it's like she was never there. Sometimes, I think it's a bad thing. To forget, I mean. Is it bad?"

"Not bad, Arif, but it would be best not to think that. You should always remember."

"I must not forget. She was my mother."

"And she will always be your mother."

"You know what I mean?"

"I guess I can imagine it, but I haven't experienced it. Both my parents are alive, and I lived with them until I was twenty-four-years old. But just like you, I don't have any brothers or sisters."

"You don't like children? Is that why you don't have any?"

What a strange question. Was he asking how she felt about him? How should she answer? "No, Arif, I like children. As a matter of fact, I love children. I just never found the right man for a husband. It's very important for a woman to be in love with the man who fathers her children. To be married." As an aside, she added, "The trick is to stay in love."

"Why is it a trick?"

She'd said too much. "It's just an expression. No trick. Bad choice of a word."

Arif tilted his head. He was thinking. "You mean like magic?"

"Well, yes, one could say it's magic." *When it works.* "I've never been married so my knowledge is limited." She looked longingly at the boy. This was not the conversation to be having over hot fudge sundaes. His face, so innocent, made her want to reach out and touch him. But she held back. This makeshift family, inherited while on holiday, as important as it had become, was temporary and would soon be ending. She mustn't forget that. "Let's eat our ice-cream before it melts."

"Then we buy more."

"From the mouth of a tycoon."

"What?"

"Eat, *bitte*."

"No German. Speak English," he said laughing.

And so it went for the remainder of her holiday. A bond had developed between Catherine and Arif, never more evident than on New Year's Eve back at the Steifel's villa because he was with her and his father. At the stroke of midnight, Unal presented Catherine with a pair of pearl earrings. Arif wanted her to know he had helped pick them out. She complimented them on their good taste, kissing each of them on the cheek.

Catherine, Unal, and Arif stood awkwardly in the tiny Arrecife Airport lounge not really knowing how or wanting to say goodbye. Three weeks had passed like a weekend. Even with Unal begging her to change her flight and stay a little longer; even with Arif's silence telling her he didn't want her to go; she had to leave.

"You write me, Catherine, and we will send postcards from Lanzarote. Arif, you can write to her in English. Catherine, you keep playing tennis." He smiled and then placed his hands gently on either side of her face. He kissed both her cheeks. His lips were close to her lips when he whispered, "You coming back. I know."

She stood frozen, her arms tight against her sides. With Arif watching, she felt uncomfortable kissing or embracing Unal. He turned away from her and looked at his son who was now tearing up. He grunted, "Why you cry? It is good thing we meet the English lady. Good thing." He kissed Catherine lightly on the lips.

Catherine flinched slightly unable to return the kiss. She moved away from him closer to Arif who was standing very still, his wet eyes never leaving her face. With her fingers, she wiped away the tears streaming down his cheeks. It was all so surreal. She held out her arms to him. He went to her and let himself be enveloped by her embrace. She wasn't sure which one of them clung the tightest.

8

London

FOGGY, DAMP, FREEZING COLD. CATHERINE IMMERSED herself in preparations for upcoming catering engagements which would soon begin, but it was without her usual enthusiasm. When she wasn't working, she moped around the flat and watched her Lanzarote suntan fade to a grayish hue before disappearing completely. She had never minded the cold weather, but now she hated it. She always loved her work, but now she hated it. She now even hated the flat that she always loved. It was just the usual winter blues she told herself. It would pass. She couldn't forget the forlorn look on Arif's face at the airport. Once again, he had lost a mother figure. First, the biological mother and then the surrogate mother. What must he be feeling? More pieces of her heart being pulled at. The ringing phone snapped her out of her reverie. She answered without enthusiasm.

"Hello, *Frau* Aslan."

It took a second and a half to get it. "Unal!" The reference to being *Mrs.* Aslan frightened her.

"What am I gonna do about you?" His voice was mellow.

The question came as such a surprise, she couldn't answer. She couldn't tell if he was drunk or half asleep. When she could get her mouth to work, she said quietly but with great feeling, "I don't know what you should do about me."

"Catherine, Catherine, Catherine."

"I've been thinking about you, too. How are you?"

"My Catherine."

"Unal, is everything all right? Is anything wrong? Arif?"

"I miss you."

"I miss Lanzarote. I miss Arif. How is Arif?" She couldn't say she missed him. She did, in a way, but she couldn't put it into words.

"He won a big tennis tournament last Sunday. He made first in doubles and number three in singles. He got beautiful cup, big cup, and one week holiday for two persons in Las Palmas valid for two years."

"That's wonderful."

"He went back to school, but he doesn't want to do the homework."

"No homework? That isn't good."

"No good. No good. Today very hot again. I cannot work between twelve and three. Can't change the weather. Better than snow and ice. What about your tennis?"

"No, it's too cold."

"See? I told you. You need sun. Catherine, what should I do?"

"I'm not really sure."

"Come back to us. We will live in the hotel apartment."

"Unal, I was on holiday. Three weeks in the hotel is different than… than forever."

"Forever sounds good. Better, I will rent a house near hotel. Good idea, huh? You like?"

"I…don't… " And then she went quiet. She had to gather her wits. What could she say to him? This was a turn she hadn't expected. Her hesitancy didn't deter him.

"I have an apartment in Germany."

"Oh?" Had he told her that before? She would have remembered that.

"Small, but nice. Near Wittlich. Small town. It isn't London, but very nice atmosphere. Me and Arif go in few months. I teach tennis to the fat ladies at the private club, I told you. Lots of money. Then we come back to Lanzarote. Next time, I will bring my Mercedes from Germany. You can drive. I can leave it here and buy cheap used car in Germany to get around. It's a good life. You will feel good with Doctor Unal. You remember? How Doctor Unal took care of you? You looked ten years younger."

The pitch. "It sounds good." And then quickly, "About the car, I mean." Was he proposing? Maybe not marriage exactly, but it was a proposal. She hadn't quite figured on this. He had slipped into his seductive tone, and she was once more on the edge of succumbing to his charms. *Remember his smell. Never mind that. Remember the way he eats!*

"Next year, Arif will go to play tournaments in Passau. You go with him like official manager."

Tempting as it was, could she really do it? How to handle this now? She'd best be honest, not lead him on. "I can't just leave my life here. My business, my parents, my friends." This was nuts.

"You are alone like me. What life is that? I ask you to think about it."

At least that was a reasonable request if he meant it. "I will think about it," she said in all seriousness.

"Okay. Now you make me very happy."

"Okay."

"Okay."

"May I speak to Arif now?"

"Arif is sleeping. It's very late here."

"Quite right. Of course. Of course. The time difference. Well, say hello to him for me."

"Tomorrow I run big tournament for island players. I will call you in two days. You tell me your answer then."

"Okay." Two days would give her some thinking time, some breathing space

They said their goodbyes quickly.

He hadn't told her he loved her. She hadn't told him she loved him. She couldn't even send her love to Arif. Had it just been a holiday romance that she would get over? That Unal will get over? But what about Arif? What about the boy? The boy. The boy. What was he feeling? At his age, is it a case of out of sight, out of mind? She didn't know. She just didn't know.

Catherine opened her eyes. Pieces of it at first, then as she focused, it came back to her. Was it a sign?

In an open space, there was a railroad track with two black trains. One was shiny and bright; the other was weather worn and faded. The grass was bright emerald green because it never stopped raining. Inside the faded train, her faceless lover and she danced naked. Rhumba, mambo, samba, cha cha, meringue. They made love all day every day. They drank white wine and laughed and danced. Then one day, without warning, she hated the rain, she hated the music, she hated the train, she hated the lover. She dressed and walked onto the unused, shiny train. It moved through tunnel after tunnel. It was dark, but she wasn't afraid. The train came to a great open, desert-like space with sun so hot the grass was the color of pale straw. A man who sported a blond crew cut greeted her. He wore a light blue seersucker suit, a white shirt, a blue tie. He extended one of his hands out to her. Smiling, she took it and stepped down from the train. In the next scene, without warning, she hated the sun. She hated the man. She missed the rain. Most of all, she yearned for that part of her that was true. She threw off her clothes and returned to the rhythmic beat of the rhumba.

The dream had rattled her. Half past six. The hour when her parents would begin to stir. Without as much as a good morning into the phone, Catherine said, "Mom, how about coming up to the big city? We can have lunch at our favorite haunt. Please don't say no. I need you."

"Just what every mother wants to hear. Her daughter needs her. I gather you prefer I come up rather than you come down?"

"Yes. I have an event this evening in Mayfair."

"Say no more. It's been months since I've been to London. Your dear father can manage without me for half a day. I believe there's a late morning train. Let's say half one at the restaurant."

Simultaneously, they entered The Fountain Restaurant in Fortnum's on the corner of Duke and Jermyn Streets and greeted one another with a fond embrace. Catherine was always amazed at how young her sixty-five-year-old mother looked and prayed she had inherited her genes. In a gray pantsuit, a black woolen coat, and black patent leather boots, Mary Stewart was a cut above the ordinary. Her blue eyes sparkled, as they always did. She'd worn the same short hairdo that framed her heart-shaped face ever since Catherine could remember. And she was lucky because when red hair starts to fade, it takes on a blonde hue rather than gray.

Newly refurbished, but still offering Fortnum's classic dishes, the restaurant had a special meaning for them both for nostalgic personal reasons. When Catherine was a child, whenever they went up to London, it was where they would have lunch. The restaurant's dining style was casual elegant, the cuisine was British and could always be relied on.

Once seated, menus didn't have to be consulted because they never wavered on their choices. For Catherine, it was Fortnum's Welsh Rarebit with herbed tomato and char-grilled back bacon. Even she, with her culinary skills, could never quite replicate it. For Mary, her favorite was seared salmon salad with mint mayonnaise. Still water with lemon, no ice, was the choice of beverage for them both.

Catherine didn't waste any time getting into every detail about Lanzarote, about its weather, about tennis, about the people, about the hotel, about the food. And finally, about what was really on her mind.

Her mother listened without interrupting.

"That's it. That's everything."

Mary was still.

"You're very silent."

"There is a time to speak and a time to listen."

"I don't know what to do, Mother. Do I go back? Do I forget the whole thing ever happened? Do I do a long distance thing? I'm not really asking. I know I'm the one who has to ultimately make the decision, and I want you to tell me what that decision is going to be."

The arrival of their food was timely as it gave Mary a chance to pause and think of her answer. Mother's opinion wouldn't count for much in a situation like this. She took a sip of her water. Was this the time to be truthful or diplomatic or a meddling mother? She cleared her throat before speaking. "You know, my darling, all I want is for you to be happy. That's all any mother wants for her children."

"I know that." Catherine wasn't sure what her mother was getting to.

"And you know I've always thought you were a bit too fussy when it came to men."

"Yes, you've always said that. That's why I need your advice now."

"Yes, I know." Mary sighed and shrugged a shoulder. She tilted her head slightly and studied her daughter. She knew nothing of this man in the Canaries. What could she say? She could hardly give advice, but she had to. Her daughter was waiting.

"Well? Surely, you have an opinion. What do I do?"

"I can't answer that immediately." She took another sip of water. Avoiding the topic at hand, she changed the subject. "I must say, Christmas wasn't the same without you."

Conversation waned for a few moments while they took a slight respite to finish their meal.

Mary looked at her daughter who seemed so forlorn. There wasn't anyone more confident when it came to business, but when it came to her personal life, she just couldn't seem to ever make it work. "What about that nice British chap, Will Waddington? From Cornwall, isn't it?"

Catherine shook her head. "Uh-uh. No way. No way. No way. Acute alcoholism."

"Dear Catherine, haven't I taught you that we all have our isms in some form or another?"

"It isn't possible. He's in love with the bottle. I mean, seriously in love."

"That can come from being a product of inherited wealth."

"What?"

"Sometimes one doesn't realize one's own worth; therefore, one must imbibe. Fortunately, that was not the case with your father growing up with all that money and then finally inheriting it. He never had to work at a real job in his entire life; yet, he was a solid chap when I met him. Still is. He knew who he was. Still does. As for Will, he might change. People do change."

How could she put this to end the subject of Mister Waddington? "I didn't like the *me* that came out when I was with him."

"And you think this Lanzarote love can develop into the real thing? Oh my, I've made a pun. *And* an alliteration. I don't do that often. Love for tennis. Lanzarote love." The look on her daughter's face told her she may have gone too far. "Sorry, luv. I mean, sorry, Catherine. Just trying to cheer you a bit."

"I know."

"You think something could develop with this man, this… Unal?"

"I don't know. Maybe. I don't know."

"You don't really know him, do you?"

"I know enough. I know I was happy. Lanzarote has a peaceful air about it. I read that Agatha Christie went there in the twenties for rest and relaxation."

"You were on holiday, Catherine darling. Everyone's happy on holiday. Let me remind you in case you've forgotten, darling, London hasn't exactly run out of eligible men. You're bound to find someone here. You know so many people. It might be someone you already know." While only wanting her daughter's happiness, she didn't trust this new infatuation. Surely, that's all it was. She didn't want her Catherine to move away to the Canary Islands to join up with a tennis coach, no less one with a young son. It didn't sound like a stable situation. "Will you live together? I mean in the same place? At the hotel? You've never lived with a man. I always naturally thought it would be with a husband."

"I guess that's the idea. Yes." And it hit her. She would be living with a stranger and his son.

Mary looked worried. "You mustn't settle. Life is a book. You don't know what's on the next page until you turn it.

"I know."

"It's the boy, isn't it?"

"I don't know. No. Yes, he's a big part of it. Yes." And there it was. She had to admit it was Arif. She didn't want to be without the boy.

"Oh, luv, you have to rethink this. You were there for only three weeks. Way too short a time to make life-altering decisions."

"You always told me that you and daddy didn't know each other very long."

"There is a vast difference between two young Brits who meet in a train station on their home turf and an educated British woman and a Turkish tennis coach meeting at a hotel off the coast of Africa on her holiday."

"Is it really so different?"

"The two can't be compared."

"My head knows that, but my heart doesn't."

"This is one time you must listen to your head."

"How many chances do we get in our mid-thirties? At any age? You know what I want, and you know what I've been through to find it. Something's always missing."

"But there's the business. You've worked hard to build it."

"I can get the girls in. There's Brett and Jill and Carolyn. They've been dying to do more. I'm booked for the next six months. Regulars. They can handle it. They'll love it."

"But clients expect Catherine Stewart in person."

"I'll notify everyone personally. They will still get the same service and the same quality. The girls are well-trained. If I've done my job, *Elegant Tastes* should be able to carry on without me."

"It won't be the same, and I guarantee you will lose some business. Maybe the entire business."

"This is something I have to do, Mother, don't you see? I've discovered there's more to life than just planning meals and cooking for other people." Talking it out with her mother helped her get closer to her decision.

"You will regret it."

"You can only regret what you don't do."

After a slight pause, Mary said, "I don't believe you believe a word of what you just said."

There was another pause during which neither of them spoke. Mary Stewart wanted her to daughter's happiness above anything, but this new… she wasn't sure what to call it… thing… was too much to grasp. Her daughter was old enough to make her own decisions, she knew that, but this was beyond anything expected. Mary blamed herself. If she hadn't supported and encouraged her daughter to go to the Culinary Institute, she might have remained in Hampshire where women married their daughters to the sons of neighbors. Sensible matches, keeping it in the family, so to speak. Not literally the family, of course. As for love? Love could come later. Children would be their mutual bond. It was still love. The employment of cooks and nannies would allow time for real family togetherness. A kind of blissful ignorance.

Catherine wasn't saying anything. Mary got the message.

"It appears you've made up your mind. What about the flat? What happens with that? Will you sell it?"

"No." Catherine had it figured out. "The business is based there. Staff will do the prepping and most of the cooking there. It won't sit there empty."

"Are you really allowed to do that? In the flat, I mean?"

"Clients don't come in and out. I own the flat. You know all that, Mother. We've been doing it for years. It's perfectly legal. I'm not running a restaurant in the flat. Why question it now?"

It was true. She knew all that. Her tone softened now. "Well, that's settled then, but I just don't know, luv. I'm concerned about you all alone on a strange island."

"I won't exactly be alone."

Mary looked at her daughter almost as if seeing her for the first time. "I'll look in on the flat, if you like. I could do that from time to time. That will be my holiday. Your father won't come up to London. He hates the city. I like London, but in short bursts only."

"I can always count on you, but are you sure you want that responsibility?"

Her mother nodded. "Of course. Well, then, you'd better get on with it and make the flight arrangements." Mary didn't like the sound of any of it. "Best to make it an open return ticket, don't you think? You know… just in case. I believe the airline gives you up to a year to use it. And you never know. You might have to pop back suddenly for something or other. The business. A doctor's appointment."

Catherine hadn't thought of an open ticket, but it was a good idea. "I'll do that. Thanks awfully. You're wonderful. I mean it."

"I can't imagine what your life will be."

"I'm going to play tennis and do the rhumba."

"The rhumba is a Latin dance. What on earth are you going on about?"

"A dream I had. I'll tell you about it one day."

"I shall look forward to it. Well, then, shall we concentrate now on the pressing issue at hand?"

"Pressing issue?" Catherine was of the opinion the pressing issue was her quandary about oh, nothing much, only her life. Apparently not.

"Food, my darling. Dessert."

"What?" Catherine was astounded. In all the years she'd known her mother, the woman never ate pudding or sweets of any kind. It was the secret to maintaining her girlish figure.

"Don't look so shocked. People can change."

They both forgot their waistlines and ordered the popular chocolate brulee with cinnamon shortbread.

Catherine loved her mother very much and valued their relationship. The ideal existence would be to lift up everything and everyone she had in London and Hampshire and move it and them to the Canary Islands.

9

On Being Noble

THRUST INTO DOMESTICITY IN THE SPACIOUS APARTMENT Unal had rented near the hotel, Catherine's role as lover, mother, cook, and let's face it, charwoman, was instantaneous. It came as rather a surprise as she hadn't really thought it through. It was hardly the same as when she was a guest at the hotel on holiday. This package deal, to put it bluntly, had come with major responsibilities. It certainly was a new experience. She wondered if this is what marriage was like. In fact, wasn't this a marriage? No legal piece of paper, but still, a commitment. Patience would have to be the keyword now. She was in the process of a reinvention. Her own.

During one of their weekly phone calls, Catherine told her mother, "I've never looked better. I play tennis every single day, my skin is turning a gorgeous bronze tone, I lost those few extra pounds I could never lose. I'm as firm as a twenty-five year old."

"And no one sees you." Mary Stewart didn't mean to be unkind. "Sorry. It just slipped out."

Catherine took a slight offense at the remark. "That isn't true. I see tons of people."

"Of course, you do. Lots of people holiday in that part of the world. You're being careful in the sun, aren't you? With your fair skin? And what about your hair? I hope you wear a hat during the day."

"Yes, not to worry, I know how to do it. By the way, how is daddy taking all this?"

"If you must know, darling, he doesn't know. I've told him you are working on a special assignment on an Italian cruise ship as some kind of presenter and instructor. That sort of thing. I thought it best for now, don't you?"

Catherine kept in close touch with the business. Her assistants didn't seem to have any problems with running things in her absence. The Spanish language came surprisingly easily. German was a little more difficult. Her daily routine fell into a pattern. During the week, after walking Arif half a mile to school in the morning, she did a few general household chores before walking the quarter mile to the hotel where she played tennis with hotel guests and then joined Unal for lunch. It was all very pleasant, but it was the after school part she cherished when she could spend time with Arif. She prepared meals in the evening for the three of them at the apartment when they didn't eat at the hotel or at a restaurant. In the evening, Unal would often return to the hotel for public relations, as he called it. Catherine knew he was drinking with his tennis students, hanging out at the bar, probably going into the nightclub. It didn't worry her in the least. She was happy to be alone with Arif. They read, played cards, or just chatted. It was the time she liked best.

Whatever the routine during the week, the three of them would spend more time together at the weekend, working around Unal's instructing schedule. Unal and Arif tried teaching Catherine how to play Skat, the national card game of Germany. It was so complicated that she never really got it, no matter how many times they explained that each player is dealt ten cards, each hand begins with an auction, the winner in the bidding becomes the declarer and plays against the other two. Thirty-two cards are used. She listened, she tried, but it was beyond her.

"Is easy," Unal said. "Two of us against person who makes game. If that person loses, score is doubled. Contra. Means double. Thirty-two cards, ten each. Two on table for person making game. He can take the two and turn two down or if he does not take, he gets points based on his call. Jack is normal card, not trump."

"You lost me an hour ago." She absolutely could not understand what the hands meant or who was doing what to whom. She never minded them making fun of her inability to pick up what to them came as second nature. At least, they were all laughing. Finally, they gave up and settled for *her* favorite game. Scrabble. Unal hated it. Arif loved increasing his English vocabulary this way.

It was an appealing package for this single, childless woman. How could she explain it? The whole thing had become quite addictive. When the honeymoon, so to speak, was over, and that more or less had happened when she was on holiday, she realized conversations with Unal were either about sex, tennis tournaments, the new tennis ball machine, Arif, or how good looking she was in her new life without business worries and with sun, thanks to him. The more intelligent conversations were with the boy. The truth was she was painfully conscious of the fact that she was caring less and less for Unal. They made love and laughed and danced and played tennis, but she was aware that Arif was her main reason for being there. He had started calling her *mutti*, the German word for mommy used by a child. Catherine didn't object. She liked it. The boy's grasp of the English language was almost flawless. He read books only in English. He made lovely little gifts for his adopted mother at school. His speech was gradually becoming British English, with a trace of a charming European accent.

Arif and Catherine were discovering how similar they were. Neither of them cared for the nightlife scene, both were morning people, they liked to walk and swim and talk a lot and read and play tennis, and they both absolutely loved hot fudge sundaes.

One evening, he confessed unashamedly, "I wish it was just the two of us without my father."

"Arif, you can't mean that." Catherine was shocked at his admission.

"He eats like an animal. You see it. I know you see it. Everyone laughs behind his back. It embarrasses me."

Feeling very uncomfortable with Arif's shift of allegiance, not to mention her own shift, she listened to his complaints, saying nothing. What was there to say?

Another gorgeous Sunday. Blue sky, not a ripple in the sea, peace all around, hotel guests enjoying Sunday brunch. The three of them were splashing around in the hotel pool. Playfully, Unal pushed Catherine under the water. Only a few weeks ago, Arif would have joined his father in the game against Catherine, but not this time. This time, Arif turned against his father, lashing out at him in German, trying to force his head under water. Unal was too strong for his son and laughed it off. But Catherine knew it wasn't a joke.

The man that Arif had depended on for his very life was becoming insignificant to him. Catherine was concerned. She wanted to believe it was just a part of adolescence and would pass, but she wasn't convinced. Although her feelings for Unal hadn't developed into love, her feelings for the boy had. He needed her. And she needed him. She had found the missing ingredient. She was the mother. He had become her child, but the last thing she wanted to do was turn son against father. The so-called game ended with Unal trotting off to mingle with hotel guests, leaving Arif and Catherine to their own devices. A sly look towards her from Arif and she knew that's exactly what he wanted. So did she.

Something was happening that wasn't right, and she was haunted by the turn of events. She wasn't sure if she should talk to Unal about it. About Arif's shift of allegiance. Would he understand? How much would she say? He would probably brush it off saying it was part of growing up, that Arif was still a baby. Best to say nothing. But she did tell him what was going on, and she was right. He brushed it off as totally insignificant, not in those words, just as Catherine knew he would. How misguided his thinking was. It didn't forebode well at all.

Shortly after the pool incident, something else happened. One afternoon Catherine and Arif were at the tennis courts watching the players. Unal was teaching. He asked for Arif's help to pick up the balls.

Arif's answer was uncharacteristically terse. "I must do a book report for school." It was the first time he had openly disobeyed his father in public.

Unal's temper was short. He turned on Catherine, shouting, "You're making Arif into a goddamn girl."

Arif's face went white. His whole body clenched. He was angry that his father had shouted at her. He looked at her. She gave him a look that said to say nothing.

Unal got over his explosion quickly. "Okay. Okay. Better he does the homework. I can get tennis student guest from hotel to help pick up tennis balls and run ball machine. Is okay. Okay, Arif? You concentrate on school and your tennis game. Is okay?"

Arif shrugged and mumbled under his breath, "Okay."

"*Gut.*" Unal seemed satisfied. He smiled and said, "Oh, sorry, English only. I mean good. You're gonna be champ, Arif. All okay."

Arif shrugged again. "Okay."

To Catherine, it didn't sound okay at all. The issue had not been resolved at all, but she didn't think it was her place to interfere.

After school one Friday afternoon, Arif and Catherine were having a snack in the apartment.

"Let's go for a swim, *mutti.*"

"What about homework? Best to do it today so you can be free Saturday and Sunday."

"No homework this weekend."

"All right then, we'll go to the pool at the hotel."

"Aw, come on, not the pool."

"I thought you liked the pool. It's water. Swimming is swimming."

"The pool is boring. I mean the ocean."

"The red flag is posted. It's too dangerous."

Swimming in the ocean was one of their favorite pastimes and something they did often. They were both strong swimmers, but today, Catherine was against it. It was more than dangerous. The flag was a warning that absolutely no one was to go in the water.

"They always do that. If it rains a little, they put up the red flag," Arif said, pouting to make his point. "It will be all right. We can do it," Arif insisted.

"Today we should swim in the pool."

Once Arif got something in his head, it was difficult to dissuade him. It had been drizzling and Arif was right. They did tend to post the warning sign as a precaution sometimes even if it wasn't needed.

Catherine was cautious. "I don't know. What if this time, they mean it? Something might come up suddenly."

"Come on, *mutti*. You will be safe. I'll be with you. I'm strong."

It was difficult to say no to Arif, and he seemed to want to do this today really badly. Reluctantly, she agreed. As they walked the short distance down to the beach, Catherine eyed the red flag. She laid out the rules. "We must stay close to shore. We must stay together. And we mustn't stay in a long time."

Arif raced into the water ahead of Catherine. "See? It's very calm," he shouted. "Come on in."

Catherine waded in, staying close to shore.

"Come on." He swam further and further away from her. "That's far enough."

If he heard her, he wasn't listening because he kept going.

"Come back. Arif, come back." She never took her eyes

off him. Was she being too cautious? It seemed calm enough. The calm before the storm?

It began as a gentle flow coming in tiny gentle waves. She kept calling out to him to come back. When he didn't reverse, she swam out towards him, struggling to ride the waves, calling out his name. But he couldn't hear her. The light breeze quickly manifested itself into a gale. Light wind to turbulence in less than a second. The waves were gigantic, higher and stronger than they'd ever been. The red flag warning hadn't been an exaggeration today. She saw it. The large raised ridge of water moving across the surface of the sea directly in her path. She couldn't swim out of the way and didn't know how to swim into it to ride the waves.

And because when it hits, it hits angrily with blinding speed, too quick for any human to escape. She slipped further and further away, half in and half out of the cold water. Helpless and drifting with only one thought: *No, God, please, not a watery grave.* Then it went black. In and out of semi-consciousness. A voice she could barely hear telling her everything was all right, telling her to relax, telling her it was okay. A vise-like grip on her wrist pulled her along.

Arif swam the long distance to the shore, guiding her limp, barely-conscious body, every few seconds checking to make sure her face stayed out of the water. He dragged her over jagged rocks onto warm wet sand where they collapsed and lay panting. Slowly, Catherine opened her eyes. She coughed and gagged; eyes stinging. It was difficult to speak. Then, finally, something that sounded like, "What happened?"

"You put your arm up out of the water. I swam to you and pulled you in."

She remembered none of it. They lay side by side on their stomachs without speaking, their eyes fixed on one another. Neither cared that their legs were scratched and bleeding. The crashing waves were just a faint sound in the distance now. Mature adults know that eventually all storms subside. Somehow, by the grace of God, they had outwitted the red flag. Their lives had been spared. Arif's quick thinking and fearlessness had saved her life and probably his own. What if she had drowned? What if he was out there alone? And then it struck her—he might have died. What would have happened then?

After a few moments, Arif said firmly, "Now that this adventure is over, we will not tell my father." It was not the voice of a child.

Catherine had stopped coughing, but her breath was still labored. "I don't think that's a good idea." Their faces were nearly touching. Her speech was faltered. "We should tell him. We must tell him. He's your father."

"It will be our secret," he pleaded softly.

She couldn't give him the answer he wanted. She was breathing a little more evenly now. "You know, Arif, when I went under, my eyes must have been open because I remember it was all black. I don't remember raising up my arm. But somehow you were there. You saved my life."

"Were you frightened?" he asked.

"I wasn't frightened exactly because I wasn't aware of the seriousness of what was happening. Because I must have been unconscious or partly unconscious. I think that's the explanation. But I'm frightened now." Not tell Unal? What was she to do?

"I was never frightened. I only had the one thought to save you."

"I was swimming out to you. I thought you had gone too far. I thought you were the one in trouble."

"Please, *mutti*, we must not tell him."

She wondered what punishment awaited him if his father found out what had happened. The boy would certainly suffer for it, and who knows what price she would have to pay. She couldn't bear any of it. Going against every part of her belief system, she agreed. "It will be our secret."

"That is good," he said. "Oh, look, there's a rainbow." He was a little boy again.

In a few weeks, they would be leaving Lanzarote for a small town in Germany. Arif would be playing in tournaments in Germany and Austria, and she would be expected to accompany him. Unal would be teaching tennis at the local tennis club. Where did Catherine Stewart fit in this picture? She was the illegitimate mother, the reluctant lover, the misplaced person. What had she done here? All of it had been her choice. Was her father right about her? If there were ninety-nine normal men and one aberrant in a room, he's the one she would gravitate towards. She knew what she had done; the question was what was she to do?

While Arif was at school, Catherine would walk down to the beach and when the sea was calm, she swam and swam and swam. The physical acts of walking and swimming were a blessing. That's when it came to her. There was only one solution. With the coolness of an actress playing a starring role in a play, Catherine announced casually to Unal and Arif during dinner one evening, "I have to go to London to take care of some business." Keeping her delivery light, she served up dessert, explaining it was a new twist on an old recipe. She couldn't look at either one of them.

"What business?" asked Unal. There was a hint of mistrust in his question. "You told me you have people running business." His eyes narrowed as he looked at her.

"Oh, not with the catering business. It's to do with the flat," she lied, not looking up from her apricot crumble. "It's an owner's association meeting I must attend in person. I... I won't be long."

She was beating around the bush. She couldn't tell them she was leaving. So she lied by telling them she wouldn't be long. "I have to sign some papers." She was being cruel to be what she hoped would be kind.

"They can send papers to sign."

"I know, but apparently I have to do it in person. It's because I run a business from my residence." Her voice cracked. Lying had never been her strong suit.

Unal was silent. Then he spoke. "No problem. You can go and be back in three, four days tops. I will pay for your ticket. You not worry."

Arif hadn't said anything. He was sulking. And then he let it all out. "I don't want you to go, *mutti*," he shouted, slamming his fork down on the table.

His harsh behavior surprised Catherine. Had he sensed the true meaning behind her words? Surely he was overreacting to her being away for the alleged few days. They had developed a closeness these past months. He knew. He had to know she was lying. She picked up his fork and held it out to him. Arif grabbed the fork and threw it violently on the floor. It missed her bare foot by an inch.

"Arif, don't, please don't," Catherine said loudly. Immediately sorry that she had raised her voice, she repeated the words quietly. "Arif, don't, please don't." She was in physical pain.

Unaware of the dynamic going on here, Unal began to laugh. Pumping his fist up and down in an obscene gesture, he said gruffly, "I will have good rest."

Catherine ignored the meaning of his racy suggestion and blurted out, "Come with me, Arif. You can come with me." The words hung in the air and seemed to be coming from somebody else.

"I...I can't miss school...I..." He looked at his father for help.

"School will be finished," she continued without giving any thought to what she was saying.

"And the tournaments. I have tournaments," a confused Arif continued.

"In London, they have real schools." Her chest hurt so much, she thought it must be her heart splitting in half.

"What the hell are you talking about?" Unal asked, raising his voice. "Are you crazy? Weather is bad. He won't be able to play tennis."

"The weather is good now," Catherine said. It was hardly a discussion about a four-day trip. Nothing had been said about her not coming back; yet, that's what it had become without the actual words. Arif and she were having one conversation while she and Unal were having a totally different conversation. And there was the third silent conversation between Unal and Arif.

"Don't be stupid. He cannot go with you." Unal dug into his food. He was the only one who was having no difficulty swallowing.

"I don't want you to go," Arif said again. He was on the verge of tears. His face looked blue to her. Catherine had never seen him like this. These were not the tears he shed at the airport the first time she left after the holiday. This was not the brave boy who had pulled her out of the ocean to safety.

"You're overreacting. Both of you. I'll be back. I'll be back." What else could she say? It didn't even sound convincing to her. What must it sound like to a thirteen-year- old?

"You won't come back." Arif was wild with fury. He said it again, this time in German adding a nasty, *"Das ist mir egal."*

Catherine was lost. There it was, out in the open. His biggest fear. She wasn't coming back. He had nailed the truth. It was his "I don't care" in German that hit below the belt.

"Nicht gut. Nicht gut. It is joke, Arif. Catherine is coming back," Unal said, looking at Catherine for the first time.

"Yes... I'll... I will... " She couldn't finish the sentence.

"You're not coming back!" Arif ran to the wall where the congratulatory poster she had made for him after he won a

Sunday tournament was hanging. With a fierce gesture, he pulled it down and ripped it into a thousand little pieces, all the while crying out, "You are not my friend. I hate you, I hate you, I hate you."

"No. You don't mean that. You don't mean that. Arif, please listen." She couldn't go on. What was she going to say? That she was running out? That his instincts were spot on? That he knew she was lying? That she wasn't coming back?

Arif turned on his father next. "I hate you, I hate you. It is because of you she is going away. She hates you. It is your fault. You are a stupid man."

"*Nein*," Unal growled, leaping up from his chair. He grabbed Arif by the shoulders and slapped the boy hard across the face.

Arif began to sob uncontrollably. Catherine gasped. She knew his cries weren't just from the pain of Unal's hand across his cheek. She wanted to reach out to him, but her arms just hung in the air. How she longed to go to him, but she couldn't. Couldn't and mustn't. So she didn't. She was crying now, too. Unal shouted at both of them to stop the goddamn crying as he stormed out of the apartment. Arif looked at Catherine with blistering hate before he ran to his room and slammed the door shut with such force that the whole apartment shook. She tried talking to him through the door but to no avail. How did she think this was going to play out? She went into the room she shared with Unal and sobbed into her pillow. Too tired to get undressed, from sheer exhaustion, she eventually fell asleep.

It was light out when she opened her eyes. She had never felt so completely drained. Only then was she aware that she had actually slept. It came back to her. The scene. The horrible scene. It was quiet in the apartment. Too quiet. She opened her door and peered out. The door to Arif's room was wide open. She was alone. She quickly showered and dressed. It was now or never. She threw some vitals in two suitcases, purposely leaving all the tennis gear, bathing suits, anything remotely island-ish behind. Without checking flight times, she rang for a taxi to take her to the airport, enormously grateful for the open return ticket that had been her mother's suggestion. It was of no consequence how long she would have to wait at the airport for a flight. As it turned out, it would be a five hour wait for the next flight out to make her connection to London. It would feel like twenty-five hours, but it didn't matter.

Periodically, she checked the entrance to the terminal. Would they come after her? More fearful that they might. Suddenly, she was afraid of Unal. Of his volatile temper, of what he might do to the boy, to her. But now it was *them* against her. Now, *she* was the outsider. Wasn't this the whole point of her action? Wasn't that as it should be?

10

Home Again

ELEGANT TASTES WAS BOOMING, AND SHE WAS GRATEFUL for that. It felt good to be good at something. And yet, the hole in her heart was evident, looming greater than before. What everyone wanted, couldn't find, didn't cost anything. Love.

Of course, London hadn't changed. London never changed. It was a sobering revelation. Life more or less resumed. At least, the business side of her life. Friends were intentionally avoided. She just wasn't ready for socializing. The parents welcomed her back. Alone with her mother, Catherine let it all out and cried a little and felt relieved to be able to talk about it where she felt safe. There wasn't any, 'I told you so,' from Mary Stewart. She chose a more rational path.

"Darling, blood is thicker than water. Always remember that. Eventually, they would have turned on you. This way, you left with your dignity. You behaved appropriately, however dramatic a turn your exit took. In this situation, you put others ahead of yourself. That's a very Stewart thing to do. A very noble thing. The boy will get over it," she said, hoping to ease her daughter's pain. "It may seem harsh, but he needs his father more than he needs you. Unal is probably courting another woman as we speak. I'm not saying that to be unkind, but from all you've said, he strikes me as that sort of man."

"I know you're not being unkind."

"You need a nice sensible English chap." And as if it were an afterthought or perhaps something she just discovered, "Like your father. That's the ticket. Just start looking in the right places. If it's meant, and I'm sure it is, you will meet someone. You really will."

"I know all that, but it isn't what I mean. Don't you see? It was the boy who made my heart sing. It's the boy." And with that, a flood of tears escaped from somewhere deep within and drenched her lovely face.

"Oh, I see. I see." She handed her daughter a clean white hankie from her pocket.

Catherine took it and dabbed. In the midst of all this, she was very aware that fancy Swiss handkerchiefs were still a part of their lives. There was elegance to who they were. Who she was. She mustn't forget that.

"Perhaps you could volunteer at a children's home or a school. You could teach them cooking. Even better, get involved with Jamie Oliver's outfit. *Fifteen*, I think it's called. Juvenile delinquents are being taught how to cook. He's saving lives. You know him, don't you? That would be a wonderful thing for you to do, wouldn't it? In addition to *Elegant Tastes*, of course."

"Mother, for godsake. Don't. Please!" Catherine was outraged by her suggestions. It was the most insensitive thing she had ever heard her mother say.

Understanding the look on Catherine's face, Mary said. "No, of course not. Sorry. I don't know what I was thinking. Please stop crying. I just can't stand to see you so unhappy."

"I'm a mess."

"You're not a mess."

"I feel like carrot puree without the carrots. I'm salad Niçoise without the tuna. Rosemary country bread without the rosemary. Cheese and crackers without the cheese. Scrambled eggs without the eggs."

Before she could listen to anymore of this self-deprecating talk, Mary interrupted. "That's all a bit dramatic, don't you think, luv?"

"No matter what I do, there is always something missing in the love department."

"You just haven't found the missing ingredient. You will." At least her daughter had stopped sobbing.

"In my professional life, I shine." Her father was right. She was attracted to the only man on the lake rowing with one oar. "Will I ever be able to stop talking and thinking about Arif, about Unal, about Lanzarote? Will this chapter ever be behind me?"

Mary chose her words carefully. "It leaves a hole when one loses someone. A break-up, a death, a divorce. Loss. Nothing brings them back. One has to keep going and believe in time the picture will become less like a sharp photographic image and more like a Monet painting. Rather fuzzy. There, but not so prominent. Does that make sense?"

"In other words, we carry on. Life goes on."

"One door closes; another opens."

11

Recovery

It took every bit of discipline not to write or ring Unal, not to get on a plane and go back. Not for him. For Arif. For that beautiful boy. Was he winning tennis tournaments in Passau? Had Unal found another *frau*? Did they ever discuss her? What if Unal rang? What if Arif wrote? Would she respond? She prayed her dilemma would never be tested. And she prayed she could one hundred percent believe she had done the right thing, not only for herself, but for them. She prayed Unal and his son would be getting on with their life without her, just as she was getting on with hers. It takes years to know if one's choices have been the right decision. When the emotions are raw, it's impossible to know. It takes time. All she knew for sure was she could not be the one responsible for causing a permanent rift between a boy and his father. It had become ugly and ultimately it would have become uglier and uglier, just as her mother predicted. No matter what the circumstances, blood is thicker than water. And she would have been the one left behind. The experience had added another dimension to her character. In the end, it wasn't going to matter one iota if her soufflés won prizes or not. Somewhere inside her there was a little voice that told her where it mattered, really counted, she had acted morally correct. She had done the noble thing.

When she could bear it, she looked at the photos of the three of them and remembered the time in Lanzarote when she was suntanned and pencil thin and when she was utterly and totally needed by a young boy on the threshold of manhood.

For a long time, it lay in an envelope in her jewelry box. She had stuffed it into her hand luggage that final morning. The green and white enamel and mosaic cross. She could wear it now without shedding a tear as she remembered. 'For my mother and best friend,' Arif had said when he gave her the pendant he made at school.

Consolation

1

HE LOOKED AT HIS WIFE ACROSS THE BREAKFAST TABLE, exactly the way he had looked at her for the past thirty-some years. The not-so-gentle telltale signs of time don't jump out at you when you see someone every day. Not like meeting up with a person you knew in your youth and then see thirty years later. Not like that. She had taken to wearing turtleneck tops now to cover the slightly sagging skin under her chin. Being a vain woman, she was terribly bothered by her neck and the lines around her eyes and mouth, but not enough to undergo elective surgery as many of her friends were now doing, male and female. Instead of the knife, she experimented with different moisturizers promising anti-aging properties and twice monthly facials at the local, aptly named European Spa. Aptly named as all the estheticians were German, Swiss, or French. Collagen facials, vitamin C facials, wrinkle-reducing facials, brightening facials, pumpkin enzyme peels, seaweed facials, and microdermabrasion treatments with the promise to remove dead rough cells of the outer layers of the skin and diminish fine lines and wrinkles. She wasn't sure if she did it all for her husband, for herself, or for her women friends. At between a-hundred-and-twenty and a-hundred-and-fifty bucks a session plus a substantial tip, she hoped it was all working.

While she was aware of these changes, he wasn't. Well, maybe he was. He chose not to dwell on it. He knew he wasn't a prize, either. So he decided that she looked like she always had. Maybe that was love. He loved her. He knew that much. He also knew it wasn't in a deeply "in love" way—he always knew that, wasn't sure if she knew or not, but they had made it work. Maybe it was just luck because he didn't think he had been working at it. So maybe that was love. As a younger man, he had longed for that hopelessly in love feeling—the way it happened in the movies and with celebrities. He once read that the musician Sting felt that way when he first saw English actress, film producer, and director, Trudie Styler. They married and stayed married.

But that kind of love wasn't in the cards for Bud Brown, hardly a celebrity. Did he love his wife at all? Did he ever love her? It drove him nuts the way she used her teeth instead of her lips to take cereal off the spoon. It drove him nuts that she used a fork to take the cherry jam (she had never even tried another flavor) from the jar and spread it onto her whole-wheat toast. He would have liked the jam to be spooned out of the jar and put into a little serving bowl with a serving spoon before it was set out on the table. It's what he had grown up with. It's the way his mother did it. Not that he was against progress. Or a mama's boy. It was just that some things should stay the same. But these things had nothing to do with love. Or did they?

Back to the beginning, if only he hadn't taken that phone call that day. Before that. If only he hadn't visited Los Angeles that summer. Before that. If only he had never been born. Ah, there it was, and here he was. And there she was. Mrs. Bud Brown. It was summer and she still wore turtlenecks.

Burying his face behind his newspaper, his attention went from his plate of scrambled eggs and English muffin to the financial section. These days, the yo-yo stock market didn't help anyone's digestion, but facts were facts. Anyway, hiding behind the paper was just a way of avoiding morning conversation. But more than that, a way of letting his mind wander freely. Where had it all gone? Thirty-five years ago he was so young. Everyone was young, so they claimed. But he really was.

2

"BROWN RES'DENCE," MARY DONOVAN SPOKE INTO THE phone, sounding very much like the Hattie McDaniel character in *Gone with the Wind*, even though she and her parents arrived in the States from Dublin when she was ten. She liked the phone part of her housekeeper's job with the Brown family best because it gave her a chance to spout different accents, based on the latest viewed movie or television show.

"Is Bud… Bud… Bud Brown there, please? I mean, if he is, can he talk? I mean, is he home now and if he is, is he able to come to the phone now? That's what I mean. Meant." The female voice sounded young and unsure.

"And with whom am I speaking with, dearie?" Mary tried out a type of posh British accent a la the tea lady in the tearoom at the train station in Noel Coward's *Brief Encounter*.

"Oh… well, ah… could you just say it's a friend? It's sort of a surprise," the timid one replied.

"He won't come to the phone, luv, if you won't be givin' me a name as in your first and last." Her movie accents were history. Now she was just plain Irish and quite irritated.

"Well okay," the voice said. "Just say, it's the girl who was on the Mister Toad ride with him. Did you understand? The Mister Toad ride."

"Child, this is the Brown household, not the petting zoo." The kids today were all sex mad.

"Well, oh, I don't know. Just say it's a friend." And she quickly added, "From the past. Please."

"Hold on." Mary was not thrilled. The information was too vague. She prided herself on details, whether it be in preparing and serving her perfect Irish Stew or taking phone messages.

"Thank you," the voice said.

Bud was the only kid in America who didn't have his own phone so Mary had to page him which meant she had to holler up the stairs; something she thought was beneath her. Standing at the foot of the stairs, she hollered in the direction of the floor above, "Master Bud. Phone. Someone 'bout a frog." Having hollered once, one time being her limit on hollering, she disappeared to her well-appointed quarters behind the kitchen to watch her beloved soap operas before tackling the menu for the family dinner.

Bud was well into a weightlifting session in front of his bedroom mirror and had worked up a good sweat when he heard the call to the phone. It was not a good time to take a break. He liked to be dripping, and then jump right into an ice cold shower. Stopping in the middle of a routine drove him nuts. Why hadn't he ignored Mary's summons? He wondered if she could be trained to take messages.

He grabbed the terry towel from the floor, where he had dropped it earlier, and put it around his neck. He had to leave his room and come out into the hall and walk down the back stairs to the kitchen because his mother refused to install a phone in the hallway upstairs, and he was sure he was the only guy in America without his own phone—a totally embarrassing situation for a middle-class teenager. For Pete's sake, it was practically the seventies and he didn't have his own means of communication. His mother said he could have his own phone when he started college. Fortunately for him, only a month away.

Wiping his hands on his cotton shorts, he picked up the receiver from the counter. "Yuh?" he grunted into the mouthpiece, somewhat flatly.

"Bud?"

"Yuh?"

"Bud Brown?" The girl answered his question with a question of her own.

"If you want the handsome guy with curly black hair and hazel eyes, that's me." He had no idea why he said what he said, although it was true; nor did he have any idea who was on the other end and that made him even madder than letting sweat dry on his body. He was starting to feel cold. He hated this girl who still hadn't told him her name. Even if it was a girl he loved, right now he would hate her for making him shiver. This whole episode was bound to set his muscles back three weeks.

Imitating, as best she could the voice of an old man, she grunted, "Hey, you kids, were you just on the Mister Toad ride?"

Now there was a phrase you didn't hear everyday. Bud froze. Mister Toad. Maybe he heard wrong. Maybe this was the next door neighbor. His name was Mister Todd.

"Remember? The Toad ride?"

He couldn't believe he had heard what he had just heard. Definitely not Todd. The voice sounded strange, and yet, strangely familiar.

"Are you still there?" called out the voice on the other end.

Suddenly it clicked, and he went even colder, if that was possible. "Hey! Wow! Wow!" *Jesus*, he thought. *That horrible girl.* "Who is it?" he asked again knowing full well who the interloper on his time was.

"It's me. Ju...dy K...atz," she said as if she were announcing herself as the next guest on a late night talk show where one syllable names were stretched into two and three syllables.

It was all coming back to him. Disneyland. The Mister Toad ride. The tunnel thing. Oh, brother. "Yuh, I remember you. Judy Katz," he said slowly.

"That's great."

It wasn't great at all. "Wow! You're not here in Connecticut, are you? I mean, you're calling from California, right?"

Please, please, please. That skinny redhead with yellow teeth that he took out only once as a sort of favor to a complete stranger. That one thing that happens in your life that you tuck way in the back of your mind, an event so grotesque it can never be repeated to anyone, not even your best friends. He repeated hopefully, "You're calling long distance, right?"

The answer was an abrupt, "No," followed by a kind of giggle.

The brevity of her reply said volumes to Bud. "No, what?" *Please, don't be here.*

"Not California. I'm in Connecticut. Isn't that amazing?"

Trying to sound casual, not too interested, not too vague, he could feel the bile rising in his throat as he replied, "Amazing." What was she doing here? Was she stalking him? Would he have to take out a restraining order? He didn't think it would be difficult. He had connections. He knew someone whose father was a lawyer.

They had gone to Disneyland on a blind date. She had brought along a friend so they could make it a foursome. On this Mister Toad ride, he and his friend, Steve, started fooling around. They jumped out of their plastic toad car and scared people half to death as they jumped out from behind posts and hollered at the people in the passing toads. There was a lot of screaming going on, especially from their dates who'd been abandoned in a four-seater toad. The two boys absolutely believed it was the prank of the century; yet making a pact never to tell anyone back home. Anyone, anywhere, ever.

"So you won't, will you, Bud?"

Had he momentarily passed out? What had she said? "Huh? Won't what?"

"You know."

"I do?" Was he supposed to be a contestant on a quiz show he hadn't signed up for? This guessing game was making him nauseated.

"Forget it."

"Hey, how could I forget it? How many kids can say they were thrown off the Mister Toad ride and chased around Disneyland by the guy in charge? To be more exact, chased out of Disneyland."

After a pause from the other end, he said nervously, "That was you, wasn't it?" He didn't know what he was saying. "Where did you say you were *exactly*?"

"I didn't. But I'm at my cousin's house. Sheila Harvey. Do you know her? She says she knows you."

Everyone knew Bud Brown. He probably was the most popular guy in Greenwich. Maybe in all of Connecticut. He had enjoyed three fantastic weeks in Los Angeles during the summer, a high school graduation present from his parents before settling down to four years of college and then maybe two years of graduate school. One day he would follow in his father's footsteps as the president of the Brown Leather Company.

He and Steve Wilson had leased a suite in a residential apartment hotel on Sunset Boulevard. That is, their parents had set it up. Just as they were getting their gear out of the back of a rented Ford Mustang, there was a loud crash at the corner. They moved closer to get a better look, along with about a hundred other people who seemed more interested in seeing if there were any celebrities in the crowd rather than if anyone was injured. Three cars had locked bumpers. The drivers were screaming at one another, but no one appeared hurt.

The woman standing next to Bud began talking to him as if they were longtime friends. Talk about a small world, Sylvia Gold had moved to California from Connecticut, and by sentence four, they discovered she had once played Canasta with Bud's aunt in Greenwich. Sylvia Gold went on about her fabulously adorable niece who was visiting from

Connecticut. Maybe he knew her. Bud didn't care if he knew her or not. He hadn't come all the way across the country fifty-thousand miles to meet a girl from his hometown.

"You two will have to get together. She has a mass of gorgeous curly red hair. You have curly black hair. What a combination." Sylvia Gold's sales pitch sizzle was pretty transparent.

Bud Brown wasn't buying. "No, listen, Ma'am, I—"

"We're of the human species for goodness sake. Call me Sylvia," she interrupted.

"Listen, Sylvia, I, oh, never mind." He wasn't even going to try to win this one.

"Good. It's settled. Tonight you'll come to the barbecue at my cousin's house in Bel Air not far from where Raquel Welch used to live. I'll introduce you."

"To Raquel Welch?" he said dryly.

"You're a hoot." She slapped his shoulder, not that gently. "You'll be a big hit out here."

And that's how Bud Brown met Judy Katz. One date. That had been it. And now she was hanging on the other end of the phone. Why didn't he just hang up? His demented self rambled on. "So-o-o, you're here. How 'bout dem apples?"

"I never met anyone who says things the way Bud Brown says them," she said, gushing.

After a three-second awkward silence that seemed to Bud to be at least an hour and a half, he repeated, "So-o-o, you're here. After the holiday. The vacation is over and yet, it continues. How 'bout dem apples?" He was happy none of his friends could hear this non-conversation.

Teenage girls were all a pain in the bucket seat. Not like Sandi Fisher. Sandi with an 'i' was always made clear right up front. Now there was a woman. Older. Mature. His kind of woman. A man's woman. At twenty-five, she had it all.

Bud started to sweat again just thinking of her. He could never have taken *her* to Disneyland. Even though he knew who she was—who didn't—he might never have had the chance to actually meet her if his parents hadn't forced him to go to the Country Club that Saturday night for the tennis awards dinner dance. He couldn't take his eyes off the mean cha-cha she and the tennis pro were involved in. Suddenly, she dropped to her knees and started feeling around the floor with her hands for what could only be a contact lens, maybe two, the way she cha-cha-cha'd. Bud saw this as his opportunity and leapt onto the dance floor from his front-row table, dropped to his knees and proceeded to help the most beautiful woman he had ever seen in his life look for her contacts. He needn't have bothered. It turned out she hadn't put the lenses in that night, and that was the reason she couldn't see two feet in front of her.

Later that night, seated on a bench for two in the garden of the Club, enthralled and in heat despite a cool breeze, Bud Brown listened to pale and interesting Sandi Fisher tell her life story. She had studied in Paris, France one summer. She didn't believe in suntans because they ruined your skin; therefore, she was planning to give up tennis, but she hadn't told the tennis pro yet. Breakfast never before eleven, and then only a thin slice of wheat toast. No butter. Maybe a dab of honey or orange marmalade. Black coffee. Lunch wasn't a crummy cheeseburger and a chocolate milkshake. None of that poison for her. At two in the afternoon, following her massage, Mademoiselle Fisher lunched on cottage cheese and fresh fruit in the Grill Room at the Club. In the evening, she dined on champagne and filet mignon, whether at home or out in a restaurant. Never before nine. And she always wore black regardless of the season. She explained that her strict dieting regime was because at forty, she didn't want her *derriere* to be somewhere down around her ankles. She was sophistication itself. A romantic affair with the lady was not in the cards for Bud—he knew that—but he could dream.

"Calling Bud Brown. Calling Bud Brown. Are you there? Come in, Bud Brown," Judy Katz screamed, sounding like some kind of Naval Officer, not that Bud knew what a Naval Officer sounded like.

"Say what?" He was quickly brought back to earth by the voice from hell, which was more irritating than fingernails on a chalkboard. At the same time, the screen door to the kitchen slammed shut. "Hang on a minute. I gotta deal with something."

Ira Brown, his face streaked with tears, scuffled in and plopped down on the bench at the big rectangular pine table in the middle of the kitchen. His entire world had obviously crumbled.

"What's up, kiddo?" Bud asked. It was the first time in his life that Bud was actually glad to see his little brother.

For some reason, the question made Ira jump up, squeal, and rush out of the house, again letting the door slam. Bud figured it had to do with not being able to play baseball because at eleven, Ira was looked down upon by the twelve-year-olds. Bud had to make a decision. He didn't know whether to rush out after his kid brother, who had taken on pig-like intonations with his squeals, or go back to the laughing hyena on the phone. What a life. He was smack in the middle of an anthropomorphic nightmare, finally getting to use a word in real life that had come up and been discussed in his English class.

What to do. What to do. The dilemma was settled when he opted for the cookie jar his mother hid in the pantry which he could never understand because why bake cookies if you were going to hide them? Taking the cookie jar with him, Bud returned to the phone on the wall. He was somewhat comforted by the fact that the cookies were chocolate chip, his very favorite, and not the macaroons he despised. He took a cookie from the jar and bit into it, unbothered by the crumbs dropping down on the floor.

"Yuh, I'm back." He had to get rid of this caller. The cookie in his hand and the prospect of more to come was much more enticing. "Okay, I have to go now."

Judy cleared her throat. At least that's what it sounded like.

"What?" he asked. "Did you say something?" Bud finished the cookie and took another one out of the jar.

"Are you busy? You're not eating, are you, while you're talking to a person on the phone?"

Missing her point about it being rude to talk on the phone and eat, he said, "It's okay. I can talk and chew. I never choke." Actually, he once did. On the phone with Steve. "Can you cook, Judy?" Now why did he ask her that dumb question? Sandi Fisher said there were people who were paid to cook and if a woman cooked it was taking a job away from someone who really needed it.

"Sort of. I guess I'll have to learn, I guess."

What did *that* mean? Bud absolutely hated this girl. He did not know what to say. Why didn't he hang up? He threw another cookie down his throat. He wondered how long he'd been on the phone. Felt like a year. He raised his leg up to the counter and switched on the radio with the big toe of his right foot. He switched it off. He never knew he could do that with his toe. He bit into another cookie. "Well, Judy, it's been swell talking to you, but I gotta go now."

"Wait, wait. Don't hang up. I forgot to tell you something."

"You did?" She hadn't told him *anything*. He ate two more cookies, leaving only one in the jar. His mother was going to have a fit.

Judy giggled nervously. Finally, she said it. "Okay, here it is. I'm engaged."

"Yuh?" he said without any interest. "In what?" Like he cared.

"To be married, of course," she said with pride.

"Married?" This took him by surprise. What was she talking about? "You're not old enough to get married." And why was she telling him?

"I will be by the time it's time to get married." There was a silence on the other end that she misunderstood. "Oh, you're mad. I hope you're not mad. You're mad. I knew I shouldn't have told you over the phone."

"Mad? I'm not mad. What makes you think I'm mad? Why would I be mad?" This girl was nuts.

"I guess I better just say it outright. Prepare yourself. It's Paul Davis."

Good thing he wasn't in the middle of a chocolate chip bit; otherwise, he would have needed the kiss of life. "Paul Davis as in Paul Davis from Greenwich, Connecticut Paul Davis?" Now he was mad.

"The very gentleman. Isn't it amazing?"

"Amazing? That's your word? Amazing?" It was catastrophic.

"So I guess we'll be seeing each other."

"How do you know Paul? I mean, how did you meet Paul Davis?" He was in the middle of a science fiction movie.

"Sylvia Gold fixed us up in California."

"Sylvia Gold? What? Does she walk around Hollywood with a sign on her back?" Paul had made the same trip right after Bud when he heard how great it was. Paul had never told Bud about a date with a Judy Katz, and they told each other everything. Bud wondered if Paul knew about the Mister Toad ride. He didn't have to wonder for long.

"Listen, Bud. That's why I called. I know you and Paul know each other."

"Know each other? Know each other?" His voice went up an octave. He sounded like his grandmother. "Paul and

I are only best friends," he boasted. "That is, next to Steve Wilson," he added quickly.

"Please, please, please don't tell him about our date last summer. I'd like to keep that part of my past the part that my husband-to-be will never find out about. You have to promise. Okay?"

He grunted. It wasn't an *okay* or a *no* or *anything*; just a grunt. His life could only be described as seriously troublesome.

"Promise?" she pleaded.

Bud started to sweat again. This girl was getting married to Paul, his friend. This girl he had taken out once in Los Angeles. He had never told Paul about taking this girl out. If it came out now, Paul would wonder why Bud hadn't told him before when they told each other practically everything. And why hadn't Paul mentioned the engagement? Maybe it was a secret. Maybe it was a figment of this girl's mind. It was a tangled mess and precisely the reason why Bud preferred working out alone in front of the mirror in his bedroom. People were just too complicated. *Oh, boy. Oh, boy. Oh, boy.* He muttered a barely audible, "Dilemma."

"Huh?" When Bud didn't say anything, she asked, "Are you still there?"

He looked down at his shrinking body. "Still here, what's left of me."

"You won't say anything to Paul?" There was a pause. "Bud? Promise?"

All those questions. He was really under pressure now. "Judy, listen, Paul is a very good friend of mine. I don't know if I can promise. I'll just have to see how it goes."

And then she started to bawl, real loud, and it made Bud feel like a jerk. He told her not to cry, that it would be their secret. And when he said that, *he* nearly started to cry.

She stopped crying. "Oh, Bud, I knew I could count on you. Well, that's it. That's why I called. I better go now. I'm cooking supper for Paul tonight. I hope he doesn't break off the engagement. Ha, ha. I'm making meat loaf. Do you know if he likes chocolate or vanilla ice cream? Never mind. I guess I shouldn't be asking you under the circumstances."

"Jesus." *Under what circumstances*? Bud's brain was positively bursting. Veins were popping out of his skin from everywhere. He could feel it.

"Did you say something, Bud?"

"No."

"I thought you said something. Well, see ya. I mean, you don't know me when you see me. Don't forget. Bye."

Bud heard the click on the other end. He felt drained. He vowed never to go to California for a holiday again. Or anywhere.

3

A couple of years passed, and as planned, Judy Katz married Paul Davis. Bud Brown was the best man at the wedding. Bud didn't mind being the second choice because Paul's brother was in Alaska and couldn't make it home for the wedding. He did, however, mind the formal gear. It all worked out. He knew he looked good and when he caught sight of himself in the ballroom mirror holding a glass of champagne in his hand, he was beyond thrilled with the whole appearance. If only Sandi Fisher could see him now, but he'd heard she'd gone to England and hooked up with a Duke or someone like that.

More years passed. Bud graduated and went into business with his father per the plan. Bud kept the secret. There was no reason to mention the Mister Toad ride to Paul. Maybe one day way in the future when they were old, when it wouldn't matter. But not now. His friend seemed happy with his new life. And then, the flip side of the happiness coin entered their lives. And Bud didn't have to worry about making the choice anymore to tell or not to tell.

It had been the usual kind of cold after a December snowfall in Connecticut. Clear, cold, with the dreaded lingering black ice. Roads were okay during the day, you could see ahead, but at night treacherous, and this was a particularly bitter cold night. He and Paul had planned a guy's night out; a rare occasion for them. Bud insisted on driving so he could get the new car out on the road.

Around eleven, a knock on the Davis's door surprised Judy who was in the den watching the late news on TV. It wasn't the bell, just a knock, maybe four or five raps. She thought Paul had forgotten his key. Fully expecting her husband, drunk and disorderly, whom she would have to undress, get into bed, and let sleep it off, she opened the door. But it wasn't Paul. It took her a second to focus. A policeman? Standing at her door at eleven at night?

The officer didn't hesitate. After confirming the woman standing in front of him was the wife of Paul Davis, keeping his voice low, never taking his eyes of her, the police officer told her there had been an accident. "I have the duty to tell you…" He couldn't finish the sentence, saying quickly that this was the part of his job he hated. Otherwise, he found it rewarding, even fun. As if any of that mattered.

Her mind began to race, filtering out the word 'accident.' What the hell was he talking about? It had been a call from someone in the neighborhood. Her TV was too loud. Mistaken identity on the hit and run in the supermarket parking lot that afternoon? But she knew. She knew the way a person knows. It was none of those things. None of those minor things that wouldn't change her life forever. She had begged Paul to drive. They had a sturdy SUV. But Bud insisted. She and Bud argued back and forth, Paul staying out of it. A brand new Mercedes sports car was just the ticket for a guy's night out. Just as safe low to the ground in a skid situation. Even safer. Statistics had proved that a Mercedes was the safest car on the road. Bud and the sports car won out.

"Your husband…" the policeman began, unable to finish.

"What are you saying?"

"We'll need you to come downtown and identify the body," he blurted out.

"What are you talking about? You've made a mistake. The wrong house…"

It was silent for a short time which felt like a hundred years. Breaking the silence, Judy said, "They went out for a couple of drinks. It's Christmas. Ho, ho, ho."

The officer continued. "A big SUV. Four women. The holidays. They were going fast, talking, not paying attention. Black ice."

Judy was having a difficult time breathing. *Sweet Jesus,* she thought, *what is he saying*? She heard words. Only words. Why didn't he talk in sentences?

"Their car crossed the dividing line head on into the other car. Heavy vehicle like that against a two-seater sports. The driver survived. He's in the hospital."

She preferred the words to the sentences. "So my husband is okay. He was driving." She was sure Bud would have let Paul have a go behind the wheel. She kept insisting her husband was okay. He'd walk into the house any minute now. They'd be sitting in front of the fireplace any minute now, talking about the evening. But he wasn't okay. And she knew it. He wasn't the one driving. Nothing could have prepared her for this blow. Nothing would ever make the pounding in her head go away. She felt dizzy and had to sit down. She fought back the vomit that was threatening to release itself from her inners.

After she identified the body of her husband, Judy went to the hospital to visit Bud. They both cried. She was angry, but couldn't express it. Instead, she told him it wasn't his fault. She didn't believe it for a minute. It was his entire fault. Together, they mourned. She went through the mechanics of the legal stuff, the stuff you do when your husband dies. Bud didn't know why he helped. Out of guilt probably. Or why she let him. And out of guilt or out of wanting to do the right thing, fourteen months later, Bud Brown married Judy Katz Davis in a private ceremony with just close relatives in attendance. It was a bittersweet occasion because the bride and groom weren't in love. If not *in love*, maybe a kind of love born out of an accident they both survived.

4

BUD LOOKED UP FROM THE PAPER HE HAD STOPPED READING long before he looked up. "I've been thinking, Judy."

"Yes, dear?" Taking a sip of her coffee, she waited for him to go on.

"Our thirtieth is coming up. What would you say to a trip to the West Coast?"

"California? You mean it?"

"We've never been back to Los Angeles, you know. Not since that first meeting where it—"

"Where it all started." She finished his sentence with a big smile.

She did that a lot. Finished his sentences. It drove him crazy. Maybe that's why she did it.

"This time, we'll do it up right. Stay at that fancy hotel in Beverly Hills."

"Where all the celebrities stay. I'd like that." She came around the table and kissed him on the mouth. It wasn't passionate, but neither was it like a sister to a brother.

Maybe he didn't know much about romantic love like in the movies and books. How real was that, anyway? Maybe this was better. Even with her red hair kept almost to its original color every five weeks at the beauty parlor, now called a salon, maybe she wasn't exactly a Debra Messing look-a-like, his favorite redhead, but she had grown into a very attractive woman that he didn't mind looking at. She still played a mean game of tennis and was quite fetching in her whites out on the court with her hair pulled back in a ponytail.

Her meat loaf was so-so, but it didn't matter because he didn't really care for meat loaf all that much. Not at all, actually, to be completely honest. There was her lemon chicken once a week. Not bad. Not bad. Not gourmet. Acceptable, that would be the best description. And this is what made it all possible: the chocolate chip cookies. As good as the ones his mother used to bake. She had always been a superb mother to their two children and shared his anticipation of one day being grandparents. She ran a nice orderly household. Thirty years had flown by like a week. The truth of it was being around his wife pleased Bud Brown enormously. And that was fine. It was more than fine.

"And you know, I've been thinking," he went on. "Thirty years is a milestone. How many marriages last that long these days and are still happy? Well, I've been thinking. We didn't really have much of a deal the first time. Due to the circumstances and all. How would you like to renew our vows?" They hadn't had any celebration at all. Two and a half days in Vermont for a honeymoon. He had always felt guilty about it. "You know. A real wedding. You all in white, me in whatever a groom wears these days. The kids can give us away. What do you think? Game?"

"More than game. It's a wonderful idea. We can have the ceremony and the reception at the Country Club in the remodeled ballroom and then go off to California for our

honeymoon. Oh, Bud, I love you very much."
    "Our delayed holiday."
    "The holiday after the holiday, darling."
    "I wonder if the Mister Toad ride is still in existence."

The Australian Featherweight

<u>Preface</u>

WHILE THIS STORY IS FICTIONAL, IT WAS INSPIRED BY THE life of real Australian featherweight, Albert Griffiths (1869-1927) known as Griffo. He was a wise-cracking, illiterate boozer who trained little, often arrived in the ring drunk, and yet was able to win more than his share of fights. At 21, he went to America as the featherweight champ, but didn't treat his boxing career seriously. Years of hard living slowed him down, and when he used up his fame and money, he was reduced to panhandling in Times Square where he died at age 56. In 1991, he was inducted into the International Boxing Hall of Fame.

Much of what happens to Jiffo is based on fact: the handkerchief trick, the fly trick, the boozing, arriving in the ring drunk and winning, the Push, and running down the gangplank of the ship on his way to America. Flo Berry, however, is an imaginary character who typifies what it may have been like for a prostitute with higher ideals who wanted to rise above the no-hope existence. The flying cab is a total invention and years ahead of the real thing. Much more than a boxing story, we witness the coming into manhood of an illiterate street brawling slum hoodlum, when Tom Riley, the retired heavyweight champion of Australia, invites him to join his boxing academy. Through the sport, Jiffo learns skill, character, and courage leading him to rise out of the no-hope existence in Sydney in 1900.

The full-length stage drama adapted by the author can be accessed through Heartland Plays, an online play catalogue.

<u>About The Rocks, Sydney, New South Wales</u>

THE ROCKS BECAME ESTABLISHED SHORTLY AFTER THE colony's formation in 1788. The original buildings were made mostly of local sandstone from which the area derives its name. From the earliest history of the settlement, the area had a reputation as a slum often frequented by visiting sailors and prostitutes. During the late 19th century, the area was dominated by a gang known as the Rocks Push. It maintained this rough reputation until approximately the 1870s. In 1900 bubonic plague broke out. Thousands of houses, buildings and wharves were inspected and hundreds demolished, but the continuation of these plans was halted due to the outbreak of World War I. During the 1920s, several hundred buildings were demolished during the construction of the Sydney Harbour Bridge. However, the outbreak of World War II once again stalled many of the redevelopment plans, and it was not until the 1960s that serious attempts to demolish much of the area were revived.

Today, the area is a bustling tourist attraction with its close proximity to Circular Quay and the views of the Sydney Harbour Bridge. It features a variety of retail shops, art galleries, restaurants, pubs, and a lively night life. There are numerous historic walks through the area including visiting historical buildings such a Cadmans Cottage, the oldest house in Australia. Two of the many pubs in The Rocks claim to be Sydney's oldest surviving pubs: the Fortune of War and the Lord Nelson.

1

JUST A HAPPY FAMILY OUTING. THAT'S ALL IT WAS MEANT to be. Just another pleasant Sunday afternoon stroll for the three of them. But this time, they were having too much fun, weren't paying attention, and walked further and further into the woods away from the safety of the center of town. Less than a split second before Mr. Jiffiths spotted the pack, the wild dogs had smelled the trio. Faster than lightning, the filthy dingoes sunk their teeth into the two large meatier figures. Mr. and Mrs. Jiffiths never had a chance as the ferocious dogs chomped and slurped their way through flesh and bones. The petrified child stood rigid as he witnessed the gruesome mauling.

"Run, young Bert, run," the dazed Mr. Jiffiths weakly called out to his son. His last words before he was gone from this life. It was a brutal end for the pair and something of an unexplained miracle that saved the life of the youngster.

The townspeople always would say that it was this tragic incident that turned a soft-hearted boy into a hoodlum, a reckless boozer, and an angry and malicious fighting machine.

2

"PASS THE BREAD, YOUNG'UN," JOHN EDGAR SAID TO HIS fostered son, Bert Jiffiths, Junior.

Bert. He hated the name now. Too much of a reminder of that day when his father called out to him to run. His mates down at the docks and the gang members called him Jiffo, short for Jiffiths. He passed what was left of the bread after four mouths to feed.

"You goin' out again t'night?" Jack asked.

Three years older than his illiterate foster brother, Jack, the Edgars' eighteen year old son who had some schooling was forever nagging the loose canon who had been adopted into their household five years earlier.

At this moment, Jiffo preferred to concentrate on his potato pie.

Jack mistook the silence as an opening for him to continue. "I know about you hangin' out with them larrikins down at The Rocks."

That got Mr. Edgar's attention. "Larrikins? You're not runnin' around with that wild bunch, are you?" Larrikins didn't wait for trouble to come to them. They made the trouble. The Rocks area was known for its slums, sailors, convicts, prostitutes, pubs.

"That gang's nothin' but two-legged dingoes, Pa."

Jiffo stiffened at Jack's words. The sound of mashing and crushing flesh and bone rang in his ears until all that was left was a pulpy mass. The sound was nothing more than his own sound as he ate his supper. He pushed the plate away.

Mrs. Edgar said, "Now boys, I won't have any fighting in our home."

Ignoring his mum, Jack continued his tirade trying to be persuasive. "You gotta use your time better, Bert. I left the Push 'cause there ain't no future in it. Knives, switchblades, fists, broken bottles, roaming the streets at night, robbing innocent people, killings. It's dangerous."

That's when Jiffo finally spoke. "You're an apprentice barrel-maker," he spat out with obvious disdain for the profession.

"I admit it doesn't bring in as much as the mob activities, but it's regular and honest without the law breathin' down your neck."

Jiffo had better things to do than listen to Jack. "I gotta go." He moved quickly out the door without so much as a nod to his foster parents.

"Missus, I dunno what's to become of him and with no schoolin'. That most unfortunate incident left him scars for

life. I reckon havin' to watch yer mum and dad go like that..."
Mr. Edgar's voice trailed off.

John Edgar looked much older than his years. He was a fair provider who took care of his small family, concerned for their well-being, trying to set good examples for living, doing the best he knew how. He had a good heart and took in his distant cousin's child, but the sadness in his eyes clearly revealed he was apprehensive about young Bert's prospects.

Attempting to reassure her husband, Mrs. Edgar said, "He'll be all right, Mister Edgar. A bit headstrong, he is, that's all."

"Two poles apart, they are, our Jack here and the other one. Should have changed his name to Edgar when we took him in. Maybe change his luck." He shook his head. "I dunno."

"Never you mind, Mister Edgar. He'll turn out just fine."

"I dunno," he repeated, still shaking his head.

"Now, Mister Edgar, finish up yesterday's apple pie, and I'll buy some fresh blueberry and strawberry extract from Sanders and Sons."

"Left-overs is good 'nuf for me and Jack here and half the time, Bert don't finish his supper. Don't you go tryin' out them extracks. Ya never know what's in 'em. And I'm standin' firm on that subjek." Mr. Edgar had definite opinions on how his laborer's salary was going to be spent.

"Aye, Mister Edgar." Under Elizabeth Edgar's mild and drab exterior, she was a pillar of strength who knew when to yield in a matter.

3

THE MAJORITY OF INHABITANTS IN THE ROCKS AREA OF Sydney in 1900 were poverty stricken, no-hopers with short life spans, bad diets, little or no education, poor medical facilities and overcrowded, unsanitary living conditions. Cheap, easily available liquor assisted their escape from the hard reality of their surroundings. It was a harsh, violent world with few second chances, as witnessed by the prematurely aged faces, sullen expressions, and the commonplace physical deformities.

Being a part of the Push offered a false sense of security to its members who believed the gang was their only refuge. They roamed the alleyways and dimly lit streets after dark looking out for other gangs. Mostly they waited for drunken patrons to pour out of a tavern with their defenses down, not expecting a mugging. Their cruelty didn't stop with humans.

It was an almost deserted night when a mongrel of a mutt sniffing for food wandered into the alley behind the Fortune of War. Drawn to the odors wafting out from the open rear door of the pub, the creature became confused by another odor—its own fear welling up in him when he saw the gigantic, distorted shadows thrown up on the wall of the building. Yapping loudly, there was no escape as his tormentors surrounded him.

Nelson, who was second in command under Jiffo in the Push, already had his knife at the ready. Craving Nelson's approval, Shorty, another Push member, grabbed on to the howling dog and pinned him down. Shorty's name had been given him, not because he was particularly short of inches in height, but because he had a permanent limp having been born with one leg shorter than the other. Typical of his species, being part of the Push meant to him acceptance in society. He didn't have the intelligence to know that nothing was further from the truth.

"I never had no mutt soup. Reckon this'll shut it up." Nelson held the knife to the dog's neck as Shorty held on to the trembling dog.

Having had his final pint for the night, Jiffo appeared at the back door of the pub in time to witness the impending doom unfolding. He held up a hand and called out, "Hold up, lads. This ain't a kangaroo drive. We don't kill or torture animals for sport. Put the knife away, Mister Nelson. Now!"

Jiffo was captain of the Push and like it or not, when the captain gave a directive, the others had to follow or suffer the consequences of punishment.

Shorty obeyed Jiffo and let go of the dog that was either too stunned or too stupid to run. "I'm gettin' outta here," he said, clearly as frightened as the dog. "Let's go, Nelson."

After a moment's hesitation, Nelson grumbled, "Right. We got better prey to hunt." He adjusted the black patch over his left eye as if to make his point.

No one knew if Nelson wore the patch to look sinister or if he really had lost an eye. No one would dare ask. He slipped the knife inside his boot and looked at Jiffo with deep contempt. "One of these days..." he muttered under his breath. He started to wave his fist in the air, but thought better of it. "One of these days..." he whispered. Although he was proud of his high position in the Push as lieutenant, second in command wasn't what he craved.

It wasn't the first time that Jiffo had heard the threat from Nelson. Each time, he let it pass. He looked at Nelson and firmly but quietly said, "Go on I told ya, get outta here." That was a trait about Jiffo that was feared and envied. He knew when to shout, when to speak low, when to speak firmly without raising his voice. It was that firm, low tone that was the most menacing.

With the full moon as the only witness, Jiffo picked up the trembling mutt and held him in his arms. "No worries, I'll take care of ya."

4

Early the next morning, Jiffo was very convincing about finding the half-starved dog at the side of the road. The Edgars agreed to keep the stray provided certain conditions were met.

Mr. Edgar said, "You feed him and keep him cleaned up, ya hear?"

Mrs. Edgar said, "You keep him outside. I quite like the idea of having a dog as long as it don't come in the house."

"Keep him away from me." Jack sneezed for the tenth time in five minutes.

"I think it will be good for our Bert to have a pet so he can learn responsibility, don't you, Mister Edgar?" It wasn't a question that needed a reply. In the spirit of it all, to Jiffo, she said, "What's its name?"

Jiffo shook his head and shrugged. "Ain't got no name. Nameless, I reckon," he said and laughed.

"You ought to give the poor thing a name," Mrs. Edgar said with enthusiasm. "Is it a boy or a girl?"

"Ya ain't keepin' it," Jack whined.

Ignoring Jack's protests, Jiffo said, "Like, well, I found it down at the docks in Sydney." He thought a few seconds. "It's a boy dog so I'll call it Sydney." At that, the little dog yelped wildly. "It's definitely Sydney, then," confirmed Jiffo, feeling quite pleased.

Mrs. Edgar's smile didn't go unnoticed by Mr. Edgar. A conservative man, he said, "Not so frivolous, Missus Edgar."

Mrs. Edgar lowered her eyes and covered her open mouth with her hand.

"I thought you said you found it at the side of the road," sniveled Jack.

Jiffo responded with a curt, "Blow yer nose, Jack."

"Remember our deal, young'un." Mr. Edgar had to raise his voice in order to be heard over Sydney's non-stop yapping.

"Or I'll drown the thing," added Jack whose burning eyes were an intolerable fate.

"I can take a hint. Ta ra all. Come on, Sydney."

"Bye, son," Mrs. Edgar said lovingly.

Jiffo sighed. "I must be gettin' soft. I never heard of the captain of the Push havin' a pet."

And after that, wherever Jiffo went, Sydney was sure to go. Except at night when Jiffo joined up with the Push at the pub. For reasons known only to Jiffo, Sydney was dead scared of that part of town.

5

ON A HEATH LOCATED IN THE GROUNDS OF A LARGE PROPERTY with a magnificent estate as the background, two professional boxers, covered in dirt, sweat and blood, were battling it out, struggling to stay upright in the outdoor ring. A weedy looking youngster standing at the back of the crowd of well-dressed gentlemen, wearing an ill-fitting shabby jacket, baggy trousers, worn out shoes, and accompanied by a dog on a makeshift lead of rope and twine, was invisible as all eyes were on Tom Riley, the father of Australian boxing, fighting his last bout. Jiffo was mesmerized by the scene.

"Defend yourself, old man," declared Sandy Lynch, rushing at his opponent.

Despite the fact that Sandy was younger and larger than Tom, Tom sidestepped each punch and repeatedly landed a left into Sandy's midsection. This was the trend for the next ten rounds with neither of them able to put the other away.

A voice in the crowd shouted, "Finish him off, Tom."

Another voice cried out, "Show him why you were the heavyweight champ."

Tom was exhausted. He knew it was time to end it; time to put his fifteen years of experience behind the next few punches so he could move on to the next chapter of his life. Every inch of his body was focused. He lashed out with bloodied bare knuckles until his opponent went down. The jeers and cheers from the crowd lasted a good twelve minutes. Not even a bucket of ice water thrown over the fallen fighter could revive him. A large number of Tom's supporters broke through the ropes to get to their hero. They hoisted him up on their shoulders and burst into an old familiar tune.

"Did ye hear the news that's goin' round?
Old Tom's mashed up Sandy's spleen
and beat him to the ground;
This Sandy is an Orangeman,
a mighty tough spalpeen,
while Tom Riley is the greatest
Champion of the Green."

6

"Bare-knuckle champion Tom Riley retires," Jiffo screeched in his unschooled voice. Six days a week, Jiffo sat on an orange box outside the Town and Country Journal office and sold its newspapers. Whatever Jiffo's activities were at night, by day he held down a legitimate job. Each morning, the editor would read the headlines to his illiterate employee and at periodical intervals, Jiffo would hold up a newspaper and from memory, he would declare the big news of the day. With each announcement, his voice got louder and shriller as he recalled the fight on the heath.

A rather obese boy tiptoed up behind Jiffo and forcefully shoved him off the orange box solely to provide a laugh for his mates who were standing nearby. Along with the newspapers and pennies, Jiffo went sprawling onto the footpath.

If Sydney hadn't been tied up, he would have certainly attacked his master's attacker.

Jiffo picked himself up and adopted a boxing stance. To his known assaulter, he commanded, "Put 'em up, Charlie Scott." This was Jiffo's language now. He didn't need a newspaper editor to feed him the line.

Charlie's mates gathered around wondering what Charlie was going to do.

Jiffo repeated, "Put 'em up, Charlie Scott." He circled around the scared Charlie, in the same way he had seen his hero, Tom Riley, circle around Sandy Lynch.

Charlie's mates were fired up. They knew Charlie wasn't a fighter, but still, they egged him on, their sadistic cries overlapping one another.

Jiffo peppered Scott with a series of telling blows. More frightened than enraged, Charlie, head down, charged into Jiffo, but Jiffo was ready. He stepped aside, looped up a right into Charlie's nose sending his bleeding opponent into a run. Despite his bravado, Charlie proved himself to be a gutless wonder after all. The boys dispersed as quickly as they had gathered, losing interest in the newsboy who sat back down on his orange box and calmly restored his papers and coins, continuing periodically to shout out the headline, while day-dreaming about the fight on the heath.

7

After a day's work, it was Jiffo's custom to stop in at the Fortune of War down at The Rocks, the pub where the locals hung out. This evening wasn't just a social call. He had Push business to attend to.

The tavern's proprietor greeted Jiffo with a mug of beer. "Hiya, mate." It was no secret that Dave preferred staying on the good side of Jiffo.

"Howzit, Davo?" Jiffo took the mug. "Cheers," he said, taking a gulp.

Tobacco smoke filled the air along with odors drifting in from the fly-infested lavatories just outside the open rear door. Unwashed bodies reeking of rum, whiskey, and beer lolled about. Drunken sailors slumped over the bar. Half-asleep floozies in colorful, cheap low-cut bodices and full skirts waited cross-legged on chairs and wooden benches for the next customer. Near the door, a group of four larrikins, propped up on a bench against the wall, were looking out for their next unsuspecting drunken victim to roll out into the night. They acknowledged their captain with a nod. Jiffo reciprocated in the same way.

Jiffo spotted her sitting sidewise on a chair in the corner and approached her. Knowing this meeting was strictly business, there was no attempt at social chit chat by the pretty girl who handed her boss a large sum of money. Without counting it, he took a couple of notes off the top and gave them to her.

Taking the money with no particular flourish, she said, "Ta. See youze later?" Flo Berry, a few years older than Jiffo, was in love with him and had great hopes for a serious relationship developing.

"See youze later," he responded casually.

"See youze later," she repeated, making sure she had his attention, but his interest waned as he looked around for his mates.

Knowing it would increase liquor sales, Dave called out, "Jiffo, mate, show us your handkerchief trick."

Jiffo never minded showing off his famous handkerchief trick. He downed his mug of beer and began his performance. First, he took a large soiled handkerchief from his pants pocket and waved it to the crowd who cheered him on. Next, with great aplomb, he unrumpled the handkerchief and carefully laid it flat on the ground near his feet. He looked at the crowd and asked for a challenger urging the lads not to be shy.

When there was no response, Jack stepped up. "I'll have a go."

"Naw, go on, Jack, you're family. You know I'm gonna win."

Jack persisted in a monotone voice, "You asked for a challenger, and I'm here as a challenger."

"Suit yourself," said Jiffo, as he stepped meticulously onto the spread out square piece of cloth. He stood as still as an upright corpse.

Jack studied him a few seconds and then aimed a punch at Jiffo's face. Jiffo swayed slightly moving only his upper body and arms. This maneuver caused the punch to hang loosely in the air while Jiffo's feet never moved off the handkerchief. It was a miraculous feat and always brought extended cheering from the spectators for the wiry fellow with massive shoulders.

"I told ya, Jacko."

Jack slipped away feeling slightly humiliated, muttering, "It ain't fair."

Still standing on the handkerchief, Jiffo called out to Dave, "Bring a fresh drink to my good sport brother."

Jack felt better with the acknowledgment and waved modestly to everyone.

A burly, gorilla-like sailor pushed his way through the crowd shouting, "I'll knock the kid's bleedin' 'ead off!"

There was new excitement at the Fortune of War. Without delay, betting took place. A newcomer came forward and placed a heavy bet on Jiffo to win. Jiffo steadied himself on the handkerchief. The challenger lunged wildly at him. Jiffo swayed slightly to one side, again moving only his upper body and arms. The sailor was angry and threw another punch. Jiffo swayed to the other side. Hoots of laughter from the crowd totally enraged the challenger who tried another punch.

"One try is all anyone is supposed to get," called out Jack, sticking up for his brother.

Infuriated and degraded, the hulk rushed at the much younger Jiffo, but despite the fact that Jiffo was at least half a foot shorter than his challenger, the man couldn't touch the speedy Jiffo who did a quick sidestep, leapt up in the air and uppercut the man sharply under the chin. The sailor sagged. He caught his breath and tried to come up for another go, but when he looked at Jiffo who was poised for another punch, he thought better of it. Trampling the man underfoot, the crowd hoisted their hero up onto their shoulders, calling out to the proprietor to bring Jiffo as much beer as he could drink.

The betting newcomer collected his winnings and headed out the exit, unaware that he was being followed by four Push members who smelled fresh money. The innocent man was out on the street before he heard the rustling sound. He turned quickly, but it was too late. Two of the gang members laid into his face and body with their fists while one of the mobsters grabbed his arms from behind. The man tried to strike out again and again, but it was a hopeless battle. To put on the finishing touches, Nelson kicked the victim with his heavy boots. The gangsters went through the unconscious man's pockets and took all his winnings and whatever else they deemed valuable. They were rejoicing over their haul when Jiffo joined them.

"Not bad for an evening's work, eh, Jiffo?" Nelson boasted, holding back the loot.

Jiffo held out his hand and waited. Nelson handed over the money.

Jiffo held out his other hand.

Reluctantly, Nelson handed over a pocket watch, presumably gold, to the silent leader.

"I'll put the cash in the Push bank account tomorrow. Nelson, for not killin' the bloke, you can have the watch." He tossed it to him. "I'm feelin' generous tonight."

Nelson caught the watch but complained about the arrangement. "This was our job, Jiffo. It didn't involve the whole of the Push. Just us four. Therefore, I reckon us four should have the money on this job, not the bank."

The other three participants were shaking as they witnessed the open defiance between their captain and their lieutenant.

"You know the rules, Nelson. It was a Push job and Push money goes into Push funds. You wanna change the rules, Mister, you gotta change me first. How about it?" Jiffo adopted a boxing stance. Nelson knew what that meant and backed away.

8

Dressed in his Sunday best, Jiffo was showing off for Mrs. Edgar. He walked backwards on the dangerously high, forward sloping two and a half inch heels. "Pretty snappy, ain't they, Mum?" He pointed out the fine tooling. His new boots were his pride and joy.

Mrs. Edgar's, "Jingoes!" demonstrated her great admiration for the black leather boots and indeed for his entire apparel. The widely-flared, tight-thigh, black bell-bottom trousers and the clean, white, collarless shirt under a loose fitting tan jacket gave him the kind of good boy air that she had prayed for. She always loved the way his shiny, dark brown hair seemed to grow every which way from his head. Most of the time it was covered up with a dirty cap, but not tonight. "Bert Jiffiths, Junior, you look dandy. Yes, indeed, just dandy."

Mrs. Edgar had never regretted her decision to foster the boy. She loved him as much as if he was her real child. She loved when he called her 'Mum' from time to time, usually when they were alone. Jiffo respected his adopted mother. What he felt was a kind of love, even if it wasn't the same as for his real mother. There it was again. Just the thought of her would bring it on. The sound of flesh being ripped from bones. Crunching. Slurping. Growling. He blocked it out, doing another little walk around. "Blimey, them's bloody hard to walk in. Sorry, Mum. I mean, them's hard to walk in." Jiffo apologized for the slip of the swear word, but the truth was, the bloody boots were killing him.

"I expect you're going out somewhere special." Mrs. Edgar didn't like to pry, but she did like to know where he was going when he was all dressed up.

"Yeah. Me and a particular Miss Flo Berry is goin' dancin' down at Blakes Buildings." It was the first time he had mentioned her name at home. To cover up his embarrassment, he immediately called out for Sydney who came running.

"Does Sydney go dancin', too?" Mrs. Edgar smiled approvingly at her joke.

Jiffo smiled, too, relieved that the part about Flo Berry wasn't questioned, the focus being on the dog. He explained, "Naw, he gets tethered up outside the hall, but he never barks or howls like some of them other dogs." Sydney cooperated thoroughly while Jiffo put the lead around his neck.

Jiffo did a last minute check on his set of clothes before saying goodbye.

"Have a nice time, Bert. Don't get into any fights now. You don't want to spoil your new boots."

9

THE FIRST FRIDAY NIGHT OF EACH MONTH, THE DANCE AT Blakes Buildings was the big event to look forward to by Rocks' inhabitants and folks from surrounding areas who felt safe because everyone knew there was a silent truce that night from all gang members. Dancing was dancing. Fighting was fighting. The two had never mixed on the first Friday night of each month.

In the center of the dance floor, Jiffo and Flo were keeping up with the best of them to a live, four-piece band made up of local musicians. Flo Berry was fond of make-up, bright colors, huge feathered hats, petticoats under big flouncing dresses, boots with four inch heels and gaudy colored stockings. Both she and Jiffo were naturally good dancers, but Jiffo was having a problem with the boots and kept taking nips from a hip flask filled with a special medicinal herb tea laced with alcohol.

"For the pain," he explained to Flo.

Flo knew what Jiffo meant by 'medicinal herb' and didn't say a word.

Several of the other dancers, as well as some onlookers, complimented Flo on her outfit as she and Jiffo twirled by. Jiffo received nods and respectful greetings, but with his feet causing him trouble and Flo turning around to acknowledge her fans, Jiffo was out of his mind. "For cryin' out loud, Flo, you dancin' or standin' for Mayor?"

Flo got the message. Not wanting to antagonize him further, she concentrated on their dancing, making sure to keep her eyes only on her partner.

When Jiffo lost the battle with his feet, he led Flo out the door with an abrupt, "We're goin'." Collecting Sydney on the way out, he led Flo out to the street. Sydney appeared happy to be on the move.

The gas-lit streets were deserted. Flo twirled the ribbons in her hair and fingered the buttons on her bodice and danced as she walked, competing with Sydney for Jiffo's attention. Her gestures were lost on Jiffo as he was no longer subtle about the pains in his feet and legs.

Wanting to get his mind off his boots, Flo didn't realize

she would be stepping out of the frying pan into the fire with the next subject. "I got a question, something I been wanting to ask ya."

Jiffo nodded for her to go ahead.

"How come you never said there was a place in Italy with my name?"

"Say what?"

"In Italy. A place like a town named after me."

Jiffo shook his head not having a clue what she was talking about.

"You goin' deaf? A place in Italy like a city with my name."

He burst out laughing. "What's that, then? Flo Berry, Italy?"

Flo didn't like being laughed at and was angry now. "Florence!" she shouted.

"Don't be stupid!" Jiffo shouted back.

"Don't you be stupid!"

"Don't you be stupid!"

"For your information, Mister, an Eye-talian business-man said so, and he should know."

"What Eye-talian businessman, I'd like to know?" He didn't like discussing the customers with her.

"From Italy. Here on business as it happens." Her tone was haughty.

"I suppose he said you was an Eye-talian Princess and you got kidnapped in the olden days, and they thought you was dead so they named a town after ya."

Not believing her ears, Flo said softly, "How'd ya know?"

Jiffo shrugged his all-knowing shoulders.

"How'd ya know?" Flo repeated with more emphasis.

Jiffo still didn't answer.

"How'd ya know?" Flo screamed.

Defending his territory, Jiffo said, "Listen, Flo, I know those blokes. My advice is, just do your work, keep your nose clean, and stay out of trouble."

Flo wouldn't let it end at that. "Why couldn't they name a town after me? You named Sydney after Sydney, Australia," she pouted.

Sydney barked twice at the sound of his name.

"It ain't the same thing," Jiffo declared with great emphasis.

Flo persisted even though her confidence was down a quart. "You don't know there ain't a Florence in Italy. Not for sure, you don't."

Jiffo said firmly, "I'm tellin' ya, don't believe nothin' those blokes tell ya and only half of what ya see. Ya hear me? Nothin' ya hear and half of what ya see."

Flo said dreamily, "But it's nice to think about. I like hearing things like that. I like thinking about it."

Jiffo spat out, "You're workin', ain't ya? You're happy, ain't ya? So whaddya need to think for?"

"Cuz it's nice, that's why," she exclaimed.

"Keep movin' so's I can get a drink." He pointed at the street.

"Where's your flask, as if I don't know what's in it."

"As I told ya before, solely a medicinal product. I need the real stuff."

The verbal battle subsided and the trio walked in silence. As Jiffo couldn't get his mind off the pain in his feet, Flo lost all interest in her earlier flirtatious gestures.

10

JIFFO KNOCKED RAPIDLY THREE TIMES ON THE ROTTED wooden door. A Judas window slid open. Eyes behind a pair of gold steel spectacles peered out of the peep hole and in a second, Madam Nicole welcomed the pair into a dimly lit plush salon of dark wood furniture and red velvet sofas.

Nicole ignored Jiffo's saucy slap on her backside. The stout, heavily made-up middle-aged woman was used to this kind of harmless physicality from clients of her establishment. While Jiffo got his cut of the action only from Flo, Nicole got her cut from all the activity. Three young, scantily clad ladies lounged on the large soft-cushioned sofas. It was a slow night with only three clients in attendance. As it happened, Flo had been given the night off.

Jiffo instantly recognized a familiar face. "Evenin', Judge," he said, smiling.

The mortified official's face turned beet color at being caught and disappeared without speaking.

From her ornate desk in a corner of the room, Madam Nicole did paper work, keeping a close eye on the proceedings. When a customer helped himself to a bottle of spirits from the cocktail bar, she noted it in a large ledger. When Sydney was left in her custody while Jiffo followed Flo up a wooden staircase to private quarters, this, too, was noted in the ledger. It didn't faze Nicole in the least when the buzz of inarticulate voices coming from behind the closed door turned into a very distinct shouting match.

"A gentleman don't leave his boots on!" That was Flo.

"He does if he can't get the bloody things off his feet!" That was Jiffo.

They went back and forth like that for a long while. First about the boots. Then about the Eye-talian gentleman. Back to the boots. Louder and louder. Then it was dead quiet for a long while with an occasional low murmur, merely as proof they hadn't killed one another.

11

There was little light in the deserted warehouse down at the docks where Jiffo and his gang were preparing to administer a Push punishment to a Push member who had disobeyed Push rules. Nelson was in charge of filling a sock with wet sand obtained from two separate wooden bowls. One bowl contained dry sand; the other bowl contained water. Mixed together, it provided a lethal weapon. A very scared Wally Thompson was lying face down on the long, rectangular-shaped, mottled oak table. Each of his arms was pinioned by a Push member, while the others looked on with relief that they were not the ones in detention.

Jiffo lifted Wally's head up by his thick, straw-like hair and, as magisterially as he could, addressed him. "Wally Thompson, you are hereby found guilty of informing to the bloody cops as to what went on down at the docks on Monday night, hereby known as the fire at the warehouse, the results of such dobbing landing poor old Ted Burke a stretch inside." Wally winced as Jiffo pushed his head down onto the table. Wally's body tensed. He knew he had done a bad thing by telling the cops who set the fire. He was lucky Jiffo didn't have him eliminated permanently.

Eager to move things along, Jiffo asked Nelson if the sand was wet enough. Nelson responded with a test by swinging the sock against his hand. He smiled sadistically at the smacking sound.

"Very well, Mister Nelson, administer the sock. Twelve lashes, if you please."

Nelson lifted the heavy sock over his head and came down hard with it onto Wally's left shoulder.

Jiffo told Nelson to start again and hit the back of Wally's neck between the shoulders.

Nelson didn't like being corrected in front of his mates. This time he slammed the sock into the back of Wally's head. The observing Push members stiffened. Wally let out a cry of pain. Nelson's sock connected again and again, eleven more times. Wally's body sagged. Nelson was just about to administer number thirteen, but Jiffo's command stopped him.

"Twelve, Mister Nelson, twelve. That's Push rules. We don't kill one of our own." Once again, Nelson had been thwarted by the captain in front of his mates. He tossed the weighted sock aside, his anger building.

As Jiffo headed out, he ordered the lads to stay with Wally until he came to. Without turning around, through clenched teeth he said to Nelson, "Just watch it, mister."

Lunging for Jiffo's back, Nelson openly challenged the leader. "Yuh?"

The other Push members froze.

Jiffo spun around. His first instinct was to defend himself with his fists, but he thought better of it and steadied himself.

Nelson repeated the challenge, this time with a more menacing, "Sez who?"

Jiffo knew he had to respond this time. "Outside!" He locked eyes with Nelson, and then he spun around and headed for the door, snapping his fingers behind him. "Now, mister!"

Nelson was a sadistic criminal with one eye who, although lacking vision and intellect, had certain cunning and experience, which helped to make him the best of a bad bunch. Bitterly resentful of Jiffo's popularity as a leader, Nelson did all he could do to undermine Jiffo's position with the lads. Nelson didn't realize that in his desperate effort to become number one, even if he won the battle, he would lose. He was never number one material and by eliminating Jiffo, he would only succeed in putting himself out of business. He picked up a bottle from the ground intending to smash Jiffo on the back of the head, but Jiffo was too quick. Sensing the enemy behind him, he stepped to the side. The bottle went flying and smashed into the wall. Nelson was mortified. Jiffo swung around and faced his assailant. Nelson pulled a knife out from his back pocket. He wanted to finish Jiffo off once and for all. He described vicious circles with the weapon, advancing on Jiffo who, in a defensive stance, stepped back. Jiffo continued to slowly back up, waiting for the right opportunity to disarm the knife-wielding Nelson. Unseen by Jiffo and Nelson, one of Nelson's mates kicked an empty chair into what he thought was Jiffo's path, but it was Nelson who stumbled over it, dropping the knife as he fell backwards onto the ground. His face contorted with defeat, he reached out for the knife, but to no avail. Jiffo's foot had connected with his kidney. Nelson folded.

Jiffo dragged him outside onto the street. "Stand up!"

Slowly, Nelson got to his feet, but it was clear the wind had been taken out of his sails. He looked around for something to fight with. Not even the lads would come to his aid.

"No knives, no bottles, mister. Yer fists only. Put 'em up!" ordered Jiffo, adopting a boxing stance. "You know the rules. If you want to be captain of the Push, you gotta take me in a fair fight."

Nelson threw his body against Jiffo, but Jiffo was too quick. He dodged the weight. Nelson tried punching Jiffo, first with his left, then with his right. Jiffo danced around Nelson, occasionally sending a punch Nelson's way, connecting each time. Nelson, unable to land a punch, became more and more enraged. Jiffo kept weaving and ducking, and then, at precisely the right moment, he sent a stream of punches against his opponent. "Double or quits, Nelson?" Jiffo shouted, hardly out of breath.

Gasping for air, Nelson rasped, "No more. No more. You win." He went down, bloodied and beaten.

Nelson's followers shriveled at the sight of their lieutenant on the ground.

Jiffo leered at them. "I should kick youze all outta the Push. Go on, get."

Only Shorty stayed to help Nelson.

No one had paid attention to the hansom cab parked on the other side of the alley. On their way home from the theatre, Tom Riley had instructed the driver to take an uncharacteristic tour of The Rocks allowing the father of Australian boxing and his official head trainer to witness the no holds barred street brawl.

"I think we're watching a potentially great featherweight, Jim," Tom said.

"A right donnybrook, it was," agreed Jim.

Leaning out of the cab, Tom called out to the young scrapper to move closer. Suspicious of strangers, at first Jiffo hesitated; then, slowly, he walked over to the hansom with his fists up in front of his face barely recognizing the occupant. When he saw who it was, he lowered his arms and started to shake at the sight of his hero.

"I'm Tom Riley. This is Jim Hall. You're fond of the knuckle, youngster, that's no mistake. You can fight, but if you're ever going to rise above a street battle, you need training. Come over to my boxing academy, and we'll have a look at you in the ring. I don't believe I caught your name."

"B—Bert J—Jiffiths, J—Junior. They c—call me J—Jiffo, Mister R—Riley, s—sir."

"The Iron Pot, that's where you belong." Without waiting for a response, Tom instructed the driver to pull off.

12

THE NEXT MORNING, JIFFO WENT TO HIS JOB AS USUAL, BUT at the end of the day, instead of joining up with his mates at the Fortune of War, he found his way to Tom Riley's gymnasium, the Iron Pot, at Circular Quay. Awed, he stood on the cobbled stoned street and looked at the sturdy building with a wooden frame and iron walls and roof. It was one thing to be outside. Now he had to get up the courage to step inside. The interior had bleacher seats and an expanse of ringside standing room. In the center ring, which was a square, two boxers were sparring for a small audience made up of students, trainers, and numerous well-dressed gentry. At the side, Tom Riley was holding court. A raconteur and king of his world, Tom was as Australian as it gets, but he would often lapse into an Irish brogue as befit his strong temperament.

"The Australian eats meat with a big—whatever letter meat commences with." Tom winked at one of his listeners. "If they're reared on meat, they are natural fighters; much better, of course, if they've got an Irish father, see what I mean, but a meat diet's the principal thing." Tom spotted Jiffo. Their eyes locked. "Excuse me, gentlemen, my invited guest has arrived." As a way of welcoming Jiffo into his world, Tom read Jiffo's mind. "Aye. We can accommodate about nine hundred people. No less than amazing, don't you think?"

Jiffo opened his mouth, but no sound came out. He wondered if he would ever be able to utter the spoken word again. He nodded his head up and down.

Tom led Jiffo over to the twenty-four foot square ring. "I'll be teaching you a great tradition, my boy. Father O'Donnell taught me the art many years ago. Yes, indeed, there's a noble tradition to be learned. Meet Jim Hall, my chief trainer." Tom re-introduced the man who had been with him in the hansom cab.

Jim welcomed Jiffo with a shake of his hand. As if the gesture would make up for his inability to speak, Jiffo didn't stop pumping Jim's hand until Jim finally pulled it away.

"Jim," said Tom, "I reckon you are looking at a future world champion. You and I are just going to speed up that event."

World champion? Jiffo couldn't believe his ears.

"Put 'em up, Jiffo," said Jim encouragingly.

That language Jiffo understood. He removed his jacket and cap and seemed relaxed as he and Jim set to for a brief spar. A hush fell over the gymnasium. All eyes were glued on the new pupil in the center ring. Jiffo was younger and more agile and weighed less than Jim. It was obvious that he was a natural fighter. Jim let Jiffo pepper him with a few punches. After a few minutes, Jim put up his hand and Jiffo pulled back.

Tom turned to those present at ringside and announced, "Listen, gents, you're seeing a coming champ."

Jiffo was beaming. He spoke his first words in the Iron Pot. "When's me first fight?"

This remark caused quite a stir of mirth among the ringsiders. The laughter confused Jiffo who was ready to fight each and every one of them.

"Steady on, youngster," said Tom. "You have to train first."

"I'm strong. I never had no training." Jiffo flexed his muscles. "I win all me fights."

"Out on the street, you have fortitude, true, but you need discipline. When I get through with you, they'll know about Young Jiffo in America." Tom had big plans.

Young Jiffo. Jiffo liked that but not the part about America. "Da Rocks is good enuf for me," he said with great emphasis.

"Not any more. You'll be moving on with the new skills I'll be teachin' and you'll be learnin'. Be here early tomorrow morning to begin your roadwork."

An opportunity to spend time with Tom Riley was sensational, even if Jiffo didn't fully understand what was implied by training and roadwork. He grabbed his cap and jacket off the floor and raced to one of the doors. Unknowingly, he exited through the entrance. Believing this to be an intentional joke, it nearly brought the house down with raucous laughter. It was a good thing Jiffo was out of ear shot. He wasn't one to take being mocked lightly.

"Looks like you'll have your hands full with that one," Jim said.

A wise man, it was Tom's hope that with professional training, his new pupil would develop courage and character along with skill and would be weaned away from a life of crime, just as he had been twenty years before.

13

NOW INTO THE FIFTH WEEK OF TRAINING, JIFFO AND TOM were jogging side by side in the stylized, upright manner of the day, wearing new training gear: Singlet, long white wide-legged pantaloons down to the knees and laced up running shoes with no socks. Despite Jiffo complaining about the early morning training interfering with his nightly Push activities, he hadn't missed a day, and he was still able to get to his newsboy job.

"I feel like a bloomin' idiot with these things," Jiffo grumbled, hoisting up his pants over his spindly legs.

"You'll be getting used to them, my boy, not to worry. In my day, we used to wear work-trousers. At least pantaloons free you up and let you run more easily."

"I been lucky so far no one has seen me," babbled Jiffo.

No sooner had he uttered the words, they went around a curve and came upon a friend of Tom's out for a morning stroll. Jiffo was extremely embarrassed. He held his cupped hands over the front of his lower body.

Sir Harold raised his hat in a greeting. "Morning, Tom," he said cheerily. "See you have a keen pupil."

Tom touched his forelock without breaking the running pace. "Top o' the mornin' to you, Sir Harold."

As they passed by Sir Harold, Jiffo quickly switched his cupped hands to his rear.

"Concentrate on your breathing, Jiffo. That's the important thing. Your breathing is everything. Don't be worrying and thinking about other people."

"Oh no," moaned Jiffo with his next breath. Three Push members were idling up ahead at the side of the road. "We gotta turn back."

"Keep going. You're going to be a public person, so no difference now if your mates see you in pantaloons."

"Maybe they didn't see me yet," said Jiffo, slowing down. "I had enough for today."

Maintaining his pace and encouraging Jiffo to do the same, Tom said, "It's no use stopping. The lads have seen you now. Just carry on."

Jiffo and Tom passed by the trio. Without batting an eyelid, Jiffo touched his forelock mimicking what he had heard earlier. "Top o' the mornin' to you, lads."

14

THE ROAD ROUTINE CONTINUED EVERY MORNING BEFORE Jiffo went to his job at the newspaper. After work, he practiced bag-punching, jumping rope, and sparring with Jim Hall at the Iron Pot. At night, he drank with the Push at the Fortune of War and frequently spent time with Flo. Despite warnings from Tom about Push activities and his boozing potentially undermining the training, Jiffo kept up the rigorous schedule. Tom thought he had seen it all in his time, but he hadn't seen anything like this phenomenon. No matter how much Jiffo caroused, none of it interfered with training. He would come to his morning workout as if he'd had eight hours sleep instead of the two or three he somehow managed to fit in.

After twelve weeks, part of the development of a pupil was a brief spar in the ring with Tom Riley. Walking to the center ring, Jiffo spotted a wooden cask. More curious about the added feature than what Tom was holding in his hands, Jiffo dunked his head in and took a big gulp of the dark liquid. Immediately, he spat it out. "Blimey, what kind of establishment are youze runnin' here? I never tasted no drink like it." He wiped his mouth with the back of his hand.

"It's for the face and hands, not for drinking. Walnut juice imported from New Zealand to toughen the skin."

"Never heard of no walnut juice. I survived every fight I ever had without no walnut juice," protested Jiffo.

"You never fought inside a ring."

"I ain't puttin' that stuff on me face. It stinks."

"You leave me to do the instructing. Now come on, we've got work to do. Let's get these on you." Tom held up the pair of six-ounce, thinly padded, leather mitts he'd been holding and called out to Jim for assistance.

"What's this, then?" asked Jiffo.

"Bare knuckle days are over, my boy."

Jiffo studied the gloves. "I ain't fightin' with feather pillows on me fists."

"Feather pillows be damned. You can cut a man to pieces with these."

Jiffo jiggled about as he was being helped into the boxing gloves.

Tom's Irish temper was getting the better of him. "For Chrissakes, stand still!"

Jiffo didn't know when to be quiet. "Wouldn't be any good down in da Rocks. Me enemy is about to clout me from behind and I say, 'Hold on, mate, would you mind helping me into me gloves first?'"

"If I were you, I'd be saving all that energy for the ring."

Jiffo corrected himself and waited while Tom got help

with his gloves from Jim Hall before they climbed through the ropes into the ring. Tom put up his gloved hands and adopted a boxing stance. Jiffo hesitated.

"Come on, big shot, what are you waiting for?" Tom swayed to and fro.

The challenge ignited an excitement in Jiffo, but he was unable to resist clowning for the spectators who had gathered ringside. Acknowledging them with a sweep of his head, he said, "Ta very much, everyone. Ta."

"You can thank them later." Tom was not happy with Jiffo's delay tactic. He raised his voice to get his pupil's attention. "The prize ring ruffian's had his day. Boxing is an art form like painting or music or writing. Come on." Tom threw out a few punches into the air.

"You'll be makin' me play the violin next."

"Let's see if your fists can match your mouth."

Now they were just two fighters, sparring lightly, finding it difficult to hit one another. Jiffo was slightly unsure on his feet and with the gloves on, he had the habit of dropping his left before throwing his right, but there was no question that he was a natural boxer. Tom was the better fighter, but he had trained Jiffo well. Finally, when Tom penetrated Jiffo's defense, he stopped the sparring. Jim Hall climbed into the ring and removed the gloves from teacher and student. Jiffo stretched his fingers.

Tom put his arm around Jiffo's shoulder. "Almost there. Not yet." He stepped out of the ring followed by Jim. "He's a natural, Jim. Just look around. I've never known this many folks flock around to see a fighter train. It's a good sign."

A pupil overheard the remark and said, "Why are you wasting your time, Mister Riley? Jiffo don't need any training."

"Listen up, son. You're wrong about training. Boxing is a science now. In my day, the emphasis was on the power of the punch. Footwork was practically non-existent. Now, with padded gloves, it's all about skill. Once in a while, a potentially great one comes along who needs all the mentoring he can get because he doesn't know what he's got or even if he did know, he wouldn't know what to do with it. Young Jiffo is one of those."

Tom heard loud giggling coming from inside the ring. He turned and was shocked to see Jiffo acting as referee to a mock boxing match between two girls while a third girl watched. The girls, dressed for a night on the town not a gymnasium, had managed to slip in unnoticed. Jiffo singled out one of the girls who happened to be Flo Berry, while the other two stood aside to witness the upcoming lesson.

"Pow, the jab. Pow, the hook. Pow, uppercut. Pow, pow, pow. Bop, bop, bop." Jiffo danced around demonstrating each call.

Flo punched out at Jiffo with her left fist. "Wham, bam."

"Southpaw," Jiffo called out, still dancing around, fists out in front of him.

"Huh?"

"Left hand. When someone leads with the left, it's called a southpaw. Come on, put 'em up."

Flo danced around, swinging out at Jiffo.

"After you swing, don't drop your arms." He showed her, glancing at the girls to make sure he still had his audience. "Keep 'em up. Always protect your face."

"You're movin' too much."

"S'pose to. That's how it's done. The idea is not to get hit."

"I would think it isn't the hit; it's how you come back from the hit."

"Says the authority."

"It's like dancin'. What's so dangerous about it?"

"A fighter can get injured. Brain damage. It's very medical."

"Brain damage? No fear of that, Jiffo."

"You a doctor all of a sudden?"

"You bin fighting practically your whole life out on the street. Don't see the point of all this training."

"Cuz inside a ring it's professional. Your opponent don't sneak up from behind."

Into the spirit now, Flo hit out with her right. "Pow. Pow. Pow."

Jiffo countered with small light jabs. "Pepper, pepper, pepper."

"Salt, salt, salt." Flo broke into gales of laughter.

Tom had seen and heard enough. "Hey, hey up there, this isn't a circus." Hands on his hips, Tom leered at Jiffo while he waited for an explanation.

The laughing ceased instantly. Jiffo introduced Flo and her two girlfriends, Lizzie and Mary. Terrified, the two girls leapt through the side of the ropes as far away from Tom as possible and without looking back ran out of the Iron Pot in a flash.

Flo realized she had done the wrong thing. She dipped into a low curtsy and, in as syrupy a voice as she could muster under the circumstances, she said, "Oh, it's an honor, I'm sure, Mister Riley. Sir Mister Riley. Sir."

Jiffo cleared his throat nervously and said, "I was just showin' Flo Berry and her friends the ropes, so to speak."

Realizing she was Jiffo's girl, Tom regretted he had been so abrupt and changed his tone. "I trust you are in full feather, Miss Berry."

Flo curtsied again. "I'm very well, I'm sure, thank you very much, sir." Lacking good breeding, it wasn't her fault that she was unable to suppress her giggles. She saw the disapproving expression on Tom Riley's face, clammed up, curtsied, jumped through the ropes and headed for the exit without looking back.

"Sorry, Tom," Jiffo said. "I'll tell her not to come down again."

"Anyone can watch as long as they behave themselves."

"I'll tell her."

"I've got something for you, Jiffo. Come with me."

Preparing himself for the worst, Jiffo followed Tom into the office. He was sure he was going to be dismissed from the training at the Iron Pot. He couldn't have been more mistaken. Tom picked up a fancy looking white card from his desktop and after hesitating a split second, picked up a second one. He held both of them out for Jiffo.

"What's these?"

"Invitations to my home. One for you and one for Miss Berry."

Jiffo took the cards from Tom, mumbling a thank you, even if he wasn't quite sure what he was saying thanks to.

"I hope you can make it," Tom called after Jiffo who was on his way to the locker room to change.

Jim Hall saw it at the same time Tom saw it. Jiffo caught a mosquito mid-air between his forefingers and thumb, let it go, caught it again, and let it go again.

"Never seen anyone do that before. Tom, with that kind of agility, I reckon your boy's ready for his first match." Jim was astounded.

"Maybe he is and maybe he isn't." Tom was thinking about the boy's unusually thick upper arms and shoulders for one so slight in frame, about his agility, how quickly he had adapted to the training. "And maybe he is." Tom always liked to have the last word. Especially when he knew he was right.

15

JIFFO AND FLO WERE ENJOYING A PICNIC ON THE BEAUTIFUL grounds of Hyde Park, a blissful and peaceful part of the world, not their accustomed habitat. While it was not too far from The Rocks, life was a three-hundred-and-sixty degree turnabout from their frenetic lifestyle. Being amongst the elite made Flo feel like a real lady. And Jiffo thought it was good for Sydney to stretch his little legs in the green grass.

"Remember that Eye-talian businessman I told you about?" Flo asked.

"Whaddya go spoil it for? I was enjoying the quiet." Jiffo wasn't too thrilled about hearing about *him* again. "Yeah, I remember. What about it?"

"He give me this," she said, patting her hat. And in her best Italian accent, she uttered, "*Kah-pello.*"

"How many times I tell ya, cash only? You're gettin' too matey with the customers."

"It's Eye-talian for hat," she went on, ignoring his remark.

"You got all the words ya need to know without learnin' no foreign ones. Take that stupid thing off your head." He flicked his finger at her hat.

"Well, sir, what about when you becomes a big famous boxer and you're fightin' a famous Eye-talian or Frenchie and what if they don't know no English and you don't know nothin' but Australian, you won't know how to talk to each other." Flo adjusted her hat which had become somewhat askew.

Jiffo made a fist with his right hand and waving it wildly back and forth, he said, "This'll do me talkin', I reckon."

"You're in a right mood. You're always in a mood. Something must have happened you ain't told me about."

"Nothin' happened."

"I mean when you was a lad, not immediate."

"Don't know what youze is on about."

"A boozer. A fighter. A hoodlum. That's you. You can be real mean sometimes. Something must have happened to make you like you are."

"Nothin' happened."

"For instance, take me for instance. I'm a Rocks whore. My mother was a Rocks whore. Until she run off. Then it was just me and him." She stopped talking.

"The silent treatment now."

"Every night for six years from when I was ten. He said it was okay cuz it was a sisterly brotherly love thing and was special."

"I heard enough."

"I was just showing an example. Events that happen to us in our past shape our future. It's just conversation."

"Could you converse a little plainer?"

"It's how people talk sometimes. I told you mine, now you tell me your story."

"Ain't got no story."

"Everybody's got a story."

"No story, I tell ya."

"Come on. It's just us. Sydney don't talk."

"No story, I tell ya." Jiffo hemmed and hawed before he went on. "I got somethin', but don't like talkin' about it."

She waited.

"It was a summer's evening. Mild, like now. Me mum and…naw, forget it."

"Go on."

"Don't remember."

"Fightin' must have erased it from your brain."

"I wish it had. You don't understand what it was like. Me mum and dad and me was strollin'…" He couldn't go on.

"Something happened."

"Never mind. The Edgar family took me in. Jack was their real lad. Until I came along, he was king of the castle. End of story."

"A mum, a dad, a brother." It was a wistful look on Flo's face now.

"They ain't my real family."

"Still…it's a kind of love."

"That's the time I tasted me first drink. I liked it."

"How old were you?"

"Dunno." He thought a minute. "Ten maybe."

Flo winced at the thought of being ten years old because of what had happened to her at that age. But it was too beautiful a day to spoil it with bad thoughts. She moved closer to Jiffo and began moving her fingers playfully over parts of his body, repeating the corresponding word in her best Italian.

"*Testa*, head." She caressed his head.

"What's this, then?"

"*Fahchia*, face." She got closer to him and moved her fingers lightly around his face. "*Naso*, nose."

"Quit it, Flo." Jiffo shifted uncomfortably.

She put her hand on his arm. "*Brachio*, arm." Then she kissed him lightly on the mouth. "*Bocca*." Next, she brushed her fingers across his lips. "*Labbro*."

Jiffo didn't like a public display of affection. "Don't be stupid." He removed her hand from his face.

"*Gamba*, leg." She continued her exploration. "*Coscia*, thigh."

He squirmed. "Not here, I tell ya."

Ignoring his protests, Flo continued to explore his upper body. "*Cuore*, heart." Through his jacket, she felt a slight bump and placing a hand inside his pocket pulled out the two white cards and held them up in front of his eyes. "What's these, I'd like to know?"

"Tom give 'em to me."

She read one of them. "Wow!" She looked up and saw a stone-faced Jiffo.

"You know I can't read it, Flo." Jiffo's voice cracked. It was the first time he had said the words out loud to anyone. Now it was real.

"I know, I know," Flo said softly.

"Well, what is it? What's it say? Both of 'em."

Sensitive to Jiffo's frustration and embarrassment, carefully she rattled off, "You are invited to a Morning Reception next Saturday afternoon at the home of Mr. and Mrs. Thomas A. Riley in Randwick. R. S. V. P."

"What's that?"

"*Ree-spondey seel voo play*," Flo explained in her best French accent which sounded very much like her Italian accent.

"What's that?"

"Let 'em knows if ya can come. It's French."

Jiffo thought a second. "Yeah, but how come they has a Mornin' Recepsun in the afternoon?"

"Because it is what they do on Saturdays, them folks what is upper class," Flo replied all-knowingly in her version of a posh English accent.

Jiffo was slightly dazzled by the information. "Never heard of it. Pretty stupid."

"Well?"

"Well what?"

"There is two invitations." Her four words said volumes as she stared into his eyes.

Jiffo got the message loud and clear. "No worries. I ain't goin' without ya." He quickly added, "I just don't know if I'm goin.'"

16

THE RILEY HOUSE WAS TASTEFULLY AND EXPENSIVELY furnished with the best furniture and décor money and taste could buy. Mary Riley was a painter and a true lady from whom a subtle magnetism seemed to exhale. Tom made no secret of the fact that he knew he had *married up*.

Once, he asked her what she thought about all the parrying in the ring that was in fact a square.

She thought a moment before replying. "Tom, life is a struggle done in private by most folks. A boxer is open about his struggle, taking the blows that come his way. It inspires both repugnance and admiration in the observer. The writer, the painter, the sculptor pick up pen, brush, or chisel and stay in one place. The boxer has to keep moving. Perhaps because the physical act is the exact opposite of the artist's cerebral sedentary lifestyle might be the reason why it is so fascinating." Not one to mince words, she added, "It was the reason I fell in love with you."

Up to that time, Tom thought he was just a brainless hoodlum turned boxer. After Mary's explanation, he saw himself as a kind of artist. And he liked who he was.

The eighteen invited guests mingled, adapting their conversation to the company and the occasion. The men wore the customary formal daytime suit of a black cutaway, striped black pants and vest while the ladies had on muted colored high-necked, long sleeved dresses. Their bonnets were plain with no frills. By contrast, Flo Berry was painfully aware she was the fly in the ointment with her bright multi-colored feathered hat and low cut yellow satin dress, beautiful by gaslight, hardly appropriate for daylight. What she lacked in social graces, she made up for with a swift mind. For most of the time, she chose to observe this new world from a corner, determined to study the art of proper etiquette. Dressed in his larrikin Sunday best and his now worn-in boots, Jiffo was oblivious to any class distinction and in an unconventional way, appeared to be somewhat of a fascination to the ladies.

The refreshments, including tea, coffee, punch, ices, custards, fruit cakes, and a cold collation made up of a variety of meats, were spread out on a buffet table covered with a snow white damask tablecloth. When Jiffo attempted to eat a part of the decorative fruit and flowers, the *faux pas* didn't go unnoticed by one of the gentleman.

"That is a centerpiece, intended to be admired, not handled in preparation for an oral feast. If you insist on behaving in such an uncouth manner, you should return to The Rocks," Lord Annesley spat out. He instantly regretted his words, remembering he was aristocracy, which meant showing no malice to this inferior invited guest who was supposed to be shown the same politeness and consideration as an equal.

Jiffo retorted the only way he knew how. "Put 'em up, you bloody stuck up stuffed shirt." He put his fists up, adopting a boxing stance.

"Mind your language, boy. There are ladies present."

"Bloody good thing. Otherwise, we wouldn't be standin' here talkin' about it, if you get my drift, mate."

"Why, why I've got a good mind to…to…" Lord Annesley couldn't think what to say.

"To what, guv?" Jiffo held his fight position.

Instead of using words, Lord Annesley pulled himself up to his full height. He was considerably larger than Jiffo and that fact alone allowed him a modicum of confidence in this dicey situation.

Jiffo eyed the giant before him. "Don't let that fool you, guv. I near killed blokes twice your size with this," he replied, waving a fist back and forth under the gentleman's chin which was as far as his arm would reach.

For a moment the two froze, each one staring at the other. After a few seconds, Jiffo's cunning kicked in. He broke out into a big grin, opened his fist and offered his open palm. At first, Lord Annesley was reluctant about accepting the gesture and kept eyeing the hand belonging to the odd little fellow who was its owner. Jiffo was unrelenting and

Lord Annesley, proving himself to be a true member of the peerage, shook the outstretched hand, deeply relieved it was not Jiffo's closed fist that was making contact.

Jiffo's brand of diplomacy had been witnessed by Tom who was very pleased that a clobbering had been averted. He took the moment as an opportunity to announce that Young Jiffo's first professional boxing match would be in three weeks time against the well-known Sydney feather-weight, Bobo Quigley. An immediate buzz filled the room. An ecstatic Jiffo clasped his hands over his head in a victory gesture. Mindful of her surroundings, Flo's cheers and howling at the news were all kept inside.

"This is the beginning, my boy. Are you ready?"

"Tom, I'll knock him out in four," Jiffo stated positively. Leaning over the buffet table, his interest had switched to the plate in his hand as he set out to pile it with food.

It was one of those awkward, freak accidents that could have happened to anyone. As Jiffo moved away from the table, the edge of the tablecloth caught onto his watch-chain causing the punch bowl, food, plates, cutlery, and glasses to crash smack onto the parquet floor. Seconds before the loud gasps and groans from the guests, accompanied by the piercing scream from Flo Berry, you could have heard a pin drop. Ever the perfect, attentive hostess, Mary Riley chose this halt in the proceedings to shuffle her guests out to the lawn for a game of croquet. With great diplomacy, she gently dismissed the ladies' protests about not having on the appropriate shoes for lawn croquet.

17

WHILE ALLOWED TO WATCH TRAINING IN AUSTRALIA, ladies could not attend matches. Flo strongly objected to what she thought was an outlandish rule but, with no choice, eventually had to give in. For giving their solemn word not to stir up any trouble, several Push members were permitted into the packed out Iron Pot to join the near nine hundred excited fight fans.

Tom had picked Bobo Quigley as Jiffo's first professional opponent because he was good, but not so strong that Jiffo couldn't beat him. Tom Riley, with all his fight wisdom, couldn't have predicted what happened. The referee paced around the center of the ring. And waited. Quigley sat in his corner. And waited. Jim Hall and Tom Riley hovered in the opposite corner. And waited. A livid Tom Riley had a gut feeling as to the whereabouts of the missing fighter and in a fury stormed out of the Iron Pot.

Flo Berry opened the door to her room. Expecting it to be unoccupied, she let out a scream that could be heard on the other side of Australia. She didn't know which to be angrier about: that her man was in bed with another girl or that he was missing his first professional boxing match.

"How many times I tell ya, Flo, believe only half of what you read and nothin' of what you see," he slurred.

"But I see you," Flo hollered.

A disheveled Jiffo leapt out of bed, jumped into his pants and stumbled past her. "You ain't seen nothin'. I ain't here. Simple as that." He tumbled down the stairs where midway he rolled smack into his pursuer. "Evenin', Tom."

Tom was seething. "You're pickled, you are." He grabbed his soused fighter by the neck and pulled him the rest of the way down the staircase and out the front door.

"I'll knock him out in four. I'll knock him out in four."

"You knock him out? *You* knock *him* out? He'll knock you out in one, you little drunken bastard." Tom half-pushed, half-dragged Jiffo through the streets in the direction of the Iron Pot.

"I'll knock him out in four," repeated Jiffo who was unsuccessful in remaining upright without Tom's aggressive assistance.

"The hell you will. I've a good mind to knock you out right now." Heading for the Iron Pot, in the silence, he had a thought and was sure he had it figured out. "You punk. Is it because you're afraid you'll lose?"

"Lose? I'm gonna win. No worries, mate," Jiffo boasted.

"If you know you're gonna win, why'd you run away?"

"I'll tell ya. When I win and become famous, I'll have to live in Randwick."

"Randwick? What's Randwick got to do with it?"

"Where the rich people live like you."

"What the Christ are you on about?"

"I ain't leavin' da Rocks."

"Aye." So that was it. Tom loosened his grip on Jiffo. He was reminded of his own move from The Rocks all those many years ago. At first, he had protested, too. There was compassion in his voice when he said, "Come on, son, we need to be pulling you together. We got a fight to win."

18

After multiple dunkings in a tub of ice water, Young Jiffo climbed into the ring with the assistance of Tom and Jim. It took the two of them to guide Jiffo into the stool in his corner of the ring. The restless spectators conversed among themselves. The punters put more money down. Some Jiffo supporters switched their bets to Quigley. Some bet on whether or not there would be a fight. One thing all of them had in common, no one could take their eyes off the center ring in anticipation of the awaited event.

Bare-chested, the two boxers wore the typical attire of the day: flat, black leather shoes, white calf-length cotton tights with a crimson sash at the waist, lightweight six ounce gloves. Quigley was a tough looking pug, shorter and lighter in weight than Jiffo's trainers. Tom had told Jiffo he would have to shorten his punches, but not let up on muscle. The starting bell rang. A hush fell over the gymnasium. Infuriated by the long wait, Quigley flew out of his corner. As he approached the center of the ring, he held up his hands in a victory gesture as if he'd already won. The gesture was lost on the crowd, as all eyes were on Jiffo who hadn't moved from his corner.

Tom was beside himself. "What's he waiting for, damn it! Go, Jiffo! Go, Go!"

The crowd was now shouting, "Jiff-o...Jiff-o...Jiff-o...Jiff-o..."

There was no explaining the strange metamorphosis that came over the still slightly inebriated Jiffo as he got up from his stool and met his opponent in the center of the ring. The little fellow with bleary eyes became a remarkably skilled fighting machine with a keen concentration. He remembered everything Tom had taught him. Quigley shot out a fusillade of lefts and rights, then bore in for what he thought would be a quick kill, only to find himself swinging foolishly at empty air. Jiffo's ability to dodge punches with a minute movement of his head or a twist of a shoulder was uncanny. The handkerchief trick had been his training. As predicted, Jiffo knocked out Quigley in the fourth round. The crowd went wild. In all his years, Tom had never seen anything like it. In one swoop, he and Jim hoisted an unmarked Jiffo up onto their shoulders. Just as Jiffo had heard the crowd chanting for Tom Riley that day on the heath, the fans were now chanting for him.

"There is a fighter named Jiffo
When asked will he fight,
He says, too bloody right,
I'll knock 'im for four in a jiffo!"

"I did it, Tom. I did it. I'm the Australian champ!"

"Not quite, my boy. We've a long way to go before you earn that title."

Jiffo wasn't listening. All he was thinking about was how easy it had been. All he did was what he did down at The

Rocks, in an alley, or at the docks; only now it was inside a boxing ring wearing special fight gear with people watching and cheering, and he was getting legitimate money for it. Jiffo couldn't wait for his next match.

19

FOR THE NEXT TWO YEARS, JIFFO SPENT THE MAJORITY OF HIS time with the boxing career that Tom was carving out for him. He gave up his job as a newsboy. And although Push activities had slightly waned, to Tom's disappointment, Jiffo had not been able to eliminate that part of his life completely. Neither had he been able to give up drinking. No matter how soused Jiffo was when he stepped into the ring, when he faced his opponent, he was transformed. No one could figure it out. Not even Tom would try.

Flo had mixed feelings about what was happening with Jiffo's career. They still saw each other, they still went dancing and all that, but she was beginning to feel left behind. After an evening of carousing, back in her room, she broached the subject that had been on her mind.

"I ain't seen much of you lately with your training and fighting and all," she said.

"We was havin' a good quiet time. Whaddya wanna start yakkin' for?"

"You haven't found another girl, have you?"

He knew she knew about the other girls so there was no point making it a topic for discussion. "You know the rules. I'm keeping myself fit while I'm in training. I bin with Tom in the ring and on the road. He's got me doin' road work at the crack of dawn. Plus me other responsibilities."

"The docks you mean."

"What about it?"

"I heard."

"My motto? Believe nothing you hear."

"You're a successful boxer now. On your way up. Why do you still need the Push?"

"Cuz one day these hands ain't gonna be able to make a fist no more." He made a fist with his right hand. I need somethin' what to fall back on."

"You could run the Iron Pot Boxing Academy. Later on, I mean. Be a trainer."

"Like Tom? Naw. That ain't me."

"Why not?"

"I ain't a role model kind of bloke."

"That's not true. Everyone looks up to you. I could be your…your helpmate."

"Say what?"

Not sure what to say next, she changed the subject. "You seem on edge. And you're drinkin' more than usual.

"Don't you start. I get enough from Tom."

"What about after?"

"After what?"

"When you're a big champ. You'll emigrate to America like the other fighters before you. I'll never see you again." That's all she thought about. And now it was out in the open.

"Not me. Sydney and da Rocks is good enough for me."

"You say that now."

"Repeating…Sydney and da Rocks is good enough for me."

After a slight hesitation, unable to keep it under wraps, Flo blurted out, "What about us?"

"Us as in you and me?"

"You know what I mean."

Jiffo did not like the direction of the conversation. "You're one of my girls."

"That it?"

"Dead right. Youze is part of the team. A big part.

Anyways, how come youze is askin' all these questions all of a sudden? You never asked before. My advice? Stay out of my business. Do what you do best."

"And what is it I do best?"

"It ain't interrogation, I can tell ya that."

"I'm getting older. These looks ain't, aren't guaranteed to stay forever."

"You got somethin' to say, say it."

"I been thinking about my life."

"Thinkin' again. Never a good thing."

"The Rocks. The docks. The Push."

"If you want more money, we can talk about that."

"It ain't, isn't the money. Nothing's changing."

"Changing? Youze is under a misconception. Places don't change."

She took a deep breath. "The brothel. The smell of the bed. I want one man in my bed."

"Blimey, Flo, if that's what you want, youze is established in the wrong business."

"I want a fortnight's holiday at the beach every year. I want tea every afternoon in a real china cup. I want to eat beef every week."

"Higher wages. I thought so. I can fix that."

"It's more than that. I'm gettin' fed up with second hand goods."

"Youze is takin' it too personal. Like fightin's my business. The Iron Pot's Tom's business. Your business is your business. Youze is there, but you ain't there. You know how to do it. You're a pro. It ain't personal. It's business."

"I have a chance." Flo's voice was low now. "A chance."

"What chance you talkin' about?"

"An opportunity."

"Now it's an opportunity. I don't know what youze is talkin' about."

"An engagement." She studied his face.

"Engagement? What kind of engagement?"

"There is only one kind of engagement."

Jiffo was silent.

Flo went on. "Like in marriage. Maybe I can get married to someone. Someone you don't know, as it happens."

"Jeez, Flo, if you want outta the game, can't ya go into domestic service like a regular girl?"

"Who says I'm a regular girl? You ever think about marriage?"

"I think about it. I think the hours would be too long."

"I told you about that Eye-talian businessman. He wants to marry me and bring me to Italy." It was out now. Once out, there was no taking back the words.

"We have a rule about that. No fraternizin' with the paying customers outside of shaggin'."

"We never had no rule about that. What about you and me?"

"I'm holdin' me tongue on that subjek. I recommend you do the same."

"So assassinate me."

"This conversation is distinkly unconventional."

"If you must know, I've been helpin' with a kind of business idea this bloke has. You wouldn't understand. Never mind. I said enough."

"Quit wafflin'. Spit it out." Jiffo was more curious than angry.

"It's like what they call an experiment. Early stages for a machine that can go up in the air. A flying cab."

"A what?"

"I can't explain."

"Use your words."

"You won't get mad?"

"Dunno. I ain't heard it yet."

"It's a machine made of a kind of mixture of different

metals. A pilot drives passengers. It's got an engine you crank up with a handle on the outside and everyone wears goggles. Them's big glasses."

"Flo, I got a serious query."

"What?"

"You on opium?"

"Don't be daft. Listen to me, Jiff. It's a vehicle for transportation that can go up in the air. This Eye-talian businessman I been tellin you about is doin' it." She wanted desperately for him to get it. For him to be impressed. For something from him.

"He's on poppy juice. Never thought nothin' of them foreigners. Sounds phony."

"It's legit."

"So whaddya tellin' me for?"

"I thought you…you might…never mind."

"Never mind is correct. You think I'm gonna stop you? Cuz I ain't. You wanna go? You wanna go? Be my guest. I got plenty of other girls." He punched the air. No longer curious, he was angrier than he'd ever been. "As it happens, I'm takin' this as your official notice of resignation."

"My what?"

"You heard me."

"Why are you being like this?"

"You're Eye-talian bloke might be waitin'. I'm gettin' outta here." Jiffo quickly got out of the bed, put on his clothes, bowed from the waist, and left the room without saying another word.

Flo let the tears come. It was all wrong. She hadn't meant to say what she did. She did have a plan, but not what it sounded like. There was no Eye-talian engagement. She'd lied hoping to get a proposal out of Jiffo. Her plan hadn't worked. She dressed and raced over to the Fortune of War where Jiffo was bound to be. She didn't want to lose him.

20

THE SPORTS REPORTER FOR THE JOURNAL ESPECIALLY LIKED when he got to interview someone of prominence. "Mister Riley, your boy Young Jiffo here has fought Tommy Warren, Paddy Moran, Frank Murphy, Chiddy Ryan, Ike Weir, and Jerry Marshall. Some as many as six times and some weighing much more than him. It seems like he's running out of opponents in his class. What's next?"

"Pete, son, there's no question you've studied your facts. Write this in your paper. Nipper Peakes is next in Melbourne for the Australian featherweight title. When Jiffo wins that one, and make no mistake, he will win, he'll fight Billy Murphy in Sydney. When he wins that fight, Young Jiffo will be the featherweight champion of the world."

Pete was impressed. "The Torpedo? Murphy nearly killed a man once. Can Jiffo beat him?"

Jiffo spoke up now, imitating Riley's Irish accent. "It's a fearful mauling that awaits Billy Murphy at the hands of Young Jiffo."

"What about after, Jiffo? Will you emigrate like Peter Jackson, Dan Creedon, Frank Slavin, and some of the others?" The reporter asked.

Jiffo wanted no part of travel and replied emphatically, "Sydney and da Rocks is good enough for me."

Ignoring Jiffo's comment, Tom said, "America's the place."

"Why America, Mister Riley?" asked Pete.

"Well, it's clear we've run out of competition here. There's big money to be made over there. They call it the Golden Age, you know. They've got horseless carriages, machines that run on chemicals, moving pictures. Aye, America's the place."

The reporter asked, "What's the purse for the Nipper Peakes fight?"

Tom puffed up his chest and said, "Twelve hundred pounds for the winner."

Jiffo piped up in all seriousness, "I ain't fightin' for less than a thousand."

Not realizing that Jiffo had not made a joke, the reporter let out a loud laugh and said, "That's a good one, Jiff." Having accomplished his assignment, Pete asked if anyone had any objections if he stayed around and watched training.

Tom said, "Be our guest. All are welcome to watch. Even the ladies. Did you know that in America, ladies are not allowed to watch training, but can attend the matches? Down under, the women aren't allowed to attend the matches."

Pete said, "That's quite interesting. I did not know that."

In jest, Jiffo adopted a boxing stance. "Put 'em up, Mister Writer."

Pete was chuffed, but declined the invitation. "Thanks, but I believe I'll leave the fighting to the Shakespeare of the ring."

"Shakespeare? He ain't so good. I knocked him out in three."

21

JIFFO WAS MOVING UP AND FLO WASN'T FITTING INTO HIS new life. She was determined to elevate herself to match his climb out of the no-hope existence. In private, she focused on the flying cab concept she had told him about. The day came when she was ready. It didn't have to be a secret any more.

Jiffo stared at the huge black lettering on the side of the outside of the large wooden structure which was open in the front and in the rear.

FLO BERRY AND HER FLYING CAB.

They were just letters to him until Flo read the sign out loud.

Jiffo was baffled. He looked at her costume. "And what the hell are you wearin'?"

Flo's customary satin, silk, ribbons, artificial flowers, and feathers had been replaced by a subdued gray service-able outfit of a light woolen material. Her bonnet was neat without trimming. She wore stout boots better fitted to endure the vicissitudes of the weather and other acts of nature.

Ignoring Jiffo's question about her clothing, Flo said, "The building is called a hangar."

Jiffo didn't know what she was talking about, and he definitely didn't care much for her new get-up.

Flo was in a positive frame of mind as she led an apprehensive Jiffo inside. In the middle of the large space sat a machine of metal. "Here it is. Two seats, an engine, some controls, and it goes up in the air and moves around when I propel it. Pretty basic. My flying cab." She moved her arms forward and back.

For one of the few times in his life, Jiffo was at a loss for words.

"I built it myself." She didn't think it was a lie to omit certain details. The fact was she had made a deal, using her strengths, with a certain Eye-talian acquaintance. As far as she was concerned, a lady must live. She was on her way to independence. To Jiffo's obvious lack of comprehension, she said simply, "Businessmen hire me to fly them to meetings in different locations locally."

All Jiffo could think about was the money she had been giving him. "Set me straight on this so's I can understand. The money you been payin' out to me these past months come from this here occupation and not the main occupation?"

She shook her head. "I wanted it to be a surprise."

"Some surprise, I reckon." After a second, Jiffo said flatly, "I don't want no more money from you. I got enough money."

Flo had reached a new plateau. For the first time, she felt his equal. He couldn't possibly leave her behind now when he went out to conquer the world. "I'll take you up for a spin."

"Maybe some other time." Jiffo could handle himself in any situation with his feet on the ground, but the truth was this flying machine scared him to death.

Ignoring his protest, Flo cranked up the large metal handle on the side of the machine. "The loud roaring sound is the engine," she shouted. She climbed up onto the flat surface projecting from the side of the machine and into her seat. She motioned for a hesitant Jiffo to get in the other side. She waited until he finally climbed up into the contraption.

She reached across him and made sure he was secure. "Always the job of the pilot to check the passenger."

"Who?"

"Me. Okay, here we go, Jiffy." Flo focused. The take-off was smooth. In no time, they were above the trees.

"Don't call me Jiffy," he shouted over the loud whirring of the engine, praying his bowels wouldn't obey his nausea and open up.

"It's easy." Demonstrating her skills, Flo said, "When I push this stick back, we go down." They went down. "When I push it forwards, we go up." They went up.

Jiffo was hanging on for dear life. This was not how he wanted his life to end. "I didn't know this is what you was doin' when I was fightin'. I thought you was busy doing your business. The other business. I thought you was over all this flyin' business."

Feeling no need to explain, she said, "You can see the other side of the clouds from here. See how fluffy they are?" Flo was in heaven.

Jiffo was in hell. "We ain't gonna crash, is we? Just keep your eyes on the road."

"I read the instructions and the maps. I know where we are." She stopped talking. It was that old thing again about Jiffo not being able to read. She changed the subject. "God lives up here."

The only god Jiffo knew was called John Barleycorn. "You ain't got somethin' to drink in here, has ya? I'm feelin' a bit queasy. I'm better off goin' twenty rounds inside a ring than sittin' in this thing. No offense, Flo. Ya gotta get me down." Jiffo was sweating profusely.

Flo switched gears and headed for the landing strip. She had proved the point that it was possible to change your life. She glanced over at Jiffo who was retching into a paper sack, always part of the equipment in a flying cab, and she knew there could never be another man for her.

22

It was Jiffo's back that Nelson approached at the bar in the Fortune of War. "I'd like a word," he stated firmly.

Recognizing the voice, Jiffo didn't turn around.

"We figure it this way," Nelson said, a little less sure. Gaining courage, he went on. "Like, they'll all have their money on you, so the story is, we're gonna put all the money in the Push bank account on Peakes." Nelson got closer.

Jiffo could feel the traitor's breath on his neck, but still said nothing.

"You give the fight to the Nipper in the fifth round, and we all clean up, includin' you, Jiff."

Keeping his eyes straight ahead, Jiffo slowly sipped his beer.

Nelson thought Jiffo didn't understand. He boldly added, "Not to worry, mate, you get your cut as member of the Push."

Without moving, without any emotion, Jiffo spoke. "I'm still the captain, reckon?"

Unable to contain his wrath, Nelson screeched, "The whole Push is behind me now."

"Is that a fact?" Jiffo remained controlled.

Nelson stood firm. At first, he didn't mind, but now he

didn't like talking to Jiffo's back. "You got exactly thirty-six hours to fix the fight," he said.

Jiffo turned his head and looked Nelson in his one eye. In all seriousness, he said, "The thing is like this, Mister Nelson, I'd like to help ya out, but it's like I keep tellin' ya, the captain of the Push is the only one who can get the money out of the bank."

Being eye-balled by Jiffo made Nelson extremely nervous, and when he got nervous, his voice went from arsehole to breakfast. He sounded like a howling animal caught in a trap. "Get it out first thing tomorrow. You know what time the bank opens, Mister Captain."

Jiffo was still calm. "From where I stand, I'm still runnin' things around here."

"No, you ain't." With a nod of his head, Nelson indicated several Push members who were hanging around the far end of the bar. "You ain't the leader no more."

"Don't think they heard you all that far away," Jiffo said.

"They're all behind me."

"Looks like them's standin' behind the bar, not behind you."

Nelson opened his mouth, but having run out of his clumsy repartee, nothing came out.

"You know the rules, Lieutenant Nelson. How many times I keep sayin', if you wanna be the captain of the Push, you gotta take me in a fair fight. Then you can be the leader. Now that seems very fair to me." Jiffo turned as if about to walk away, but in a swift movement, he spun around and breaking a Push rule, he punched Nelson hard in the stomach. Nelson went down without knowing what hit him.

Jiffo picked up his beer from the bar counter, raised the mug to Nelson's so-called supporters. "Cheers!" He downed his drink and walked out, leaving a mortified Nelson on the floor.

23

WHILE JIFFO WAS AT THE IRON POT RECEIVING GOOD WISHES for his coming fight in Melbourne, Nelson planned his revenge where he knew it would hurt. Flo Berry.

"Look who's here as pretty as any sheila could be all by her lonesome." Nelson couldn't believe his luck as he swayed from one foot to the other.

"I'm waitin' for Lizzie so's we can go over to the Iron Pot. Shouldn't you be over there wishin' your leader good luck and farewell and all?"

"Looks like I'm the one in luck." Nelson didn't waste any time with his purpose. "Bein' as we works for the same organization, so to speak, I could use some relaxation." His tone was all sugar.

"Join the queue." Her tone was all vinegar.

"You don't seem keen." He reached out for her, his hand just brushing her shoulder as she stepped away. That didn't sit too well with him. "Wowser," he cursed as he closed in on her.

"Jesus! Get away, you snake." Wowser. Hardly an apt description, but through his eyes, she certainly was behaving puritanical. She knew what he was after and quickly defended herself, trying to remember a boxing position that Jiffo had taught her.

As her arm came out at his face, he grabbed it with his hand, almost twisting it off. She was breathing hard as she lashed out with her other arm.

"You like it rough, that it?" He grabbed her arm. Now he had both her arms pulled behind her back as his body covered hers.

"Get away from me, you no good crim." The smell of stale liquor all over him flew up her nostrils making her slightly woozy. She struggled to free herself.

"This ain't friendly, Flo. Ain't ya gonna invite me into your establishment? I reckon this ain't the way a professional Rocks prostitute welcomes a customer."

"I got another business now and you ain't a customer. Piss off. I'll call Jiffo."

Nelson's one good eye looked like it would pop out of his head. "He can't hear ya, Flo. It's just me and just you." He twisted her around with such force that they both fell backwards down on the ground with a thud.

24

Outside the Iron Pot, final farewells were in progress. Patrons, pupils, and other fans were confident that their hero would return from Melbourne with the title.

Lizzie came running towards them interrupting the pleasantries shouting at the top of her lungs, "Flo's been attacked outside the hangar by that hood with the eye patch."

Jiffo tensed. Only twice before had he had this kind of sick feeling in his gut. Once, when he rescued a helpless little dog from a near fatal beating, and that Sunday when he couldn't rescue his mum and dad.

Tom reminded Jiffo they were ready to leave, but he knew Jiffo couldn't be stopped from going after Nelson; not when Flo was concerned.

Nothing appealed more to an Australian than a good fight. Led by Jiffo, with Tom and Jim along side, an immediate procession formed in a march down Pitt Street. On the way, pub crawlers, pedestrians, sportsmen, shopkeepers, butchers still in their aprons, and members of the police brigade joined them, all of them with one goal in mind.

"We'll get the lot of 'em," said the marching chief of police. "It's time we cleaned up that mob. Come on, lads, get the lead out."

Jiffo knew in an instant his Push days had come to an end. All he wanted was Flo to be alive; then he would personally put Nelson out of business for good. He stepped up the pace. As the crowd approached Flo's wooden shack, Tom warned Jiffo against using up his energy in a street brawl. Tom needn't have worried. On the ground lay Nelson out cold. Flo was standing upright next to him.

Happy to see Jiffo and half the townspeople, she raised her arms in a victory gesture the way she'd seen Jiffo do and quickly explained, "I've been experimenting with a thin metal shield that can be worn under clothing to protect the upper bodies of me and my passengers in case of a crash. I was wearing it. I'm wearing it now." She pounded her chest with her fists. "It was this shield that protected me from Nelson. He flung himself up against me, I forced my upper body against him, and the impact knocked him out." She was delirious with happiness. "Guess my invention works, don't it, Jiffy? And it didn't hurt that Miss Lizzie here happened along when she did."

Lizzie smiled and waved at the crowd who let out a little cheer for her.

For once, Jiffo didn't mind being called Jiffy.

The human side of Tom was glad that Flo hadn't been hurt, but the businessman side was more relieved that his boy was in one piece and would get to the Melbourne fight in time.

While the police were busy doing their job of handcuffing a dazed Nelson, Jiffo had something he wanted to say to the crowd. It was now or never. He held up his hand to get their attention. In a loud voice, he said, "I hereby announce the official end to all Push activities. All the money in the Push account will be shared out to the poor who never had the good luck like I did to meet the great Tom Riley." His voice never cracked once.

25

"Young Jiffo, new featherweight champion of Australia," shouted the young newsboy who had stepped into Jiffo's place at the Journal.

At the Edgar home, stumbling over only a few words, Jack read an account of the fight to his parents. "In the sixteenth round, Young Jiffo weaved and ducked, and then sent in a stream of punches against the weakening national champion who sunk to the floor. By the count of five, Nipper Peakes was out cold. The Melbourne crowd cheered the new Australian champion for a full ten minutes."

"Jingoes!" said Mrs. Edgar, proud as she could be. "In Melbourne. Did you hear that, Mister Edgar?"

Sydney, who was now allowed inside the house, barked and jumped up and down as if he understood every word about his master.

Sneezing at the proximity of the barking dog, Jack continued. "Torpedo Billy Murphy is the world champion in the featherweight class. If Young Jiffo can take him—and he hasn't lost a bout yet—then he will own the title."

"Title?" asked Mr. Edgar.

"The featherweight champion of the world," Jack replied with great pride.

"Our Bert in the world. Did you hear that, Missus Edgar?"

Mrs. Edgar nodded. She knew he'd turn out right.

26

"Young Jiffo, featherweight champion of Australia fights Torpedo Billy Murphy, featherweight champion of the world," shouted out the newsboy who couldn't imagine doing any other job in the whole world.

The Iron Pot could comfortably hold nine hundred. This night, nearly double that number had squeezed in. Amidst the frenzy of the last minute betting, no one paid attention to the young man with the eye patch, carrying a folded up newspaper and wearing a long coat, who worked his way through the crowd and jammed himself into a seat half way to the front. The escaped prisoner was clumsy and, as he sat down, his coat fell open just enough to reveal a pistol stuck in his belt. Quickly, he covered himself, looking around. All eyes were on the center ring. It didn't appear that anyone had observed Nelson's mishap.

It was no man's land between the Murphy supporters and the Jiffo supporters, each side calling out for victory for their favorite. When Jiffo and Billy Murphy entered the ring, fist fights between the two factions broke out. For a few minutes, no one knew who was fighting whom. It took a full fifteen minutes to restore order. Tom warned Jiffo to keep his focus on Murphy, not the crowd. The referee announced loudly that this was the fight for the featherweight championship of the world. He called the two boxers to stand with him in the center of the ring. Briefly, he went over the rules, emphasizing that the fighters were to break clear any time at his word, that his word was final, and the bell was to be obeyed as a starting signal and as the signal to end the round. He then ordered the fighters to their respective corners to await the official start of the fight.

The starting bell clanged. Before Jiffo moved out of his corner, Murphy rushed at him and led with a jab to the top of his head. It failed to connect. Jiffo skipped around to the other side of the ring. Murphy rushed in again. Again, Jiffo sidestepped; this time, with accompanying insults.

A ringsider jumped off his seat and shouted, "Hit him with the right, Jiffo."

Jiffo made the grave mistake of turning his head. "What say?" he shouted.

Murphy grabbed the opportunity and with split-second timing and precision, he jammed a right hook into Jiffo's head that was strong enough to knock Jiffo onto the canvas. The crowd went wild.

"Jesus." Tom hadn't expected that to happen. At any rate, not so immediately. "Get up, Jiffo," he shouted. "Get up! Get up!"

It took a few seconds for a stunned Jiffo to get to his feet. Murphy didn't waste any time. He hit Jiffo repeatedly with a series of effective punches to the head and face. Only the sound of the bell ended the brutal beating. Jiffo staggered to his corner where Tom and Jim cleaned his bloodied face with cold water and liquid antiseptic.

It was a combat zone. Tom didn't know how long Jiffo would be able to take it. Billy Murphy was capable of killing a man in the ring. If Jiffo could keep dodging, somehow get Murphy fatigued, maybe he would at least live.

Round seven. Murphy sneered at his challenger and went in for the kill. He threw a right at Jiffo who sidestepped the blow and countered with a right to Murphy's middle. Murphy doubled over in pain. Out of the corner of his eye, Jiffo looked at the cheering crowd. Next, he prepared to hit Murphy with a looping right to the chin. He swung his arm and threw a punch, but his grandstanding threw off his timing and when he looked back, Murphy was gone. Now on Jiffo's blind side, Murphy threw a series of unexpected punches into Jiffo's ribs. Jiffo was out of breath, but retaliated with a flurry of punches into Murphy's middle. The bell sounding the end of the round didn't stop them. When the referee stepped in, he only succeeded in copping a few loose blows from the fighters. It was Tom who finally pulled the two boxers apart.

Rounds eight through thirteen went much the same. Ignoring the protocol, they were two street punks battling it out.

Round fourteen began with Jiffo dodging punches from Murphy. A frustrated Murphy turned his back on Jiffo, then swung around suddenly and threw a jab at Jiffo's head. Instinctively, Jiffo moved his head slightly to the left, causing Murphy's arm to carry on straight through in mid-air. Jiffo half-smiled at the missed shot, but before he realized it, Murphy brought his elbow back to connect with Jiffo's jaw. The blow that sounded like a champagne cork being popped knocked Jiffo flat on his back and out cold.

One ringsider climbed in the ring, grabbed a bucket of cold water to hand, and threw it over Jiffo. The fallen fighter opened his eyes, but couldn't stand up. Tom dragged a soaked Jiffo back to the corner. Jim dried him off and held smelling salts under his nose while the referee took special care to wipe the canvas clean of all the water.

Tom didn't think he had been wrong about Jiffo's abilities, but he knew it was time to conclude this bloodbath before his boy got killed. He could end the fight, but that was a last resort. There was still a chance; that is, if Jiffo could comprehend his directive. Just as the bell clanged, Tom whispered something in Jiffo's ear. Something major. And then he silently prayed.

Round fifteen. With one eye half closed, Jiffo staggered out of his corner and met his opponent in the center of the ring. Oblivious to the crowd, only Tom's whispered words sustained him. Murphy extended his arm out to Jiffo's head for what Murphy thought would be a straight hit, but Jiffo ducked and, with everything he had, bore in with a solid left to Murphy's right kidney. Before Murphy folded, Jiffo came in with a powerful right uppercut to the chin. Murphy was down.

The referee began the count. Jiffo never took his eyes off his opponent who got to his feet before the count reached ten. It wasn't over yet. With all his hundred and twenty-six pounds, Jiffo tore into Murphy, finally crashing into him with the knockout blow. The referee tolled eight, then nine, then ten over the fallen champion.

It was over. The crowd was on its feet. The Jiffo backers who had been holding their breath could now breathe. And that included Tom. Half the Murphy supporters were now cheering for their new hero. The other half were calling for a rematch.

27

THIS WAS THE MOMENT THE ESCAPED PRISONER HAD BEEN waiting for. Unnoticed, he made his way through the jostling crowd, took the gun from inside his coat, slipped it into the newspaper, aimed the paper at the victorious Jiffo and fired. The sound pierced through a stunned gymnasium. Not fully understanding what had happened, the patrons went silent.

Miraculously, the bullet hit the corner post with a loud ricochet, missing its target by only a few feet. All eyes were on Tom Riley as he jumped over the ropes, reached the would-be assassin, knocked the gun out of his hand, and then knocked him out. Thinking they had got double for their money, the crowd burst into a frenzy of wild excitement.

"Cor'blimey, it's more bloody dangerous outside the ring than in it," exclaimed Jiffo, still too surprised to realize how close he had come to losing his life.

The referee held up the arm of the winner and in a voice that was just audible above the clamor, very precisely announced the final decision. "THE NEW FEATHERWEIGHT CHAMPION OF THE WORLD—YOUNG JIFFO."

Tom raced back to his champ, leaving the fallen prisoner to the attending police. A beaming Jiffo acknowledged the crowd and threw his arms around Tom.

Later, in the packed dressing room, noisy well-wishers were offering their congratulations. Jiffo was the picture of health, if you didn't count one eye that had swollen shut, the other that was discolored, and a mouth that was so swollen, it appeared to expand to his ear. He was finding it a little difficult to sip his beer, but not impossible.

The Journal reporter was doing his job. With pencil and his notepad in hand, he asked, "Jiffo, tell us in your own words, how did you do it?"

Without skipping a beat, Jiffo held up his beer mug and replied, "I was thirsty." The remark brought gales of laughter from those close enough to hear.

"May I quote you?"

Jiffo held up his glass as his positive answer.

"One final question. What's next for the champ?"

Without a second's hesitation, Tom Riley shouted, "America!"

"Can I quote you on that, Mr. Riley?"

"You can bet on it." Tom began to dismiss the crowd. "That'll be all for now, folks. Don't want my boy to catch a chill."

28

Next day, a clean and rested Jiffo was in Tom's office.

Tom knew no other way than to tell it like it was. "You've won the featherweight title, there is no mistaking about that."

"Aye."

"But, son, here's the truth. It is official only in Australia."

"Aye."

"You're not getting it. To be truly accepted in the world, to truly hold the world title, you have to fight George Dixon who holds the American version of the world featherweight title. Then it's an official world title."

Jiffo was puzzled. "I almost got killed out there. What was I fightin' for if it didn't count? Why didn't you tell me this before?"

"Because I didn't know myself. It did count. You had to fight Murphy, and I always said you'd have to go to America. Now when you go, you go as a somebody."

"I'm still the champ?"

"You'll go down in boxing history as the world featherweight champion, but it's considered an Australian title only. You have to go to America. Those are the rules."

"Funny rules. A world title, but only in Australia. Ain't we part of the world?"

"Boxing has changed, Jiffo. It was different in my day, and even when you started out five, six years ago."

It was a fact there was nothing left for Jiffo in Australia. The racketeers were moving in. Boxing was not an art form any more. It was about skill and strategy and stamina. To prove the point, George Dixon had recently gone seventy rounds with Cal McCarthy in Boston, Massachusetts.

Jiffo started pacing back and forth. "I don't believe this."

"You've come too far to throw it all away. I've taken you from the street to the ring. I can't do any more." Tom was ready to let go. "Look at it as my gift to my protégé on his twenty-first birthday."

"A pocket watch is a gift."

"It is all arranged. The match will take place in seven months in New York. You'll be reporting to Bishop's Athletic Gym of New York when you arrive. George Bishop's a dinkum bloke from Melbourne. You'll be in good hands. He'll be acting as your second over there."

Jiffo wasn't sure how he felt about leaving his mates. Actually, he was sure. He didn't want to go. "I need a drink." He headed out the door of Tom's office for the pub. After all that Tom had done for him and after all Tom was telling him, that's all he could say. *I need a drink*. But he didn't go to the pub. He went to see Flo to tell her the news. Maybe she knew. Maybe they all knew but him.

Tom's spirit was not dampened. He knew Jiffo would come around and accept the privilege. He didn't want his boy fighting it out on a heath for his last match the way he had done.

29

THE FORMER HOODLUM FROM THE ROCKS STOOD AT THE rail of the S.S. Parramatta in Sydney Harbour. Earlier that morning, it had been a tearful farewell with the Edgar family who had taken him in and made him part of their family, the decision having been made that it would be best to part company at home. He had barely been able to look at his dog that by now, to Jiffo's relief, had bonded with Jack.

Jiffo waved to the throng. Even though he didn't want to leave his mates, he knew he had to chase after the crown that was rightfully his. "I'll be back sooner than you think," he shouted assuredly.

Way too soon the ship's horn sounded announcing its departure. Tom and Flo and all Jiffo's mates who had gathered at the dock waved their last goodbye and collectively retired to their favorite saloon to drown their bittersweet emotions in pints of beer.

30

TOM AND FLO SAT AT A TABLE TOGETHER IN A CORNER OF the pub. Somehow the pint of beer in front of each of them wasn't appealing. Others stood at the bar or sat at a table. It was a gloomy setting with their hero gone. If circumstances had been different, Tom would have gone to America with the boy. But he had been challenged to a re-match with Sandy Lynch from the bare-knuckle fight on the heath. This time with gloves. A fighter always thinks he has another one in him. He'd been out of it a long time and Lynch was younger. He knew if Jiffo knew, he wouldn't go to America. He'd insist on staying and training his trainer.

Flo sighed. Tom sighed. After a few seconds, Flo said, "Never known it to be so quiet around here. It'll take some gettin' used to." Her heart was aching.

"My wife Mary says if you listen to the quiet long enough, your inner voice will guide you through."

"He'll be back soon. I know he will."

Not a moment had passed after uttering those words than a familiar figure, dripping wet, burst into the pub halting all conversation.

"I didn't reckon you'd be back *this* soon!" Flo said.

"'Allo, mates. My shout," Jiffo said, offering to buy drinks for everyone.

A fuming mad Tom demanded an explanation as to why the champ was *here* when he should be *there*. "No more than half an hour ago, we left the dock with you standing at the rail of the S.S. Parramatta in Sydney Harbour."

"In truth, I missed me mates." Jiffo took center stage now. "I left the rail and raced down the gangplank just before it was raised. As you see, I caught a bit of the spray. It was a lovely moment." Jiffo pantomimed running down a gangplank.

Tom was the only one who did not find it amusing. "Don't you want world recognition?"

"I already got the title."

"We've been through that a hundred times. First, you tell me you don't want to live in Randwick, and now you don't want to go to America. What is it you do want?"

Jiffo knew what he didn't want. He had lost his real mum and dad due to circumstances he couldn't do anything about. There was someone else he didn't want to lose. He spoke now in a way he had never spoken before.

"Today, when I looked down at the dock from the ship and I saw Miss Flo Berry standin' there, wavin' and bawlin', I realized something."

It was dead quiet. Flo could hardly breathe. All eyes were on Jiffo who was gazing only at Flo. She could have held that gaze forever.

Addressing Flo directly, in a strong voice, the former Push captain said, "All the things I am, all the things I became and will become, I'm doin' it all for one reason: to impress you."

Tom's protégé had developed skill, courage, and character. He'd brought him into manhood and away from the gang. Jiffo was a champ in more ways than were dictated by the number of bouts he had won.

Flo asked, "Ain't, aren't you going to America?"

"I'm goin' to America. I ain't goin' without me girl, and that's that."

He'd said it. He'd said it out loud in front of everybody. She was his girl. She'd risen out of the no-hope existence. She had changed her life.

Seated in the corner with Flo, Jiffo was able to talk about it for the first time. He told Flo about that Sunday. About the dingoes.

"That's how you won the big fight. That's why you're the champ. That must be what Tom whispered in your ear. You were fightin' those dogs. You were fightin' for your mum and dad."

"Reckon." He felt free.

"I love you, Jiffy," Flo said sweetly.

"HOW MANY TIMES I TELL YA NOT TO CALL ME JIFFY!"

The Arrangement

It came about early one Monday evening while they were watching the telly. A program about the divorce rate rapidly approaching one in two marriages in Britain just like in America.

Casually, Brett said to Robert, "If it works for unmarried people to live together, would it work for married people to live apart?"

Waiting for the financial report, he wasn't really paying much attention and mumbled, "What did you say, darling?"

She repeated the question.

"If you're asking my opinion, I don't see the point. Why be married?"

"Would you ever want to try it?"

"Living apart?"

"You never gave up your Holland Park flat. There had to be a reason."

"I thought I was coming up in the world coming to Chelsea," the man who grew up on an estate in the south of England joked and then seriously added, "It's real estate, darling."

He hadn't answered her question. Now she'd lost him to the stock market report.

By society's standards, they each had waited a long time before marrying. She was forty-five; Robert was fifty. Both had always been self-sufficient, independent, never wanted children, and financially secure. He made his money in stocks and bonds. She owned three upscale boutiques, one in Chelsea, one in Kensington, and one in Covent Garden. They met by chance at an art gallery opening in Covent Garden and much to the surprise of all who knew them, including them, they were married eight months later.

She saw an opening during a commercial break to press her point. "Well? What do you think?"

"What do I think?"

"About married people living apart." She let out a sigh of frustration. "You weren't listening."

"Darling, I've heard every word. Are you getting tired of me after only four years?"

So he had been paying attention. "No, darling, *au contraire*. I don't want you to get tired of me."

He muted the television. "Brett, I like living together. Isn't that the point of being married? I like that you are my wife. I like being your husband."

"None of that would change. We would still be married."

He fixed them both a drink and sat down beside her on the sofa. "Now what's this all about?"

"Proximity breeds contempt. I don't want that to happen to us."

"All this from a silly television program about divorce. Do you really believe that by living apart we will stay together?"

"We can see each other every day. We'll talk. We'll still be in each other's lives." Her voice softened.

"It sounds as if you're telling me, not asking."

"I think it will keep it-us—I don't know—fresh."

"I think you've lost your mind. No more talk shows for you, young lady. Watch cartoons."

Determined to get what she wanted, she went on. "With one proviso."

"A proviso? Perhaps this is more serious than I imagined."

"This is the deal. The arrangement. We must tell each other everything. No secrets. Best friends."

"It is my belief we do that now. And we certainly have grown into the best of friends." When she didn't say anything, he continued. "Should I leave now or may I stay the night in what I thought was my home?" He went over to the window and looked out. After a pause, he said, "It stays light later and later. Have you noticed that?"

"Please, Robert. Let's just try it. I know it will bring us closer."

Brett remained in the flat in Chelsea where she had lived most of her adult life. Robert returned to his residence in Holland Park. They saw each other four or five times a week for lunch or drinks or dinner or the theatre. The word 'separation' never came up, but in reality, wasn't that what it was? There were long telephone calls at odd hours of the night and morning. There were weekends in the country. There were walks in Hyde Park. Sometimes Robert would stay the night. Friends thought they were absolutely barmy and were sure they were headed for divorce.

Brett didn't need another person to make her happy. She had learned that lesson early on, thanks to her mother. One evening, Brett was watching her mother dressing to go out. Brett was bored and asked what she should do. Her mother replied, "Pretend I'm not here." And thus began Brett's journey of independence.

Brett's father died while she was in her final year at university. Her mother said she had nothing to keep her in London; that a grown daughter wouldn't miss her. Shocking her friends and her daughter, she sold her flat in Hampstead and took off for Portugal where she'd always wanted to go. She never returned. Not when Brett graduated; not even when Brett and Robert got married. Brett always meant to visit her, but somehow it never happened.

Until the funeral.

Brett rang Robert as soon she returned to London. In an icy tone, she said, "It's urgent. I want you here now." In the seven months of their arrangement, she had never said anything remotely this intense.

She was standing at the fireplace gulping a gin and tonic when she heard his key in the lock. He kissed her on the cheek and asked how she was, the way he had always done. He went around the room and switched on the lamps, inquiring why she was sitting in the dark.

"I'll light a fire, shall I?" he asked while fixing himself a drink.

"It isn't cold enough."

"Have it your way." Oblivious to her brittle tone which he took as fatigue, lifting his drink, he said, "Cheers. Good to have you back, darling. I missed you."

She took another gulp of her drink without acknowledging his toast. She knew he was waiting for her to open up the discussion. "You'd better sit down." She sat on the chair closest to the sofa.

He sat on the chair opposite her. "I should have gone over with you. It was too much of a strain for you on your own."

"It's done. I'm back. A few formalities still, that's all. No need for two of us there. She was dead."

He repeated, "I should have gone with you."

"You've said that, Robert." She couldn't control the bite.

"I should stop saying should, shouldn't I"

Brett was not amused at his attempt at humor. "What's the matter? You're looking at me as if I look funny. Old."

"Never old."

"I said odd not old."

"No, you said old."

"Didn't, did I?"

"If you must know, I've never seen you looking more beautiful."

"Oh, yes, death becomes me."

She was a handsome woman, not what one would call beautiful. She was surprised at his use of the word. Her skin was perfection; the stereotyped English Rose. Her eyes were too large for her face and too close together. Her nose was narrow. Her lips too thin. But the overall picture was attractive. Her style was always chic. And Robert found her attractive. And he, being over six feet, liked the fact that he could almost look her in the eyes, not down at the top of her blonde head; although her blonde hair was what he loved most about her. That, and the fact she was nearly his height. It's what drew him to her at the art gallery before they knew one another. What drew her to him? His thick salt and pepper hair, his tailor made gray pinstriped suit, and of course, his height. She learned during their conversation that it was against his nature to appear anywhere without a suit and tie. And that included what he wore at home. She could never understand his sitting watching television in a suit and tie. He preferred it, he told her. It's what they had always done at home, his parents being very formal and rather rigid.

Brett was sipping her drink and looking forlorn.

Finally, he said, "All right, out with it, Brett. Say it. You're being very mysterious."

She blurted out, "I'm not the mysterious one, Mister Mysterious."

"Pardon?"

"Pardon?" she mimicked his tone. But her 'pardon' was peppered with nastiness.

He waited unable to figure out her mood.

Then she totally broke in a shrill tone neither of them had ever heard from her. "I know. I know everything."

"Brett, what is this mood you're in? Ever since I arrived. That phone call…"

"When I was going through her personal effects. The letters. The correspondence."

"What letters?"

"What letters? Beatrice's letters. Your letters. What damned letters do you think I'm on about? Did you know she made copies of the letters she wrote you? Who does that? She paper clipped them in the order they were sent. I know everything."

His drink went down the wrong way and burned his throat. A coughing jag followed. Caught with his hand in the cookie jar, when he could speak, he said, "She should have had more sense."

"She wrote to both of us that she had married. She didn't approve of living together without marriage. She gave us a vivid description of a small ceremony in a chapel. But those other letters—those letters to you personally, not to me, to you—say they never married." Brett was up and pacing now.

Robert was at the drinks trolley a second time where he fixed himself a good stiff Scotch without offering her a refill. "You're in shock. Death does that."

"Oh, shut up, Robert. I haven't finished. This Julio person was a widower with a son. And this boy was growing up fast. Just the right age for a woman whose live-in lover pretend husband was away on business all the time." Brett was having difficulty breathing. "Light the goddamned fire. I'm freezing."

Robert did as he was told.

"So the young man and his step-thingy mother started fooling around. And then one day, he saw her in bed with his father, and she was doing to his father what she did to him."

"That's enough."

"I'm sorry if it's inconveniencing you." And in her best American movie line imitation, she said, "Fasten your seat belt. You ain't heard nothin' yet."

But Robert already knew the story.

"So the young man ran to the kitchen and grabbed a long, sharp knife and ran back to the bedroom. But he was no match for his father. And something happened. Just like that. Just like that they turned on her. The men from Portugal didn't like the lady from England after that. They moved her out of the big *hacienda* into a tiny *pied a terre*. Kicked her out would be more to the point. A case of blood is thicker than water." She stopped talking. "Would you like to finish the saga, Robert?"

He raised his hands in a gesture that indicated she should continue.

"Not knowing where to turn, she got in touch with her son-in-law, Robert. Did you sleep with my mother?"

"Have you lost your mind?"

"Did you sleep with my mother?" She shouted.

"Beatrice needed a friend. It didn't concern you."

Utterly shattered, with hot hate, she screamed, "Didn't concern me? My husband and my mother?"

Robert was searching for words now. Nothing would sound right. It was true. She had turned to him, not to her daughter, not to them. "She had no one else."

"She had me. She had me. I want to know, did you and my mother?" She couldn't say it.

"Your mother had a vivid imagination. She could turn a kiss on the cheek into a torrid love affair. She fantasized about a lot of things. Surely, you know that. Don't believe everything you read."

Brett couldn't let him get away with this. He had violated their arrangement. Their arrangement was that they told each other everything. "When? You never leave England. Unless you lied about that, too."

"I never lied to you."

"Omission is as good as a lie."

"All right. All right." He practically jumped out of his seat. "That time I flew to Geneva to set up the bank account.

One time. I flew back via Lisbon. It wasn't about, for god sakes, sex."

It was the not telling that was eating her up. Bizarre, though it may have been, she didn't give a flying fig about what happened between her mother and her husband. It was that he hadn't told her. They weren't supposed to keep secrets. That was the deal. That was their deal. "If we have a new arrangement, I'd like to be informed."

"There is no new arrangement."

"What now? A divorce?" Brett didn't know which of them was more surprised at hearing the word. She felt insane.

"Stop it. Stop now!"

"You should have told me. I had to find everything out in those letters. My faith in you is completely destroyed." Jesus. Were they breaking up? Is that what was happening?

"No one breaks up over a little…" The word wouldn't come.

Was infidelity the word he was looking for? She couldn't say it. It didn't matter. "We are supposed to tell each other everything."

"Yes, I know." Robert took a clean white handkerchief out of his pocket and wiped the perspiration off his brow. "If you want me to leave, I'll go. But if I walk out that door, and I mean this, if I walk out that door, you will never see me again."

"Is that a threat?"

"It isn't a threat. It's a fact."

Brett, who had always prided herself on being an independent woman, was now face to face with her biggest fear: Life without Robert. She ignored his declaration. She had to keep talking so he wouldn't leave. "Let's be honest, Robert. My mother and I weren't exactly the best of friends, but did you think that I wouldn't find out?"

"I'm only guilty of not telling you. Nothing more. And for that, I'm deeply sorry."

Brett could handle anything she knew about—even deception. Provided she knew, she could handle it. If she heard something as simple as a creak in the flat, she wouldn't rest until she could identify the source. The creak could keep on creaking. It wouldn't bother her after that.

Her silence now said volumes. She had never felt this way before. She had never given him the silent treatment. Had she learned this from her mother? Often, she was a witness to her mother's frostiness towards her father. No. No. No. She was not her mother.

"I'm sorry. Terribly terribly sorry," Robert repeated.

They were British through and through. Embarrassment was their deepest emotion. Sorry. Sorry. How many sorries were uttered in a lifetime? Years of conditioning in the stiff upper lip school of life. Easier to sweep it under the rug. At that moment, she wished she had a shred of hot Latin blood in her and could throw something at him. Without thinking, that's exactly what she did. She picked up the nearest object and threw it at Robert's head.

Robert saw it coming and ducked. The porcelain vase hit the wall and broke into hundreds of tiny pieces. "Good Lord," he said. "How ironic."

Brett looked down at the shattered vase on the floor. "Her wedding gift to us." She put her hand to her mouth. She began to laugh. Really laugh.

And then Robert laughed, too.

When he could catch his breath, he spoke. "Can I take our, operative word, our, laughter as forgiveness?"

She wasn't quite ready. She wanted him to suffer a little longer. "Not yet."

They were civilized people after all. She would forgive even if she wouldn't forget. But what else hadn't he told her? Was this living apart really a good idea? What was she really expecting from this arrangement? She held out her empty glass.

He appeared to welcome the non-verbal request. Physical activity and silence seemed to be just the ticket.

She sat down on the sofa.

He handed her the refilled glass and sat beside her. "We've come too far, luv, to throw it away. What do you say, old thing?"

The soothing voice she had come to rely on was there once again. His charm she so adored was there, too. She needed him. Miss Independent needed a man. She almost choked on the thought. But it was true. She looked at him a long time, and then at the crackling logs in the fireplace. "Until death us do part." She touched his glass with her own.

They kissed on the mouth. It wasn't passionate. It had never been passionate. That wasn't their thing. It was comfortable. Brett thought it was a miracle that she had met someone who felt the way she did about marriage. About togetherness. That it didn't have to mean strangulation. And at the same time she knew, death would be preferable to divorce.

"You know, Brett, I was a bachelor until fifty before you, doing quite well on my own."

"The same for me. Single for forty-five years. I was fine. Were you fine, Robert?"

"I was perfectly fine. But now, the way we are, I couldn't bear it without you."

"I don't know how I would live without you." She snuggled into his neck.

They stayed that way for a little while longer, just holding on to one another.

Robert broke the silence or rather the rumblings in his stomach broke the silence.

Neither felt like kitchen duty, so Robert went around the corner and picked up an Indian take-away. They ate on trays in the living room in front of the fire. They went to bed and made gentle love in the early dawn light. After a light break-fast, he went back to his flat in Holland Park. Brett tidied up the Chelsea flat. They had plans to meet at the Grosvenor House for drinks that evening.

Maybe it was all wrong, this arrangement of theirs. Maybe it wasn't the way marriage was supposed to be. But who was to say? Wasn't the whole thing supposed to be between the two parties concerned and no one else?

To love is so startling it leaves little time for anything else.
—Emily Dickinson (1830-1886)

Try to keep your soul young and quivering
right up to old age.
—George Sand/Amandine Aurore Lucille Dupin (1804-1876)

The Would-Be Virgin

PROLOGUE

TOPIC A
(From A to Z)

A—If you have to ask what Topic <u>A</u> is, you shouldn't be reading this book.

B—Since I am mentioned in Omar Sharif's <u>book</u>, "The Eternal Male," it is only fair that he get a mention in mine.

C—Pharyngeal laryngitis can be <u>cured</u>.

D—Some are born to defecate. Some learn how to defecate. And some have <u>defecation</u> thrust upon them. When the recipient of the latter is wearing handcuffs, it is the ultimate experience.

E—My text message to him read: "Feeling new woman. Staying at the Spa an <u>extra</u> week." His text read: "So am I. Stay as long as you like."

F—He likes to line about six of us up and watch us slip our <u>feet</u> into high heel ankle strap shoes made of green snakeskin. As he's color blind, I can't see what he gets out of it.

G—The <u>G-Spot</u> is not a stain on the carpet.

H—<u>Home</u> is where the hard is.

I—He's 6'2" and I'm 5'4", but when we're lying in bed together, we're the same height. Where do the extra <u>inches</u> go?

J—The back seat of his Jaguar was like doing it in a basket of leather gloves.

K—The modern day knight in shining armor doesn't appear on a white horse and hover outside your window like a jerk. He rings the doorbell and states his intentions. It adds up to the same thing.

L—I always know wherever you are, we loved each other for a little while.

M—If it works for unmarried people to live together, would it work for married people to live apart?

N—When that old familiar feeling of nausea overcame me, I knew I was in love again.

O—Every time he had an orgasm, I wanted to notify his next of kin.

P—There are three men in my life at the moment. All of them are played by Peter Lorre.

Q—We each filled out the questionnaires at the Make-A-Mate Agency. I lied. He lied. It was a perfect match.

R—The king and queen went into town to fetch a bottle of Liebfraumilch. Then they went ice skating. The king fell down and broke his crown. *Vivat, vivat Regina.*

S—My profile on the dating website read: Resting actress, will screw for food.

T—It's his mother who keeps us apart. She's titled. Heavyweight champion of the world.

U—He undressed me quickly. He called my name and then died. I called 911. I made a mental note, in future, to get the money up front.

V—He's the one you slim for, oil your skin for, wear perfume for, manicure your fingernails for, pedicure your toes for, shampoo the dog for, cook for, dress for, wait for, yearn for, sneeze for, cough for, blow your nose for, wheeze for, take antibiotics for. Don't kid yourself. You're not in love. You're just <u>very</u> sick.

W—I've always been the other woman. If I become a <u>wife</u>, will there be another woman? Can I be both the wife and the other woman?

X—Happiness is making love with a doctor. If you accidentally break a hip, he can <u>x-ray</u> you at the same time.

Y—When you fall in love with <u>yourself</u>, you will never be lonely.

Z—<u>Zees</u> is za vay ve do it in my country, my leetle beetroot.

1

CHARLOTTE
(Dating Therapist)

As soon as men hear I'm a dating therapist, they run the other way. And fast. Are they thinking I'm analyzing everything they say and do? Don't know. Because I don't know doesn't mean I don't care. I like men. I'd like to be in a relationship—I'm not now. So I'm trying a different tactic. I'm lying. Yes, I said lying. My new title: Counselor for At-risk Teens. Apparently, it works like a magnet. Can't keep the men away. But nothing seems to lead to a permanent relationship.

<u>THE SWEETIE</u>. We were each writing a column for the same publication; two different people said we really needed to meet. I was the one who made the call.

We met at a local restaurant; at first in the bar. I liked his looks. There was the faint smell of garlic, cigar smoke, and booze with a splash of Ralph Lauren's Polo, but you had to be standing close, very close, to take it in. So close I could feel his breath, his warm breath on my face and my neck. I brought his left hand to my lips which to him and to any onlooker appeared to be a romantic gesture. It was my way of checking for a wedding ring.

We had a couple of meetings and I remember telling him on our third date, the picnic, that all I could handle now, all I wanted now was regular sex with a regular guy. Another lie because I wanted more. Here now seemed to be the real deal. It was an opportunity to learn, to grow, to cry my tears, to love, to let go of the past. For four years, we traveled, we shared intimacies, we shared my bed and sometimes his.

But I found the Sweetie (our names for one another) sometimes cold. I wanted more togetherness so we could really get to know one another.

His response was always, "How will we get to know ourselves?"

Still I wailed and hollered and cried. There was so much I didn't know. I knew how he liked his coffee, where he had his hair cut, what he liked to order in an Italian restaurant, that he loved Chinese food more than anything. He hated going to the dentist. I liked neat and clean and uncluttered; he liked cluttered. Leaving his bread crumbs on the table didn't bother him; drove me nuts. He didn't like affectionate gestures in public. Kissing the top of my head was it. Fore play: He liked to wrap me up in Saran Wrap. After play: Eating chocolate fudge ice cream. He hated cats and dogs. He worried about money, even though he had plenty. He slept on his back. That seems a lot to know about someone, but it wasn't. I didn't know him.

"From me, you will get strength," he said. "It's very Zen."

"It's very bullshit," I said.

I started to feel abandoned even when I was with him. And yet I stayed.

I continued to wail and cry. Somehow, I realized the tears were not for this Sweetie. The tears were too intense. The tears couldn't be for now. So I let the tears come, and I knew they were all the unresolved tears, fears, anger, frustrations from before. Way before. Daddy dying when I was seven. And that's when I surrendered and allowed a Higher Power to take over. I had nowhere else to go. I allowed a Higher Power to guide, to protect, to carry, to love me. All the things I wasn't getting from the Sweetie; couldn't get from *any* Sweetie. Slowly, slowly, fear subsided and I knew if the Sweetie left or died or just didn't show up one weekend, I had me and my one constant—the ever loving presence of God. And when I finally told the Sweetie I couldn't see him any more, he didn't protest. He didn't even ask why. We were at an airport returning home from a trip. While waiting for our luggage, I said a heartfelt goodbye. Just a look. But he knew and I knew.

"Goodbye."

"Goodbye."

For someone who was paid to help others, I needed a lot of work on myself. It was time to take stock. The men, the tears, the loneliness, the sadness, the choices I was making—it had to change. And only I could change it. Somehow I had to break the pattern. Was this what I needed as a wake up call? Was this the gift from God I'd been chanting for? How would I know? Would I know? I could see improvement in my clients, why didn't I see it in myself?

KINDRED SPIRITS. A chance meeting as we were seated next to one another at a psychiatric luncheon. Instant chemistry. Two therapists talking about therapy. But the vibes were strong. I felt I had met the one I wanted to spend the rest of my life with. He was easy on the eyes, easy to talk to, intelligent, and obviously into me. There was an instant connection that transcended lust and libido. Cautiously, I inquired about his "family" status. Ah, there's the rub. His *wife* couldn't make the trip with him due to her own professional commitments. I put him away in my *married* file and immediately shut off the faucet. I was rather good at that. I was training myself to protect my heart.

We were saying our goodbyes at the end of the conference when he took my hands in his and said, "I've met my kindred spirit."

If he had been single, the romantic in me would have driven off with him and never looked back. If, if, if, if. The lover in me saw me in his house, saw us attending mutually satisfying cultural events, imagined us traveling to new lands together. End of fantasy when the elevator arrived to take him to the garage where he would pick up his car and drive home to his wife. To his life. A kiss on either of my cheeks a la French style and that was that. I hoped he hadn't seen my eyes moisten. Back to reality, the cynic in me wondered if it was just two creative minds gathering fresh material.

I thought about his words for a long time. Shouldn't his wife; for wife, you can read partner; be his kindred spirit? Maybe that was the puritanical New Englander coming out in me. Maybe not. Maybe I learned something today. Maybe you can be married or ensconced with a partner, love that person and all that, but still find an outsider to fill out the missing piece of the puzzle. Doesn't always have to be about sex. The more I learn, it seems the less I know. Is that what they call maturity?

THE POLITICIAN. He was in a loveless marriage and I was in a loveless life. Loving yourself didn't count. I admit I encouraged him. I sent out signals. Maybe, just maybe he and I—we—

One day, on the phone, he told me he loved listening to me talk—about anything. He said he wouldn't trust himself to be alone with me. Did I listen? Did he listen? It went on for about six months. Usually at my place.

One evening, he said, "There's always been something between us."

"Yes, your wife," I snapped back.

He laughed.

I hadn't meant it to be funny. Why are all the good ones married? Or gay.

We would see each other at public events around town. In public, there was the hug he gave everyone; but I sensed a special look, a yearning from him. And then as quickly as it heated up, it cooled down. On my part. And I knew the power I had in me. I knew all the work I had done on myself hadn't been in vain. I knew who I was. I knew I could live without immediate gratification. I knew the value of being able to take a stand about morality without worrying about being a prude. I knew I could think about how I would feel after. I knew the value of not buying into the old cliché, 'Life is short. Go for it. Now is all there is.' That was just the point. Life is short. Why waste it on a guy—a public figure—who wasn't thinking straight.

<u>THE CLIENT</u>. From Rumania. Studying medicine at the local university. As he was leaving my office one afternoon, he took hold of my shoulders with his gorilla hands and planted a really big wet one on my mouth. I was too surprised to move away right away. And besides, he was a good kisser.

"You're great. You're great," he said, between kisses.

Well, one 'great' led to another and there we were. On the floor, on my desk, against the door, on the floor, on my desk, against the door. Totally inappropriate. I know. I know. But he was so handsome, and I wasn't thinking. Therapists are human, too.

He left and I had to deliberate whether to see him again. Client versus lover. Couldn't do both. After all, I'm a professional. Guess what won out. Wrong. He returned for another appointment. Remember, I'm a dating therapist and he needed advice. So we went at it again, this time as soon as he entered my office. Again with the "You're great. You're great."

Some kind of sense entered my mind and my mouth, enough for me to say, "This isn't appropriate." I had to repeat it a couple of times for him to hear. Then we got on with our session where he needed advice about his current girlfriend.

I knew it couldn't continue, but I didn't want to lose a client. I had worked out how I would handle it. I would sit down with him and say something like we have to talk before our appointment. I would praise him; say things to preserve his dignity. And then say something like if we were going to continue with our sessions, we couldn't be able to repeat the sex part, we would have to be professional. "We're both professionals." So on and so forth. Stuff like that. But I never got to say all that. He didn't return for another appointment.

He was gorgeous.

THE FAN. I was in pink. A good color for book signings sitting out there behind a table in the middle of a bookstore feeling excited and hopeful; and yet, rather vulnerable. Will anyone buy my book? My second one. It is said you should write what you know. So I write about my business. Erotic accounts of the battle of the sexes. Based on actual cases, with a change of names, of course. Took me two years. And sitting out there behind a table in the book store was the reward for all the reclusive hours. Showtime! Time to sell the words. Talk to everyone. Anyone.

"Hello. I'm signing my book today."

"Hello. What kind of books do you read?"

"Hello. Do you write?"

"How would you like this inscribed?"

I didn't see him approach holding a mug of coffee, curious about the author. "Hi, is this your book?"

His thick, dark hair framed a sculpted face. Attractive. His eyes bothered me. They didn't quite focus. My questions revealed: He wasn't a writer. He wasn't a reader. He wasn't a buyer. He wasn't even a resident. Just visiting a brother and family. He picked up one of my flyers. Too late, I realized my phone number for the whole world was on it. I got that sinking feeling in the pit of my stomach when you know you've done something wrong and it's too late to take it back.

"Are you finishing now?" he asked.

"No, just starting."

"May I call you?"

At least he asked. Nothing came out of my mouth and I was relieved when others came over to my table. He walked away, returned, saw I was occupied, walked away.

When I got home several hours later, there was a message from him to call him. Do I ignore it? Do I nip it in the bud?

I decided to nip it in the bud. I called him. Voice mail. Good.

"WE are busy this time of year. WE will return your call if you let US know what you would like." Emphasizing that I was part of a team or partnership I hoped would dissuade him. It did. I never heard from him again.

People get a crush on your talent. I know that. You just have to know in the future to replace the pink 'come on' outfit to serious black and remove personal info like a home phone number from all flyers.

Still looking for Mr. Right, so back to the drawing board. Was there something wrong with me? It seemed everyone had someone. Why not me.

HER. Just had to get out and go for a drink somewhere. A little local near me. And I meant that. Just one. A glass of red. So I went to a bar. I knew it was a gay and lesbian bar, but honestly, I just needed the experience. And maybe to see if I was batting for the wrong team all these years. You know what I mean.

I was sitting on a stool at the bar sort of minding my business but looking around, too. A woman began talking to me. Very attractive. Well-dressed, well made-up. Very intelligent conversation, nothing flirty or fake. You know, the way you do with a guy you just met. She smelled good, too.

She suggested we go to a club where we could dance. Since I was new at this, I let her take the lead. We took a cab. She insisted on paying. Well, we danced, had a few more drinks. And danced. And naïve me was sure that was it. We strolled back to her apartment—it was nearby. Bottom line: I spent the night. And what a night. I drew the line at videoing the event. But hey, what did I know? I was a virgin.

In the morning, after a breakfast of coffee and croissants and a shower together, I went home and thought that was the end of it. My one night stand with a *her*. She called. How did she get my number? Oh, that's right, I gave it to her. After a few drinks, you're liable to do anything. I kept avoiding the issue with different excuses. I was busy, I had to attend conferences, my parents were coming to town to visit, my ex-husband was visiting.

Well, I finally told her the truth. My truth. Said I was doing research for my next book and told her I was sorry I misled her. I said if I was that way, I'd be the luckiest girl in the world to have met her. I think I might have got that line from a movie. And I decided I wasn't a lesbian. I like men too much.

NEW OLD LOVE. Years after the romance was over, I decided to write him a letter thanking him for the good stuff. Well, I was going through a dry spell so that was the reason. Did I want to get back together? I mean we lived two thousand miles apart, so it wasn't like he would be around me all the time. Anyway, I wrote, as I said, thanking him for the good times. I told myself I wasn't expecting a reply. But I lied because when he wrote back, I was glad.

So a new chapter began. It was different after all the years apart. Different in that we were different. There was a new freedom we never had known. Free to say anything without having to walk on eggshells lest one or the other took flight over some unacceptable behavior or remark leaving the other perplexed or angry or feeling abandoned. Here was an opportunity to neaten up past misunderstandings without the dreaded 'you said, I said' for an argument. An opportunity to show each other the real people we had turned into mellowed by time.

We spent a week together sharing our shared past. After seven days, there was nothing left to talk about. And there was the title for my next book: "There Is No Future in the Word *Past*."

2

KATE
(Widowed Heiress)

HUSBANDS ARE MY CAREER. I'M LOUSY WITH MARRIAGE, BUT love the ceremony; great on divorce. Currently, I'm between husbands. I've had three or four. Sometimes, it's hard to keep count. I've got plenty of money. And I've come to the conclusion, what good is money if it isn't spread around doing things for you? The last husband, Tom, was twenty years older and ill when I married him and rushing towards old age. I stayed by his side for eleven long years. Believe me when I say that anyone who marries for money deserves what they get. Now it's my time to live. A little skittish about getting out there after so many years, I knew I had to do it or risk being alone in my old age. A few procedures, fillers, regular facials, and I looked twenty years younger. Fifteen. Okay, ten. Ten is good. I joined a City Club hoping there would be single men there. I went to Club Med. I even went to church. In short, I went kind of wild after years of being marooned.

<u>MOVING GUY</u>. How do you explain that first attraction? That feeling that you could share secrets with this stranger? This twelve years younger stranger. Maybe it's just a momentary high. Maybe it isn't. Lust and love. The same? Different? So easy to misinterpret. He sent flowers. He wrote love letters. Real stationery. Beautiful paper that felt like silk. Postage stamps on the envelopes. I'd peel them off and lick them where he had licked them. Oh, wait. Self-adhesive wasn't licked. Who cared? He wanted me in the same way I wanted him. At the same time.

Then I reminded myself I was in my independent stage now. Learning to travel solo again and almost liking it. Who was I kidding? That *but* kept creeping into my mind's vocabulary. Am I really happy? Did I really want *alone* all my life? I had to give it a chance. *It* and *him*. A week became a month. One month became three and a half. When you start counting halves, you have to pay attention. We were exclusive. At least, I was. When you start sharing your dreams and fantasies, you have to pay attention. When you see each other every day, you have to pay attention. And when before you know it, *I* becomes *we*, you really have to pay attention. Being in love, being a lover, letting love in, isn't as frightening as I thought it would be. I believed him when he said he loved me.

He moved in with few possessions: Toothbrush—electric; toothpaste—extra strength whitening; boots—leather; shirts—a hundred percent cotton; cd's—lots of mixed categories; jeans—five pair. Three blue, two black. I believed him when he said he loved me.

On the street, in the park, at the beach, we pass those younger, slim, pretty little things. Once, I looked that way, too. Why didn't he know me then? He reassures me he wouldn't have liked me then. What a nice thing to say. Did he mean it? He knows what I'm thinking as a not quite twenty-year-old gives him the eye. He puts his arm around me. He whispers in my ear, "Plastic. I've got what I want." And I'm reassured. Until the next time. Until the next walk in the park.

It seemed fine for a while, and then the more I gave, the more he pulled back. "I can't do it on cue" replaced "I want you. I need you." So I bought him another shirt.

"We're mirrors of one another. You are the most important thing in my life." I don't remember which one of us said that. Doesn't sound like me.

Food replaced the bed. Did he always slurp when he ate and drank? Didn't he used to shave? When did he start to smoke cigars? Is that my hair or his in the sink? When did silence replace conversation? Who is this man living in my house? The electric blanket on high all night was a dead giveaway. I used to be the blanket.

He moved out eleven months, five days, three and a half hours after he moved in. He moved out with thirty silk shirts, ten pairs of boots, two leather jackets, twelve brands of cologne, a case of champagne, a pair of corduroy pants, sixteen pairs of jeans, three suede throw pillows, lots and lots of CDs. The expanded inventory was the result of my generous gift-giving. I believed him when he said he loved me.

Then somewhere down the road, I heard he had a new lady. No proof, just hearsay. But I believed the hearsay. Does he write sexy scripts to act out for her, too? Does he massage her feet, too? Does he take pictures of her in all kinds of poses, too? Does he whisper sweet everythings in foreign accents in her ear, too? Does he cook for her, too? Does he make her laugh, too? Does he travel with her, too? Does he share secrets with her, too? Does he warm up the bed on cold nights for her, too?

Does she buy him gifts? Does he still have that leather jacket I bought him? Does she know about me?

<u>THE ANTIQUE DEALER</u>. My blurb read: 'Moving.' (I wasn't, really). 'Must sell furniture.' I'd heard it was a good way to meet men, and after the last fiasco I needed a distraction. I read that the best way to get over a man is in the arms of another man. This ad about furniture was something different than the usual true/false confession on lie-dot-com. *Love walking in the rain, but it would be better with you by my side holding my hand. Love dining out, holding hands across the table. Love cooking, but cooking for one isn't fun. Love movies, but want to discuss it after.* That kind of crap.

Sandy haired; well-dressed in a pair of gray flannel slacks, a white shirt, a navy blazer, no tie; well-spoken; age appropriate. A dealer of rare antiques. There was nothing not to like. The vibes were good. If I squinted, he resembled the early Michael Caine as in *Alfie*. As I said, nothing not to like. He came, he saw, he conquered. The antique dealer, not Michael. The antique dealer glanced around the house, commenting on my décor, but he didn't seem interested in a purchase. Not too much time was wasted on preliminaries. Foreplay turned out to be everything that went on before we met; if you get my drift.

After…he lit up a cigarette.

"I don't allow smoking in the house. In bed," I said, drinking my glass of water with electrolytes.

"Never set fire to a chick's bed yet," he said, adding, "at least not with a cigarette, if you get my meaning."

I let the reference to *chick* go. "I get it, I get it," I responded only because he seemed to be waiting for an answer or a comment or something.

After the *after*, he took me to dinner. During a gourmet meal at a very pricey restaurant, he presented a business proposition. His business card said he had a shop. And I believe anything in print. He explained that antiques sell better from a private home. He would furnish my place with his inventory, pay for all the ads, so on and so forth, and, of course, I would be reimbursed. My stuff would go into storage, all paid for. That was the deal.

It sounded like an okay idea. It sounded like fun, something different. Nothing else was going on in my life. Money wasn't my problem. Companionship was. And I relished the thought of being surrounded with beautiful things that kept being replaced by more beautiful things. And I was convinced we would see each other often.

We parted that evening as business partners and in my mind, lovers, too, even though one swift lay can't really be considered anything other than just that. He told me he would be in touch for the next step. All I had to do was wait for his call to set it all up.

I waited.

And waited.

And waited.

Finally, I couldn't wait any longer. I called the number on his card. A woman answered. I asked for him. I was informed he was in Canada visiting his son and wouldn't be back for a couple of weeks. She didn't seem flustered about the call from another woman. She didn't even ask what the nature of the call was. Maybe I only assumed it was a wife, a girlfriend. I didn't know. Maybe the housekeeper. Maybe his sister, his daughter, his cousin. Maybe his business partner.

I knew the truth the way you know, but don't know. My hopes and aspirations to be an antique furniture entrepreneur and have regular sex were dashed. Mister Wrong was never going to turn into Mister Right. In fact, he was a louse. So what did that make me?

Men and their needs.

Women, too.

<u>THE EMBEZZLER</u>. Not my name for him. It was his public name. I caught the piece in small print, as if reading about a stranger, not a lover of nearly two years. Off and on for two years.

A prominent, liberal politician with homes in London, Germany, Luxembourg, Spain, Liechtenstein, and Palm Beach; and with a passion for skydiving and racing cars; has been found guilty of tax evasion, fraud, embezzlement, illegal use of party donations.

What? Was I that naïve? The man I knew was generous, humorous, intelligent, private. I actually thought he owned a small bank somewhere in London's financial district in addition to his political duties. He never took a penny from me. I wasn't there for his money. Okay, maybe the two weeks, two times, at Lake Como were part of the appeal. Never saw George Clooney. I'm doing very well financially, but next to him, I felt like a pauper.

A bigger than life provocative figure who captured my mind and heart even when he told me he was married and couldn't get a divorce. I had a choice to stay or go in the beginning, but not after it all got going. What's that saying about having to kiss a lot of frogs before finding the prince? Something like that. It was time to get moving. Travel, travel, travel. What good is the money if it isn't doing anything?

<u>GREECE</u>. Never heard the call at the airport to board. I'd been lost in the duty free shop making purchases. Just made the flight. Plane was half empty. No one wants to leave this place. I even learned a few Greek words. I love you. Honey. Good morning. Coffee. Thank you. Yes. Please. This chemistry between a man and a woman. It either is or it isn't. Length and brevity is no proof of the depth or sincerity of an emotion. Four days and three nights. That's all it took. We may never see each other again, but we won't forget. We both

have the same memory. How closer can you get than that?

I wasn't particularly looking forward to my return home. I was spending air time writing about my Greek adventure in my journal. Silly stuff, in a way. The bank manager on holiday with whom I shared a short walk and an even shorter conversation and lunch at separate tables. I think he wanted more. The elderly woman who cooked and gave me enormous portions and liked patrons to come into her kitchen and sample whatever she was cooking. I promised to call her son, the doctor, a throat specialist in London, but needed an interpreter to get the address. The bank manager wanted to take me on a tour of a monastery nearby. I declined. Never got his name, but I did get that he was thirty-two years with the Bank of Cyprus. One evening after dinner, an open air cinema showing the film, *Cleopatra Jones*. English with Greek subtitles on the top of the screen, a huge white thing on a brick wall. Must have been a parking lot at one time.

Anyway, the guy across the aisle looked pretty cool. What a solid looking chap, I thought. How do you get to meet them like that? I was soon to find out. Nothing like turbulence on British Airways thirty-five thousand feet in the air over Athens. Athens, Greece, not Athens, Georgia (but you knew that) to get you to turn to the stranger across the aisle, as I didn't have a seat partner, and ask in that obnoxious helpless little girl voice I loathe: "Is it going to be all right?"

Seemingly unflustered about the fact we were probably going to die, he turned to me and uttered, "Don't know."

I actually thought he was Greek, until we starting talking and I learned he was as American as I was. That voice. That voice. Like amber-colored honey in a hot cup of chamomile tea.

I liked his unflappability. I really liked that about him. We would go down in flames, but he would be calm, which would make me calm. And it was his voice. Just two words. *Don't know*. Deep and smooth. We got into chatting about this and that, me pretending everything was normal; pretending my lunch wasn't fighting to escape my inners. Why the hell had I eaten whatever it was! Whoever heard of gray food?

And then the turbulence stopped, but I didn't realize it until he informed me it had and why didn't I join him on the other side of the aisle in the seat next to him and we exchanged first names and learned we were both stopping in London before returning home to New York so why didn't we cut the expenses and share a hotel room? That was him.

Did I even think about it? No, slut that I am. Great idea. A few days and nights in London. And that was the beginning with Alec what's-his-name. And the ending.

SOUTH AFRICA. In an eleven-seater plane, it's a quick trip from Johannesburg to that country within a country—Swaziland. Just the sound of it is exotic. A young man sitting across the aisle is intrigued by the American who is traveling alone. A conversation. Can't remember who started it. He is a student. I didn't say no to his offer to drive me to my hotel, The Swaziland Spa. He reassured me it was not out of the way for his driver. No need to be impressed. It's South Africa. Everyone can have a driver. In the backseat of his chauffeur-driven Volkswagen, we plan the evening ahead.

After dinner, something new for me. Real, natural hot springs under the starry sky. With only the moonlight and his hand to guide me, I lowered my naked body into the warm liquid. I'd been to spas and been pummeled after luxuriating in mud baths, but it was nothing like this. This was the real thing and like nothing else before. We embraced, and with only the slightest hesitation, I gave in to his…to his excitement. His excitement excited me. All boundaries came down. I was totally abandoned in a strange kind of safety net. He wasn't terribly smart or terribly attractive; but in the dark, if I squinted real hard, at a certain angle, he looked like a very very young Robert Redford.

It ended there as he had a lot of homework waiting for him.

<u>SCOTLAND</u>.

<u>The Golfer</u>. I bought the golf clubs, the shoes, the shorts, the shirts, the tees, the balls. All to pull him, and I did attract him. He drove the cart and was the epitome of the British gentle man. I hated every minute of it. I sold my clubs, my shoes, my shorts, my shirts, my tees, my golf balls. And I guess I should mention the Brit was a little, suffice it to say, weird.

It's important to know what you *don't* like.

<u>The Earl</u>. As soon as I step into a museum, I get shooting pains up and down my shins.

But then I met Lord Pellew. We ended up in charming hotel in a charming village overlooking a charming river with a charming waterfall. It was charming. If Scotland ever became independent from England, he would be one of the claimants to the throne. Kate, Queen of Scots, wasn't exactly what I had in mind for my future. So I let all that charm go and moved on. Queen of Scots, Queen of slut and who cared? No one was looking.

<u>VENICE</u>.

One evening, in the hotel dining room, Sheik Whoziwhatsus (not sure of the name but this is close enough) summoned me to his table through an interpreter. If they're draped in a white sheet from head to toe, I am assuming *Sheik* is correct. Summoned! I had no idea what he was saying. It didn't take long for him to propose marriage. This from the interpreter. He said I should think of my future. I told him I was in my future now. He said he would build me a house and buy me a car—even though he didn't care for my hair style. A very similar experience happened to a friend of mine in Paris last year. Probably a different Sheik. They love American women, I've been told. He told me, still through the interpreter, the first time he saw me across the dining room, his heart beat strongly and the light in the world went out for him. Maybe the word was 'on.' Not the best interpreter. I removed myself from his presence and sent him a candle. Same thing happened to that friend in Paris.

And then I woke up. On to the next port of call. Capri.

<u>BRONSON</u>. The flight was uneventful, if you don't count what happened. You see, I had

just attended the funeral of an aunt whom I adored. I was allowed to take a few mementos, all sanctioned by her son and grandson, to remember her by.

Between the two round six-inch brass cylinders holding the rolled up death certificates of my father and his mother in my checked luggage, the ticking alarm clock nestled into a nineteen-inch brown-fur bear named Bronson in my carry-on bag; and the fact that Bronson requested to visit the cockpit when we were about thirty-thousand feet above the ground, I was in a load of trouble, as you might imagine.

I took it all in my stride, prepared to enjoy whatever ride I was on. The holding room where the authorities slapped me and my luggage into when we landed was sparsely furnished. I saw it as a very feng shui arrangement, which, no matter what situation you might find yourself in, it makes you relax immediately. Especially during a strip search.

First, they practically dismantled Bronson. It was a horrible sight as they ripped into his fur like a bunch of interns on crack. He took it like the bear that he is. The result is, we are scheduled to fly to the Pet Division of the Mayo Clinic in Arizona where his badly askewed arms, legs, and hat will be repaired. No charge.

After the Bronson search caper, it was my turn. A very lovely woman; well, she seemed lovely, with curly blonde hair, I think a wig, and long fingers with platinum pink nails at least three inches long told me to undress. And so began the strip search of yours truly. Not a totally unpleasant experience, I may add. In fact, we are having lunch together soon.

One of the officials present in the holding room was a former Rabbi at a Reformed Temple in Capetown, South Africa. He actually wept when he examined the death certificates. Apparently, it was his great grandfather who was the inventor of the brass cylinders. It's a small small world. Turned out he dated my mother back in the 1950's in Boca Raton where they both were vacationing one winter.

As for the little quartz clock that Aunt Edith kept at her bedside, it was dismantled by a team of ten members of the Washingtonian Bomb Squad and the good news is, when they found out it really was only a clock, they knew how to put it back together. However, I was given a strong warning never to travel with it again, although it was a travel clock, and if I did, I was supposed to remove the battery. One of the team, a possible participant in a future Antiques Roadshow program wanted to pay me two hundred dollars for the relic, but I declined his offer.

By the way, Bronson is a delightful travel companion. He's caring, a superb listener, a marvelous conversationalist and, in my opinion, quite attractive. I simply adore the bloke. The question is, is it illegal to marry your teddy bear? It would be my fourth marriage. Maybe *that's* the illegal part.

I'll let you know how lunch goes with the blonde chick. I mean, is it really just lunch? And do I bring Bronson along?

Naw, let her find her own bear. Did I mention he's a GUND bear? Top of the line. From Lord and Taylor. A gift to my aunt from the staff at the Retirement Home on her nineti-eth. And now he was mine. All mine. So whoever becomes my next husband, he will have to take me, take my bear, as the saying goes.

I'd had enough of travel for a while. Think I'll stay home and search for my one and only online along with millions of other people. Bound to find *someone*.

3

SAMANTHA
(Yoga Instructor)

ALL THE PASSION HAS TO GO SOMEWHERE. NOT TO MENTION the ability my body has of twisting into all sorts of positions and leading others to do the same. I'm not only a personal trainer in the ancient art of yoga, I'm an artist. Okay, some-time artist. A painter. Sort of. Some say I'm a bit crazy. A bit? Only a bit? How insulting. How could I create without the madness inside crying to get out? How could I balance that? The yin and yang of my position as a fitness guru. One side is quiet, settling. Inhale. Exhale. The other is the wild side as in paint brushes, palette, and all those colors to choose from and sometimes that my hair looks like it was done by the local electric company.

<u>MENAGE A TROIS, A TROIS, A TROIS</u>. I was always rath-er fascinated about what Philip Roth meant in "Portnoy's Complaint" when he started the sentence: When confront-ed with your first threesome…so on and so forth. So I had to try it, didn't I? It's a known fact that many famous paint-

ers had their women. Notice it is plural. Picasso, to name one. For me, it isn't only the men. There are the women, too. I had this idea I wanted to know what I, a woman, felt like to a man. A reasonable question. The bank vice-president and the model. And me. The poet and the poet. And me. The ad man and the secretary. And me. Oh…so that's what a woman feels like to a man.

What it would it be like to be with two men? It wasn't hard to find the willing participants. But I have a feeling I was stoned out of my mind because I don't really remember that phase very well. The two musicians in my bedroom. Just for a laugh. Or maybe because I didn't know how to say no. Didn't want to say no. Maybe inhaling the fumes from the oil paint had infiltrated my brain. The two businessmen at the country cottage of one of them. I think. Then that Sports Awards Ceremony in Los Angeles. The two football players in the hotel. While I made it with one of them on the bed, the other one was waiting in the bathroom for his turn. I hailed a cab to go back to my hotel before realizing I was staying in the same hotel. Out in the sunlight, I started to take stock. Why? I mean I should have been elated at all the sex. Instead I was depressed. Couldn't wait to get back home to my studio and paint it out. And get into the gym and work it out.

Thank God for the lotus position.

THE HISTORY TEACHER. To this tall, handsome, light-colored Jamaican high school teacher, I was Marlboro country. Remember the ad for Marlboro cigarettes? The macho man in a cowboy hat and his horse. Apparently, I, his yoga teacher, was the epitome of serious upscale to a man of color. His first white woman. He was my first, too. An experiment, in a way, to overcome my hidden prejudices. And because I paint figures, I had to know. Were men of color different than white men? I had to know. We hooked up after class one evening and one thing led to another and before you knew it, we were an item.

It wasn't just the bed. We worked out twice a week at the gym. We played tennis, we jogged, we danced. We partied, we drank, we made love. We worked hard and we played hard.

I always painted him in the nude. Read that any way you want. I decided if he was nude, why should I be clothed? It made for a very interesting and relaxing session.

We lasted for half a year; then, he moved on. I wasn't sad. The truth is, there isn't any difference between black and white, if you know what I mean. No more than white and white, if you know what I mean.

THE BUTCHER. It was the way he hacked away at the lamb and dressed the fat purple chops with bits of fluted white paper and parsley and arranged them in a row on a metal tray. Then he cut up a hunk of liver on the wooden counter and arranged the thin slices one against the other on another tray. Next he slid his red fingers in and out of a whole chicken removing the giblets and the neck, placing the pieces in a little plastic bag.

He knew I was watching him. "Can I help you?"

"Are you new here?" I asked.

"Yeah. Fresh meat, you could say." Not getting the laugh he was hoping for from me, he went on. "I grew up helping my father in his butcher shop. He sold the shop, so here I am. How can I help you?"

He came out from behind the glass counter and stood very close to me—a little too close. The odor emitting from his once upon a time white coat was a combination of day-old blood, freshly plucked chicken feathers, and a splash of Yves St. Laurent aftershave. I liked it.

A few words later including a discussion about eating red meat versus eating fish, it was set that he would come to my place after work. Don't be judgmental. A lady's got to live. Butcher boy arrived with champagne and about three pounds of meat. The work outfit had been replaced by a nice clean white shirt, black dress pants, black socks, and black shoes. Quite respectable and quite a surprise. Simple, yet very Mick Jagger rock 'n roll. I had expected jeans and a t-shirt.

Bouncy bouncy and all that stuff. Then he lit up a cigarette. Just like in the 1940s movies.

"I don't allow smoking," I said in all seriousness, faking a coughing spell. I pulled the cigarette out of his mouth and flushed it down the toilet. It was really late, so we agreed he could stay the night. We both slept and that was all. In the early morning a strange buzzing sound woke me up. *What the hell*? His wristwatch alarm.

"Gotta go. No time for coffee."

"But it's the crack of dawn."

"I'm a working man. Gotta get everything ready."

He put on his clothes, kissed me on the forehead, and headed for the door. "I can show myself out."

The fact that he was about twenty years younger than me was not the reason we didn't repeat the episode. His product was good, but I thought it was best to change where I shopped in the future. And better still, return to my vegetarian eating habits.

THE REAL ESTATE BROKER. Of the twenty or so men and women who sat on the floor in a circle in this group session of sharing at the yoga retreat in the Berkshires in western Massachusetts, the powerful force of his energy that mingled with mine could not be ignored. Just an awareness, that's all. As strong as it was, I let it go. I was there to meet me.

Later, outside in the glorious New England summer weather, he approached me wanting to know why I had been so angry in the workshop that morning. Angry? Me? Of course, I protested. His interest in my feelings interested me. He had been preparing to go off and fly his kite. I had distracted him. He never flew the kite. And I never answered his question. He invited me to join him that evening at the satsang, a spiritual gathering based on an Eastern religion. Or as I liked to call it: Scattered minds uniting through music.

It seemed quite natural sitting next to him in our whites, the accustomed attire. There was a lot of chanting and spiritual music played on an instrument I couldn't identify; and then we listened to the speaker read from a book about love. Even if you hated the person sitting next to you, you couldn't help love him. Or her.

Later, the ex-kite flyer and I sat in the lounge and shared our stories, the way you do when you first meet someone you want to impress. My story first; and then his. He said something that changed my whole attitude about my carefree existence.

"You should be proud of what you've done. Don't be afraid to share it. It has empowered me."

He sounded so positive; and I knew it wasn't my imagination that he resembled my father when he was a young man. The smiling blue eyes; the blond hair.

It was only a total of twenty-six hours, but we bonded in this spiritual place in a spiritual embrace. It felt new and old at the same time. Did we bare all thoughts and feelings because we would never see each other again? It was stronger than any physical alliance I had ever experienced, not that I wouldn't have gone for the physical alliance. He initiated the goodbye hug and kiss. A part of me wanted to hang on and go wherever he took me. He was driving north; I was driving east. I knew that nothing I ever did again should feel any less than this, whatever 'this' was.

It never felt that way again.

With anyone.

Ever.

Not even with him. Four months later, after many phone calls, he visited me. We tossed about in and out of bed for three days. Had I dreamt the initial meeting? It was nothing. Literally nothing. Meaning, I felt nothing. Maybe it was something they put in the food at the yoga retreat. Or the setting of the beautiful Berkshires. We both felt the same way. Luckily, I never heard from him again. Boy, was I way off the mark on this one.

THE CHIROPRACTOR. For sexy liaisons, for flirting, it would be my chiropractor. He knows every inch of my body and has known it for what? Three years? Something like that. No. More like five or six years. I don't know what it is about me that men like. I must document how this all happened with DC, who shall be referred to as DC from now on.

"You'll have to stop looking so good," he said when he walked into the consulting room and saw me standing there waiting to be adjusted. Two professionals being unprofessional?

Then it just happened. The full frontal hug. We had hugged before, more or less as therapy. But this was different. This was sexual. Sensual.

"Can you read my mind?" he asked.

"Yes."

"You're blushing," he said.

I smiled. I was definitely blushing.

He adjusted me as usual, always with the most finesse. We seemed to be able to compartmentalize our feelings. I was there for my treatment. It was professional without a hint of the closeness that had just occurred. I felt completely safe with his hands on appropriate parts of my body. I felt safe and trusted him when he unhooked my bra to work on my back. And then hooked it up again. Once in a while our bodies brushed lightly, but it was professional. It would happen when I was changing from a back position to a side position. I could feel his body. Or did I imagine it?

Over the years, I had referred many clients to his practice. He always thanked me for the trust in his ability. It was always healing to just be in his presence when I went for my manipulation every four weeks. I no longer had pain, thanks to regular visits which we called maintenance.

It happened this day that I was sitting on the edge of the treatment couch; he was sitting on a stool opposite me. He suggested we go out sometime for dinner or perhaps he would bring wine and dinner to me. I mumbled something about my surprise and something about how we've always kept it professional, and yes, I'd like to see him socially. He even suggested working out at the gym together when he could show me what I need to do. Or better still, he would join my yoga class.

Then there was the hug goodbye. It was long and oh, my, God, was it beyond wonderful. When we pulled apart after the extended embrace during which I could hear a soft moan from him, he looked at me and said, "Nice, huh?"

"Nice." I couldn't agree more.

So one evening, he arrived, wine in hand, me in the kitchen wearing just an apron. Music played and in between nibbles at the dining table, we nibbled one another.

It became awkward. His recently ex-wife had joined my yoga class. Why I felt funny, I'll never know. I decided to find another chiropractor. Someone I did not find attractive. Nothing lasts forever.

<u>THE TAI CHI INSTRUCTOR</u>. At a Saturday retreat, there was a demonstration designed to ultimately recruit students to his school. I gave in to this ancient art and pretended my

body wasn't in agony from the poses very different from my yoga practice. For a demonstration of a form, he chose me for a partner. Wrists, hands, arms. Not touching, then lightly brushing, then touching. Legs bending in ways I'm sure they weren't meant to bend even though I considered myself to be very flexible. A circular motion releasing tension in our space. His energy, my energy, creating a third energy I can't explain. I hadn't ever felt this kind of connection with my clothes on. There was no question that we would ever take it beyond the class. It was just business for him. For me, it was a very heady experience.

THE ENGINEER. The smell of a New England winter lingered. Fresh white snow on the ground. His forest green Ford Mustang that had been in his family for years. The old country inn with its crackling wood fire. The hot clam chowder. Him.

I remember everything about that drive to the ocean that day.

The waves beating against the sand. The deep orange and blood-red sunset shifting into amber before fading to pale apricot. It looked and felt like the beginning of time.

Even though it was our last time.

4

LYDIA
*(Ex-pat American actress in London
in the swingin' sixties)*

THEN CAME THE MEN. WHOEVER THEY WANTED, WHOEVER I imagined they wanted, I became. Because it wasn't genuine, it never lasted. I couldn't sustain the pose. So each contact came tumbling down. And, once again, I was alone. But never for long. Never a long dry spell. There was always another role to sink my teeth into. Another part to play. Always another co-star. Another audience of one. Another performance.

I wanted them all. And I had them all. Any one. Any time. Any where. Conscience was not a word. Conquest was. What I thought was the conquest. I wanted to feel their bodies, smell their smells, get naked with as many as appealed to me, and chalk up as many notches on the bedpost as I could.

The words commitment, monogamy, and forever and ever were not part of my vocabulary. A man is called a womanizer. If a woman does the same thing, what is she? Was I a manizer? In lighter moments, I conned myself by saying it was for research. I tried doing it alphabetically by profession. Too difficult. It's hard to find, for example, a Quaker, or a xylophone player, or a Zulu. That one isn't really a profession. Then I tried alphabetically by country. That didn't work either. I decided it was better not to think about labels. Was I thinking at all?

I was blessed with an exceptional body and believed it needed to be shared. No one worried about sexually transmitted diseases, wives, husbands, the next day. The only dumb thing I did was give it away. I could have made a fortune. Bodies were firm, faces were taut and would stay that way forever. Men would fall at your feet forever.

Because of the business I was in, the men were famous or maybe just working actors. Who else was I going to meet? And I was living in London where absolutely anything went and no one was looking. It was the *swingin' sixties* and I was right in the middle of it, swinging, with miniskirts, see-through dresses *sans* underwear (thank you, dear Mary Quant). Following the mini came the maxi. And way before long pants, hot pants. Thigh high boots almost but never quite met the line of the short shorts. Imagine all that with my puritanical New England upbringing. I didn't miss a minute of the constantly evolving fashion, pop concerts, theatre parties, trendy restaurants…or the men.

Because it was something not talked about, I never knew if other women went through the same thing. Then *Oprah* happened, and everyone started talking about it and writing about it. I was just twenty years ahead of the crowd. Now everyone's caught up. Of course, they were real people while I'm an actress, a mere figment of my imagination. Or just a fun-loving slut. Ah…deep sigh. Would I ever be able to free myself to be me? Whatever the hell that means. The truth is it was quite delicious…until it wasn't anymore. Nothing lasts forever.

THE MOVIE STAR. It wasn't really an affair; more like a one night stand. Not exactly. Between a one night stand and an affair. Brief but intense. He drank Stolichnaya and smoked Marlboros. In those days, everybody did. And he made love to strangers in hotel suites. To me. And when he made love, he cried and called me 'darling.' But he never fell in love. Not with me. The problem, he said, was that I was American. He'd had his American. A long time ago. A very famous American actress who now denies it ever happened.

His commitment to independence overshadowed any need for a permanent mate. There was his still ensconced wife. Much later, a divorce. He was young, fit, debonair, dashing. His world included exhilarating places like Lake Como, Sunset Boulevard, Broadway, Paris, and London. He could have anyone. And did. He even wrote a biography about it. I think I'm "And there are the ones whose names I won't mention." Maybe it was, "Names I can't recall."

We met that April in London at the Westbury Hotel. He was sitting alone, having tea. I was ushering cousins, who were visiting from the States, out the door, saw him, and decided to go back and meet the man I had adored from afar.

"What's a big star like you doing all alone?" I asked.

He smiled. "Sometimes it happens," he said softly.

Oh, that voice. That voice. The Middle-Eastern accent. We studied one another a few seconds. He invited me to sit down. Still smarting over the ex-husband and the ex-boyfriend, I, too, was capable of making love to strangers in hotel suites. It wasn't like reaching out to a complete stranger. After all, we were in the same profession, even if I wasn't a household name. He was in London for costume fittings for the next movie. I was between plays, just having finished a role in a West End musical and preparing to do a one woman show. So the movie star and I exchanged phone numbers. A few days later, I was invited to dinner; first his penthouse at the hotel. There were a few words, and then as if it were planned, we moved into the bedroom and made love. Then we walked to a newly opened restaurant around the corner. Churchill's. We talked and talked. Then back to his suite where we made love again. And he said that one thing that changed my life. Changed my thinking about things. Apropos of our conversation, he said the thing about me being American. "The only thing wrong with you is you are an American."

"I am what I am," I replied.

"No." And this is the part that changed my life. "You become who you would like to be."

You become who you would like to be. I can never forget what I learned from him. He would never remember.

Our tryst ended cordially, ended being the operative word. Except through newspapers or magazines or on television or in a film, I really didn't know anything about his life. And then he died. And for some reason it hit me hard and I cried.

<u>THE SONGWRITER</u>. It was one of those fancy music publisher's parties at Christmas. I knew someone who knew someone who could get me in. By now I had figured out it

isn't who you know, it's who you know who *they* know. We were introduced and it was *like* at first sight with a mutual overwhelming desire to be alone somewhere else other than at the crowded party in an office in an office building in central London. He took my hand in a way that made it hard to protest. A taxi to my place. We laughed when the driver charged double when he recognized his passenger. Him. Not me.

In between nibbles from the fridge, we nibbled each other. The clock struck midnight. He decided the private party was over. He rang for a limo to pick him up and take him home to his country estate, his wife, his children, and his dogs.

Another notch on the bedpost for me and a real curiosity at what I was getting out of playing Russian roulette. Never saw him again.

<u>THE TALENT AGENT</u>. He climbed the three flights of stairs to my dressing room at the Haymarket Theatre one night after the show.

He said, "You made me laugh; you made me cry. Do you have an agent?"

"No."

"Here's my card. Come see me tomorrow. I'd like to represent you."

It was serious for a long time. Children were discussed. Steps were made towards co-habitation. The lover tried but couldn't extricate himself from the wife who threatened suicide if he left her. They went into counseling; I went into a mild depression. After months of no contact, a strong impulse overcame me one morning. A voice in my head kept repeating, *Call him. Call him today. Call him now.*

Instead of making that call, I went to bed as if I were in mourning, for the first time wearing the scent he had bought me in Paris. Paco Rabanne. I slept off and on all day into the night. The phone woke me early the next morning. A friend wanted to cushion the blow before I saw it in the newspaper. It was front page news. While I was lying in bed, my agent/ boyfriend had gone flying out the fifth floor window in the middle of a business meeting in Mayfair on an otherwise perfect London summer's day. It took months of convincing myself that even if I had made the call, I couldn't have saved him.

Months later, another actor and I were flown to Dublin to shoot a commercial to be shown in cinemas, and it had to be shot at the docks in Ireland. I had been to Dublin before and just loved being there again. We did the whole thing in one take so had the whole day before we were due to fly back to London. No, he wasn't my next affair. Conversation got around to people in the business we both knew. It was he who first came upon the dead body on the pavement of the talent agent that day. We talked a little about it, but I didn't go into my personal relationship. Churning it all up again was not as devastating as I thought it would be. Divine Grace saved my nervous system. I felt only sadness for his widow and a great deal of hate for the doctors who had prescribed the anti-depressant drugs he'd been taking for many years. No other reason could explain his suicide.

I signed with another agent. And until now, have never talked about it, have never worn Paco Rabanne, have never stopped wondering what if I had made that phone call that day. I look at the only photo I have of him in his long gray suede coat. He's smiling. And I wonder how and why such things happen. And do these things happen to other women.

THE SOCCER PLAYER. According to the press, he was one of the least tranquillized Englishman. The face was a chiseled face, a perfectly sculpted Hollywood face. The way they used to look; not like now. He was arrogant, impulsive, a womanizer, a gambler, an inveterate night clubber. Not exactly everybody's cup of tea. In his case, glass of champagne, the preferred drink. He made love to a Brazilian diplomat's daughter, to famous women, to rich women, to other men's wives. To me.

He took me to dinner, to clubs, to the movies. He introduced me to his friends who were mostly soccer players. In my loneliest hours, he comforted me. I knew sometimes he didn't know which bedroom he was in. I knew he didn't love me. I knew it was temporary.

A beautiful, complex, impossible, generous, unfair, sweet, funny, obstinate, sensual man who was deeply devoted to his sport. He told me he respectfully excluded naming me in his autobiography—the forthright autobiography of soccer's most controversial personality—but inscribed the copy he gave me:

With love to my great friend. You will always be beautiful.

He died too young in a nursing home somewhere in England in 2010 after a long illness.

THE MAESTRO. World-famous harmonica player; yet, to me, he was the man who put up with my atrocious tennis. He would often call across the net, "It helps to run after the ball." He was the one who sat in my living room in my London flat and read everything I had written before I took myself seriously as a writer, before I made the transition from acting to writing. A movie script and several lyrics which he called poetry. With his encouragement, I began to take it all seriously.

One Saturday, I had to cancel our tennis game because while running across the room from my bed to turn off the alarm, I hit my toe against my dressing stool. I mean, who puts an alarm clock on a dressing table on the other side of the room?

He wrote a note: "I've got toes I haven't even used yet, could easily have loaned you one. My main toe, which I've named ptomaine, isn't available but the others are free. At the top of this letter *mein* number so *nu*, when is better the toe, holler on me." (I think he was imitating a stand-up Jewish comedian).

A few weeks later, we met at our usual spot at Regent's Park tennis courts and I was told, "We're not playing here today. I have a surprise for you." He drove us in his car a few minutes away and stopped at the iron gate of a huge estate. First announcing himself into an intercom, the gates opened and he drove through. He asked me if I wanted to know where we were.

Quite excited, I said, "Sure." In my Acting 101 class, we were taught to always say yes, otherwise the scene is over.

"The American Ambassador's residence. I've been given carte blanche privileges to play on the tennis courts—there were two—any time I want."

Big stuff. We both thought so. I still played lousy tennis.

There was a break in our routine during a cold January and February when he was performing in warmer climes. A postcard read: "If you think I've been neglecting you, you're right. I've been in Nairobi, where I'm friends with two Jewish giraffes (swear to God!)—and to Cleveland where I hate a Jewish lawyer."

In the spring, we resumed our tennis and I raved and ranted about yet another toe injury; this time, in the middle of the game.

"You got foot troubles?" he shouted across the net. "Let me tell you about my knee. Got six hours? Maybe my trouble is I've been hitting my backhand with my knee."

It wasn't just tennis. It was in his beautiful home in the north of London where we rolled about on the floor (not the couch or the bed). But only after the drinking of his famous coffee, a ritual he felt he had to share. Oh, that coffee. Kenyan. I can still smell its aroma. Not a percolator. In a French Press. To this day, I can only make coffee in a French Press. Back to the gymnastics. The kisses, the groping, the… you know….which led to more kisses, more groping. We just rolled about, talking, and laughing about my bad tennis. I think I commented on how clean his floor was.

There was the tour of his *special* room. The archives with memorabilia, history, books, news clippings. I listened for hours to stories about Bob Hope and George Burns and Jack Benny. Remember—this was a long time ago. He knew them all; had played or opened for them at different concerts, entertained the troops overseas, lived all over the world. And there was the piano. He moved the sheet music and photos off the bench, sat down, and played. Mostly Gershwin and Porter songs. I was enthralled. If only the sex had been as exciting. How he could play that piano! Not a known fact. He played for me. Just for me. It was thrilling. A real turn on. But I guess not enough to go to the next level in the relationship, whatever that might be.

In that special room, he took something down from a shelf—a tiny gray box—and handed it to me. A miniature Hohner, made in Germany, in a little gray box. A souvenir mouth organ. It really plays. His name was printed on the outside of the box.

Maybe because I wasn't a match for him in tennis, maybe because there was a twenty-five year difference in our ages, maybe because my kisses weren't sweet enough, our time ended rather abruptly. Not on the tennis court, not in his house, but on the telephone. "Gotta go," he said, "I've something on the stove."

<u>THE USED-CAR SALESMAN</u>. On the way home to Los Angeles from Switzerland, he was holed up in his friends'

house in London's Mayfair district, following a sad, sudden, and very public break-up from one of the most beautiful and famous women in the world. We were introduced by a mutual friend. I've always said, it isn't who you know, it's who *they* know. It should have ended there with just the meeting. But he was handsome, witty, well-dressed, and utterly charming with an even more charming slightly European accent. Fleeing from the press, who never gave up pursuing him, we were unable to go out.

We talked for hours. About everything. It was amazing how much we talked. We shared wine and cheese and eventually made our way up the stairs to what, at one time, had been *their* bedroom. It was white with shades of peach. Very lovely. Very soothing. In the canopied bed, he introduced me to amyl-nitrate and made love to me the way he had made love to her. I didn't understand about the drug, that it dilates blood vessels. Even when he explained it, I didn't understand it.

He wanted me to stay. But I had to leave to attend to my dog who had been left alone way too long that day.

He called from Los Angeles. He returned to London. He wanted to meet again. I said no. And I have never been able to figure out why because he was very nice. And I liked him. I think he liked me. And we were compatible.

THE SHOE TYCOON. He looked like a Spanish matador. We met when I was twenty and he was thirty-five. He taught me how to lie to my mother, to the hotel clerk, to the elevator man, to my boss when I'd fly to New York to have dinner and make love all night. I never told anyone about this liaison that happened only in novels by Harold Robbins. Off and on for twelve years, we met secretly in Boston, New York, London, and Florence.

I was appearing in a major show in London's West End. He was passing through on the way to Rome. Another afternoon; another hotel suite. To my invitation to come and see my show that night—you can watch from the wings—was met with "I saw the show in New York."

"But you haven't seen me in it."

At first his silence. Then, "Meet me after the show."

I made a choice. A real adult choice. I did not meet him after the show. I did not meet him ever again. From him I learned that you can buy a half-size larger shoe and stuff a filler in it.

SIR WHAT'S HIS NAME. He replied to my ad for a flat mate. His father hadn't died yet so he hadn't inherited half of Cornwall and the title of Lord. He needed a place to live while he got his little art gallery going in London's trendy Covent Garden area. He was tall and lean and gorgeous. I mean, Gary Cooper gorgeous in a British kind of way. He was a bit tipsy. More than a bit. He needed food. He requested a glass of milk and while he guzzled it down, I made him a bacon, lettuce, and tomato sandwich on toasted white bread with gobs of mayonnaise. It was before the days when we worried about cholesterol or eating for your blood type or anything remotely healthy. He said BLTs were his absolute favorite and only an American could make them. One check mark for the Yanks! And so he fell in love with the American who made Dagwood like sandwiches. We rolled about. Usually he would pass out after the first kiss, so there was no sexual activity with this one. The whole thing was short-lived. He didn't move in, but one very late night, he arrived, drunk, desperately in need of a BLT sandwich. I obliged. He ate. He passed out.

Years later, I did check and he did become a Lord and he did inherit half of the South Coast of England. I also saw he was on his third marriage. Oh, that it could have been me. And so it was farewell to my life as lady what's her name and membership via marriage in the peerage.

Much much later, I married a Scottish Baron. Through his father's line, he was one of seven in line for the throne. To put it another way: If Scotland ever became independent from England, and the Baron became King, Lydia, Queen of Scots would be my title. We got divorced. My luck, I told him, Scotland will probably become independent. Don't worry, he told me, there will always be a place for you.

As it turned out, an Austrian businessman working in London rented the spare room in my flat and became an absolutely smashing gentleman lodger, mainly because he was rarely in residence. He kind of became a big brother with lots of advice on how I should rethink my lifestyle. He thought I was wasting myself not writing, not acting, not doing much of anything.

THE ANGEL. It was a new West End musical written by a close friend. The show's main backer became my angel, too. Dancing in public places, beds in private places, long drives to the countryside in his midnight blue Rolls Royce, which I sometimes drove. Drinks and lunch at the Grosvenor House. An innocent business meeting at the Savoy. Dinners with his friends and their girlfriends developed into tea and scones with his mother, who adored me. Majorca would be our future home when he divorced his wife, after the kids were older. When the wife was away, we made love in their bed. Press a button and the green velvet curtains opened. Closing was more difficult, but inevitable. Conscience, the right thing, family commitments added to the fact that we liked each other too much, contributed to the gentle drifting apart. The show closed. It had been a hit. This angel was no angel.

THE COMPANY MAN. In between acting jobs, one Christmas, I did a stint in the newly opened tennis department at Harrods famous department store before it was bought out by Mohamed Al Fayed. It was his son who was killed with Princess Diana in that horrendous car crash in Paris. Europeans flocked to Harrods that season because of the money exchange in their favor at the time. I had many invitations to play indoor tennis, go out for dinner, attend concerts. It was fun. I met a lot of people, but it was the American who, for a brief time, captured my heart. He stopped in London often on his way to Rome and the Middle East. He spoke fluent Italian and Arabic and sometimes stayed at the Hilton Hotel in Park Lane.

Together we shopped, we dined, we walked, we talked, we slept. And then I found out I was under surveillance. "Am I in danger?" I asked.

"No. They have to do that," he replied.

One night, I went to the movies with a girlfriend. We stopped into the hotel next door to the cinema for a drink. We watched a man watching us. We had a funny feeling about him. We knew. When I told my company man about it, he asked me if he had on a trench coat and loafers with white socks. "Yes," I said smiling. "Yes, you were followed." He didn't smile.

Sometimes, he would use the telephone in my flat when he didn't think it was safe to use the phone in his hotel room. He always spoke in Arabic. I never knew the nature of the calls. One Saturday, after a day of shopping, I dropped him off at this hotel and took the taxi on to my flat in Kensington in order to change for our dinner date. I had a funny feeling; call it a premonition, that I would not see him that evening. Maybe ever. My senses had been sharpened by years of studying scripts' sub-texts.

My instincts were good. I never saw him that evening. Or ever again. Years later, we reconnected when I made a call to a number he had given me if I was ever in California.

His office forwarded my message to him. He called and told me he was retired. His face was getting known at airports and had to be replaced. It was safe now to talk about that night in London. Yes. They had been waiting for him at his hotel in the lobby. "And I had to go," he said. "It wasn't possible to call you."

"Do you miss it?" I asked.

"I'm glad it's over," he said. "They got other doctors to perform their operations."

I never questioned him. He wouldn't have told me anyway.

THE LONDONER. Waiting for the 'Don't Walk' sign to change, he asked if I'd like a cup of tea. Only in London on a rare, hot summer's day does one get invited for a hot cup of tea. No explanations, no apologies, no excuses, just guilt-free tea in a nearby café. Small talk made strangers sudden friends and led to my bed.

In the late afternoon light, he looked quite handsome and seemed as surprised at it all as I was. He wanted to stay for a while. My dog wouldn't have any of it. And that was the end of that. Not only that. I began to take stock. To re-evaluate. To really, really think about what I was doing.

All the men weren't married. The married ones just seemed to be the most interesting ones at that time. And maybe on a deeper level, I knew it couldn't lead to anything permanent and on an even deeper, deeper level, maybe I thought it would. Maybe the triangle was part of the past. The father-loss syndrome. There was Mommy, Daddy, and me. So I was only comfortable when part of a triangle.

My dog was right.

SWAN SONG. Playing the role of Eunice in Tennessee William's *A Streetcar Named Desire* was my chance to flop around the stage in hair curlers, a robe, and furry slippers.

No longer the glam one, it was a big change. That first day of rehearsal, I was surrounded by youth. By bodies. By beauty. Only my play husband was a contemporary. We both silently realized we weren't young anymore. I wasn't going to be the ingénue ever again. Without many lines to learn, it was time for me to listen and watch. As I opened up to this new experience, I found that others were listening to me. My experience meant something. They came to me for performance tips. No one had ever asked me that before. They told me I had a stage presence that couldn't be taught. Then one matinée, I did the unforgivable. I was late on an entrance. Apart from the lights falling on your head, it is the worst moment that can ever happen on stage. The others were professional enough to cover with dialogue until I finally appeared.

Later backstage, a fellow actor said, "If you do that, where are the rest of us?"

It was an enormous compliment from an acting peer. And a huge lesson. I was important. I mattered. I was valued.

And I didn't have to take my clothes off.

5

From Frenzy to Peace.

LYDIA

From immediate gratification to patience. From unhealthy addictions to healthy choices. From chocolate ice cream and black coffee to sunflower seeds and natural unsweetened cranberry juice. From diuretic pills and synthetic laxatives to natural fiber and colon irrigations. From antibiotics and hospitals to holistic self-healing. From champagne for breakfast to soy milk and whole grains. From self-absorption to nurturing. From seeking love to giving love. From blaming to taking responsibility. From feeling separate to being part of the whole. From denial to awareness. From anger at the nothingness to awe at the abundance.

KATE

FROM EATING CHINESE FOOD IN CHINA, DANCING TILL dawn in Greece, and sleepless nights everywhere, to yoga retreats in Massachusetts, mud baths in California, and meditation and chanting in my own home. I feel strangely calm in my new skin. And less lonely than I ever felt in the midst of former husband's business associates at empty futile dinners and cocktail parties to further his career. I didn't like the me then.

Now I sit and do nothing. Sometimes I write in my journal. I eat alone. I'm falling in love with me. I like sitting on my balcony for hours, watching the sea. The sea. Fearful, ferocious, turbulent; peaceful, calm, predictable, wild. On my road to recovery from a marriage (make that plural) that didn't agree, from lives of quiet desperation on opposite sides of the house; into the arms of faceless men.

Forgiving myself for choosing him and congratulating myself for getting out before I was sucked dry. Wait. That was number three. Number four died and left me a fortune. I earned it. Money does a lot; but no matter how much money you have, it cannot buy back yesterday. Sometimes that's a darn good thing.

CHARLOTTE

Like standing at the edge of a cliff, you can't go back, you're afraid to go forward.

You're on the fence, stuck. It becomes stale and you know you can't stay in that place.

In order to grow, you have to take that next step. You have to move on. And you do it.

First one foot, then the other. With no net below, you are in space. It's buoyant and spongy

and it holds you up. It has a name. Faith. It was waiting for you all along.

SAMANTHA

In the pose of a child
during a yoga session
unexpected tears
welled up
and streamed down my face

supposedly grieving
for the flexible young woman
no longer evident

as quickly as they came
the tears stopped
when I remembered
to breathe

through the breath
those stiff

immovable places
softened

through the breath
I discovered a vibrant
energetic woman
and I embraced her
knowing

she is
still
ever
my child

Epilogue

CHARLOTTE: Man's entire modus operandi is to please a woman.

KATE: Life *then* was the exciting guy you date. My life *now* is like the stable guy you marry.

LYDIA: What have I learned from the frenzy? Was it frenzy? Maybe it was foolish. Maybe it was sometimes even dangerous. It was fun. The truth is I wish I had enjoyed it more.

CHARLOTTE: Men are sweetly simple. What you see is what you get. Women are full of mystery, capable of change mid-sentence. Women worry about parts of their bodies; men see the total package.

SAMANTHA: And that's what they love.

KATE: Monogamous or adventurer, be it money, sex, property, a business deal or a new suit, his every breath is only to impress her.

SAMANTHA: There's a catch. For all this she must let him know her desires so he can be sure of success.

CHARLOTTE: What delights her delights him. And that's how a man loves.

LYDIA: I miss being in love.

KATE: Is this it now?

LYDIA: But, oh, what memories!

SAMANTHA: I want more than just the memory. He's out there—somewhere. The one.

KATE: I guess what they say is true: It ain't over till it's over.

CHARLOTTE: He's wondering if he'll ever meet—ME.

SAMANTHA: Or me.

KATE: Or me.

LYDIA: He isn't into lovedotcom or going to singles bars. He's at home reading a book.

CHARLOTTE: Or writing one.

LYDIA: He still drives at night.

SAMANTHA: He cooks.

KATE: He's financially and emotionally stable.

CHARLOTTE: He will love my mind.

LYDIA: My sense of humor.

SAMANTHA: My hair, my skin, my voice, my smile.

KATE: We will talk and laugh and dance.

LYDIA: And make love.

SAMANTHA: In all kinds of ways.

KATE: I don't bend that way.

SAMANTHA: You could learn.

KATE: He comes home in the middle of the day, puts on some music, takes me in his arms, and we dance around the living room. No words are needed.

CHARLOTTE: Shit. I miss being in love.

LYDIA: In lust.

SAMANTHA: Whatever.

Small Pickled Birds and Chocolate

HOW COME AT A PARTY, WHENEVER THERE'S A LULL IN THE conversation, there is always that one person who will feel compelled to break the silence with a tidbit or two so useless and boring that it renders everyone within hearing distance wishing he or she had never been born? With mouths wide open allowing saliva to drip onto their attire or down the front of borrowed apparel, the recipients of this useless information are somehow transfixed.

How come I never knew that George Washington, the first president of the United States, did not throw a silver dollar across the Potomac? According to my first grade teacher, he did, but I keep my mouth shut for fear of more drool dripping onto my coordinated ensemble. According to our charming talkative Mister *know-it-all* Wonderful, this fact is not so. It turns out that if, indeed, President Washington did toss the currency, the river was the Rappahannock. Potomac, Rappahannock. They sound alike if you say them out loud very fast.

And how come I never knew that SOS doesn't mean 'save our ship'? Apparently, it doesn't stand for anything at all. Zip. Zilch. Zero. SOS. Isn't that some kind of soap pad for cleaning grime off of pots and pans?

He was still talking. How dare I interrupt his monologue with thoughts of my own. Did you know there are more that thirty-five thousand beehives in Cyprus? On second thought, that could be useful.

Being a nice person, I feel I must show some sort of reaction, preferably a favorable one, if not to the actual piece of news, but to the fact that the speaker, a friend in this case, has all this information at the ready, has retained it, and most importantly, is willing to share the details. "Ah," I say with utmost sincerity which was obviously taken as unintended encouragement because he went on…

"Aelos was the ancient God of *the* Wind, not God of Wind."

The 'ah' of mine was too enthusiastic. "Really?" I try to sound as if this is important to know without opening a door to more tidbits. I have failed because the dynamo encyclopedia goes on.

"Greta Garbo never said, 'I vant to be alone.' She slurred, 'I vant to be *let* alone.' "

"Oh, I see. I've wondered about that for years." I'm impressed with his use of the word 'slurred' and my use of the word 'wondered.' It's two of those words not uttered very often in public or, for that matter, in private. Like the words moron and genius. Genius is used too often and moron not often enough. But I digress.

"Humphrey Bogart's famed movie line in *Casablanca* was not, 'Drop the gun, Louie,' which is quoted often. It was, 'Not so fast, Louie.' "

"I was misinformed," I say. I thought it was utterly brilliant of me to quote another Bogie line straight out of the same movie. It went over the head of the genius…er…moron…genius. For a split second I close my eyes, hoping he will have disappeared when I open them. No such luck.

"In England, you never rinse out your underwear; you rinse out your smalls."

"Gosh. Separated by a common language, eh?" When the walking dictionary of useless facts is a close friend, the realization hits you that you never really knew this close personal friend. And you begin to doubt your own mental health.

Ignoring my semi-feeble attempt at conversation, which implies two or more people exchanging ideas, the soliloquist continued. "A Bible dating from 1539 may be seen at Panayia Khryseleousa Church, Emba."

I understood two, maybe three words and respond with, "That's enormously brilliant; that you know it, I mean."

Brilliant? Brilliant? Am I not listening to myself? What is wrong with me? It's downright useless. But by this time, to keep myself from dozing off, I have begun to focus on the way a line is accented; on the rhythm of the delivery; the tone of voice; his breathing. But I had to be careful not to miss the meat of the piece. It could be a trick. There could be questions later. Worse still, maybe I was being punked and the entire world was watching. As the pre-holiday season party hosts had recently returned from Las Vegas and were known to be a little off the wall, anything was possible. Over there on the mantel in the eye of the plastic Santa! I was sure I spotted a button of a device that could be a camera.

No doubt encouraged by my enthusiasm in the form of the fact that I was still standing there, my soon to be (as far as I was concerned) former friend continues. "Peanuts are one of the ingredients in dynamite."

My jaw drops until it nearly touches the floor. I want to scream. My lips hang limp unable to form words. My eyes open so wide that contact lenses are threatening to slip out. For the life of me, I have no idea why an image of the Grand Canyon passes before me. I've never been to the Grand Canyon.

"Tigers have striped skin, not just striped fur," spouts the annoying know-it-all.

"Yuh, well everyone knows that," I toss out. He ignores my retort. How dare I steal his thunder? But I really do know that.

"A shark is the only fish that can blink with both eyes," he says precisely.

"You mean that thing in *Jaws*, the movie?" I ask with a reasonable amount of sincerity.

"Yuh, yuh." He blinks twice and nods his head. Then without taking a breath, he spills, "There are more chickens in the world than people. There are three hundred and thirty-six dimples on a regulation golf ball; if not, they're called irregulars." He swallows a gulp of air.

I'm glad about his air intake because I don't know how to resuscitate. I'm barely able to catch a breath myself by now. Can you imagine being the person whose job it is to count the dimples on those balls? Sharks, chickens, tigers, golf balls. With this walking encyclopedia, who needed four years of college? I loathed my life.

"A cat has thirty-two muscles in each ear."

"Really?" I stifle a yawn. Why don't I just leave? How much longer can I keep up the pretense that I'm enjoying myself? Right then and there, I make the decision never ever to go to another party as long as I live.

"Almonds are a member of the peach family."

"Is that a fact? I love peaches," I lied. "And the color peach is positively my favorite color in the whole world," I say meaningfully because it's almost the truth. Peach used to be my favorite color but has been shoved down the totem pole by jade green. Sometimes chocolate brown. "And almonds are good for you," I shout, in order to appear alive (in case there *is* a TV camera around). "Peaches. Almonds. I love them both," I go on. I positively do not know who I am. I wait and watch while what's-his-name puffs up in preparation for delivery of yet another pearl. You could see it. You could feel it. I wait. I feel like the straight man in a skit on *Saturday Night Live*.

"The ambelopoulia, which consists of small pickled birds, was called *beccafiguo* by the Venetians, and the delicacy was exported to Venice in the sixteenth century."

Suddenly, I'm at attention. An expression I've never uttered in my life slips from my lips. "Holy fudge!" Some lost memory pops up in the back of my head like a ringing bell in my ears calling my brain to full attention. "How in the world do you know that?" I ask. I'm astounded that I really want to know.

An understated, "I know," is the reply accompanied with a tilt of his head and a shoulder shrug.

A thousand years of my life flash by. I'm in New York. I'm a contestant on the TV quiz show, *Who Do You Trust?* I'm standing in front of the host, Johnny Carson. This was before his reign as host of the *Tonight* show. Next to me is my quiz partner. If it hadn't been for one of our Boston University college professors being a friend of the producer of the show, we wouldn't be there at all.

We got through the rehearsal of the preliminary spontaneous chit chat—which was scripted—the format that would be used when we stood with Johnny in front of the studio audience before the actual quiz questions. *What are you going to be when you grow up? What do you do in your spare time? What will you do with the money if you win?* The answers were designed to make us look like idiots, not the intelligent, adorable, precocious college kids we were.

Okay. Time for the real questions which Johnny read from a few hand-held, light blue, five-by-seven index cards. The color had something to do with the way the lights picked up or didn't pick up white on camera. He was a good reader, if you could get past the Nebraskan twang. Johnny turned to me and asked the question that was the whole point of the quiz program, "Who do you trust?"

What kind of a question was that? Who needed that kind of responsibility? By pointing the finger at my partner, I figured I'd have someone to blame if we lost. "Him," I said with great emphasis. The studio audience applauded. This, too, was scripted. A flashing sign lit up: APPLAUSE. When the light went out, they knew it was their cue to stop clapping.

Johnny asked precisely, as if every fifth or sixth word might be a code word to a spy somewhere, "What is the name of the delicacy exported to Venice in the sixteenth century which consisted of small pickled birds?"

Huh? What language was he speaking? Did my partner know the answer? No. Did I know the answer? No. I didn't even know the question. And even if I did know the answer, I wasn't allowed to assist since I had elected for him to answer the question.

Our time was up. Johnny read the answer off his card. "The ambelopoulia, which consists of small pickled birds, was called *beccafiguo* by the Venetians, and the delicacy was exported to Venice in the sixteenth century."

Pickled? We were positively paralytic. We failed to answer the subsequent questions and lost the big money, but we were given a crack at a small consolation prize. It was a musical question. Again, coward that I am, I trusted my partner. The first two lines of a popular song were played by what sounded like a two hundred piece orchestra nowhere in sight.

Einstein next to me didn't hear the audience shout out, "*Margie*." They were firmly hushed by Mr. Carson. Eventually, my partner, who may have been deaf in the ear closest to the audience, guessed the correct title after eliminating *Judy, Billy, Myrna,* and something that sounded like *Trotsky*. "Got it," he said. "*Margie*." The applause was deafening, too loud for the rather small audience. Canned or real? We didn't know. We didn't care. Because we had been such good sports, we were awarded the consolation prize money of twenty-five dollars to split between us. In today's currency, around two and a half cents apiece; or, looking at it the other way, if we had invested it wisely in stocks and bonds and let it sit, around a million and a half dollars.

Back in the present, I ask my so-called brilliant friend, "Where were you when I needed you?"

He smirks, not wanting me to think he didn't know something. But I could tell he really didn't understand my question. Obviously, I have been too encouraging, too enthusiastic, too engaged, because it isn't over yet. The talking tome is on a roll. Does he not realize that every breath does not have to be a spoken word? Without any intro, he spits out, "Did you know that the microwave was invented after a researcher walked by a radar tube and a chocolate bar melted in his jacket pocket?"

"Really?" I cry out. "Now that's interesting."

Chocolate? My favorite food; my favorite color walls for a dining room. Suddenly, my mouth is crying out for a piece of dark chocolate. Rather than engage this person… er… genius…er…moron…er…person in anything further, I excuse myself to search for a chunk of the smooth, bittersweet delicacy.

Thinking of the health benefits of all those antioxidants, I become positively disoriented as I sprint over to the buffet table. *Please, sire, a bit of dark chocolate to soothe my craving.* Bound to be some chocolate amidst the berries and nuts; a morsel nestled in the collation of assorted cold cuts including turkey, ham, roast beef, and fancy creamy desserts. What kind of a pre-holiday party orchestrated to get everyone in the mood for the upcoming season would it be without large, fresh, juicy, red strawberries dipped in one hundred percent pure natural cocao (now Anglicized as cocoa) butter handmade by the famous French chocolatier Pascal Caffet?

RECIPE FOR CHOCOLATE COVERED STRAWBERRIES

- 6 ounces semi-sweet chocolate, chopped
- 1 pound strawberries with stems, washed and dried
- Line a sheet pan with waxed paper
- Melt chocolate on the stove in a double boiler until smooth (or in a microwave)
- Hold strawberries by the stem
- Dip a strawberry into the melted chocolate
- Line up dipped strawberries on the waxed paper
- Takes about 30 minutes to set

Susan Surman

Susan Surman—aka Susan Kramer/Gracie Luck—lived and worked in London for 23 years. Her performing credits include London's West End, Edinburgh, the Sydney Opera House, Ensemble Theatre, BBC radio, TV, and film. Writing credits include material for Tracey Ullman, two plays performed (one commissioned for TV), and a play and a screenplay optioned. After her return to the USA, she focused on writing fiction, weaving in her extensive background in acting and travel. Ask her where she gets her ideas and she will say, "Why invent? All I have to do is remember."

She lives in North Carolina.